"I don't need any help dealing with my father, Jo."

She knew a dismissal when she heard one. It seemed Neil was telling her to keep her paws off his family problems. If only it weren't so tempting to interfere, to champion his cause.

"I'll see you later, Neil," she said quietly.

Her eyes were huge and warm, but he steeled himself against noticing. "I'll see you at the office, I'm sure."

At the office? But before he went in to see his father, he'd talked about them geting to know each other better. Why this abrupt change of heart?

"Sure," she said softly. "I'll see you around. And, Neil?"

He looked up. "Yes."

"You take care."

And then she smiled at him and backed out of the oppressive Hawthorne house, hoping he understood she wasn't giving up on him yet.

Dear Reader:

We at Silhouette are very excited to bring you a NEW reading **Sensation***. Look out for the four books which will appear in our new Silhouette* **Sensation** *series every month. These stories will have the high quality you have come to expect from Silhouette, and their varied and provocative plots will encourage you to explore the wonder of falling in love – again and again!*

Emotions run high in these drama-filled novels. Greater sensual detail and an extra edge of realism intensify the hero and heroine's relationship so that you cannot help but be caught up in their every change of mood.

We hope you enjoy this new **Sensation** *– and will go on to enjoy many more.*

We would love to hear your comments about our new line and encourage you to write to us:

Jane Nicholls
Silhouette Books
PO Box 236
Thornton Road
Croydon
Surrey
CR9 3RU

JULIE KISTLER
Wildflower

Silhouette Sensation

First published in Great Britain in 1989 by Silhouette Books, Eton House, 18–24 Paradise Road, Richmond, Surrey TW9 1SR

© Julie Kistler 1988

Silhouette, Silhouette Sensation and Colophon are Trade Marks of Harlequin Enterprises B.V.

ISBN 0 373 57665 X

18–8909

Made and printed in Great Britain

Prologue

A pink neon light from the pavilion flashed "Refreshments" on and off in an annoying, irregular rhythm. When it was on, it cast a rosy glow on the blunt features of the thug-for-hire known as Ed.

Caught up in an energetic recital of his accomplishments as a lowly troublemaker, Ed seemed oblivious to the garish spotlight. His résumé consisted of barroom brawls, a few scuffles with the police and a petty theft or two thrown in for good measure. He painted a picture of a small, ugly and not very intelligent life-style.

His companion, made of more cautious stuff, slid farther into the protective shadow of the park pavilion, wishing that Ed would keep his voice down and get out from under the damn pink light. This meeting had been set up in an empty, poorly lit park with one objective in mind—anonymity for both parties. Under the neon glare, Ed might as well have shouted his identity from the rooftops.

If only a smarter criminal were available instead of Ed.

But it wasn't like there was a lot of choice in these matters. The only thug around right now was blustery, thickheaded Ed, and there was no use lamenting the situation. After all, the man had been getting into trouble his entire life. Trouble ought to be easy for a cretin like him.

Ed peered anxiously into the shadows, muttering, "I can't see you in there at all, pardner. You still there?"

"Of course," the pardner snapped.

"Well, what do you say? Am I your man or ain't I? You gonna come across with the cash?"

"One hundred up front, if I decide you can handle the job. There will be another four hundred if you pull it off okay."

"Five hundred bucks?" Ed ran his tongue over his lips and jammed beefy fists into his pants pockets. Just as the refreshments sign kicked on again, he grinned, and his teeth shone pink into the darkness. "For five hundred bucks you got yourself a deal, pardner. Now you just tell ol' Ed what you want done."

"I want you to make a big mess, Ed. You should be good at that."

The sarcasm was lost on Ed. "Where and when, pardner. That's all I need."

There was a pause, as the person in the shadows took one last moment to consider the seriousness of the situation before taking the final step. The litany was familiar— it was all for a righteous cause, the best cause, backed up by the purest of motives. Associating with a money-hungry creep like Ed was only a means to an end. It would be perfectly justified when all was said and done.

"Here's a schedule," the prospective employer said finally. "It gives you places and dates for the activities of a group called Water Works. There will be a picket march a week from Friday. I don't care what you do—you can start a fight, shout obscenities at them, throw tear gas if that turns you on. But I want Water Works to have a very public, very ugly problem. Do you understand?"

Ed's grin turned into a smirk. "A cinch, pardner. No sweat. You sure don't like these Water Work guys, do you? They do something to you?"

The response from the shadows was a terse, "It's none of your business."

"Water Works, huh?" Ed persisted. "Don't sound like much. I thought maybe nukes or abortion or something to really get the blood boiling. But water? Geez, who cares about water?"

His companion smiled grimly. If only Ed knew. That was exactly the point. Nobody cared about water, even if it was vital to their survival. If you asked people, they'd say they were for clean water, but that would be as far as it went. No commitment, no excitement.

Not yet, anyway.

But once Ed pulled his act, it would be a different story. A few small stunts had already come off successfully, and the publicity was nice. But it wasn't enough. Not nearly enough.

Soon things would be different. After the thing with Ed and some other well-timed "accidents," the name of Water Works would be screaming from every paper and TV station in the state. The world would see the righteously indignant volunteers of Water Works, uncovering dramatic examples of corporate polluters. And they would see the poor, innocent, hard-working men and women of Water Works, publicly humiliated by a thug named Ed.

The natural conclusion would be that those same corporate polluters had hired Ed to harass the people at Water Works.

Who cared if the reality was that one of Water Works' own staff had polluted the waterways and paid Ed to create a controversy? At least someone cared enough about the state of the world to try to improve it. If the methods were slightly less than honorable, who cared?

The important thing was that Water Works would prosper, and the cause of clean water would beat in the heart of every right-thinking Minnesotan.

A triumphant smile broke through the gloom in the shadows, and the person to whom clean water was so vitally important began to count out the first part of Ed's money.

Chapter One

In her wildest dreams, Jo Wentworth never would have imagined herself riding on top of a giant, crepe-paper-stuffed whale, right down the middle of Main Street. But when a good cause was involved, Jo didn't believe in saying no.

She had to admit to feeling a certain amount of terror when the huge whale float jerked into place behind the Freedom Lake Jaycees, who were riding on a fire truck. Staring all the way down at the pavement, it had occurred to her that she might fall off and kill herself, single-handedly setting the cause of clean water back ten years. But the plucky Water Works whale cruised smoothly down Main Street, and Jo's fears were laid to rest.

Her sister Kit, who happened to be in advertising, had argued that Water Works needed this kind of positive, upbeat image enhancement. Although at first it sounded silly and much too lightweight for an important concern like the battle against pollution, Jo had finally let herself be convinced that Kit was right. The group would benefit from putting itself in the public eye, and the Fish Fest at Freedom Lake was even sort of thematically related. Besides, the Water Works volunteers could use a break from the drudgery of canvassing and paperwork.

And so, just as if it were high school homecoming, they'd borrowed a hayrack and put together a float, or a whale to be precise, from yards of chicken wire and little squares of aqua-blue tissue paper. After the thing was built in the driveway of the Wentworth house in St. Paul, they trundled their whale, now dubbed Junior, down to the tiny town of Freedom Lake to hawk the virtues of keeping Minnesota's waterways free of pollution. Junior's side banner exhorted everyone to Keep It Clean.

Jo flashed a quick smile at her sister, the advertising whiz with whom she shared the back plank in what was supposed to look like a rowboat marooned on top of the whale. The two of them had gotten on last, and they'd been left with the backward seats, while the other four people in the group faced the front of the parade. One brave soul, a volunteer named Stanley, installed himself just behind the whale's blowhole, where wire and streamers approximated the water a whale would blow off its top when it came up for air. There were smiling volunteers in the pickup truck pulling the float and more volunteers running alongside, handing out pamphlets to the adults and bright-colored toy boats to the kiddies. It had all worked out spectacularly, just as Kit promised it would when she pitched the idea in the first place.

"Good job, Kit," Jo declared, and reached over to squeeze her sister's hand. "If only one person sees the float and doesn't toss their garbage into the lake because of it, we've succeeded."

"You're positively beaming, Jo. If I didn't know you better, I'd say you were basking in all the attention. It's the beauty-queen smile-and-wave syndrome, you know." Kit leaned out and pointed down to the purple Cadillac convertible behind them. "You and Miss Fish Fest," she teased. "Two of a kind."

Sending a glance from her lofty perch down to the girl in the purple convertible, Jo laughed out loud. Miss Fish Fest had a good twenty pounds and ten inches of extra bosom on

Jo. If they were two of a kind, Jo was in big trouble. "I think she's more your style," Jo offered innocently.

"Get real."

Although the sisters didn't look alike, neither resembled the curvaceous, pouting Miss Fish Fest. Kit was tall and blond and Jo was small and vaguely redheaded, but one thing they shared was a definite lack of pretense about their appearance. Unlike Miss Fish Fest.

"We ought to feel sorry for her," Jo said with a sigh. "Poor thing. The guy driving her is giving her a hard time. He keeps accelerating and braking really fast. Can you see? It's all the poor girl can do to hold on to her tiara."

Shaking her head, Kit regarded her younger sister fondly. "I can't believe that even you feel sorry for that little twit. One, she's buried under forty pounds of makeup. Two, she's all of sixteen, but somehow managed a 45Z bust. And three, she threw a fit and stamped her little foot that we got to go ahead of her in the parade. She's a menace. Her driver is probably only acting in self-defense. Maybe she threatened to slug him with one of her breasts. That could be lethal."

"Kit! That's awfully crude, even for you."

"Hmph!" Kit groused. "It's easy for you to be kind. After all, she didn't come on to *your* husband."

"I don't have a husband," Jo pointed out politely. "And I don't think she was coming on to Riley, either."

"Oh, yes, she was. Little twit."

"Well, he's safe inside the truck now, and she can't get to him, little twit or not." Jo shrugged. "Maybe she's having a bad day. It can't be easy for a person to be smushed inside a dress that's three sizes too small."

Kit raised a very pale eyebrow. "A bad day? Maybe you're just too nice for your own good."

"Maybe you're just too mean for your own good."

They grinned at each other, agreeing, as they generally did, to disagree. If Jo preferred to see the best in situations, and Kit preferred to see the worst, there wasn't much they could do about it. But it didn't mean they had to dislike each other.

"Anyway," Jo ventured, as she caught a smile from a small boy at the curb, and waved back energetically, "it's too gorgeous a day to get upset about teenagers with large breasts. I decided a long time ago to pay no attention to such things. It's what's inside that counts."

"I can see why you think that way." Kit cast a cynical eye at her sister's miniscule chest.

Feeling herself blush under her freckles, Jo protested. "Stop it this instant!"

As the words came out of Jo's mouth, she felt the oddest sensation underneath her, as if she were still moving, but the float below her wasn't. She had the bizarre notion that some higher power had taken her at her word, and promptly put a stop to the float, the parade and the entire world.

The volunteer on the front of the whale was the first to feel the impact; Jo heard him shout something unintelligible only an instant before she herself was propelled sideways. The float fishtailed and then screeched and shuddered, trying to stop. A curtain of Kit's long blond hair flew into Jo's face, blinding her completely, after which they were both unceremoniously dumped over backward into the rowboat.

Amid the tangle of limbs and clothing, she could feel her heart beating, so she knew she was okay. And then she felt the vibration of her sister's side, as if Kit were laughing uncontrollably.

"What are you laughing at?" Jo demanded, trying to pull the hem of her skirt out from under someone else's leg.

Kit hiccupped as giggles overtook her. "Didn't you see?" She wobbled into a sitting position at the expense of Jo's skirt, causing an audible rip. "Oh, Jo, you should've seen it! Miss Fish Fest toppled right over into the front seat of the Cadillac! And then—and then—"

Breaking off, Kit wiped watery eyes. "Her little legs were sticking in the air, kicking, like a guppy caught in a net."

"I hope she's all right." Jo managed to climb over to the edge of the rowboat to peer down at the purple convertible. "Oh, dear. It looks like she's really wedged in there."

That comment set Kit off again, and Jo frowned. "Get a hold of yourself, will you? You're jiggling the rowboat and scaring everybody."

After a few wheezy chuckles at the beauty queen's expense, Kit managed to behave herself. Everyone in the rowboat got disentangled somehow, sitting up and rearranging themselves as a low, agitated murmur swept the parade. What in the world had happened to cause such a mess?

The Water Works float was a few entries behind the middle of the parade, and it took several minutes for the news to get back to them. Stanley, who had appointed himself scout after pulling himself out of the blowhole, hustled back with information.

"Poor organization," was his verdict. Although young, Stanley was a very serious person, with longish dark hair and a neatly trimmed beard. He had a habit of stroking his beard thoughtfully when he spoke. "They didn't realize the parade was too big for the route they mapped out. They thought they could circle it around and back onto the same street where it started. So what happened was that the first float in the parade saw that it was going to hit the end of the parade and slammed on the brakes. Some politician's car was behind that, and I guess the driver wasn't paying attention. When he couldn't stop in time, his car plowed into the back end of the Happy Tyme giant ice-cream cone, which ended up cramming into the side of the Future Farmers of America hay wagon."

"Like a dog chasing its tail," grumbled another volunteer, this one a college student named Chris who had a knack for being in the wrong place at the wrong time. Accident-prone Chris had had the misfortune to land on the bottom of the six-person pile-up in the rowboat, with the consequence that his wire-rim glasses and his dignity were severely dented.

"Except this time the dog caught itself and had a collision with its own tail end." Taking in the spectacle of Chris's glasses slowly sinking to the left, Jo had a hard time keeping the laughter out of her voice.

With several helping hands, they managed to clamber down off the whale to assess the damage. Although Junior tipped forward more than he had when they started, and the blowhole was bent, there was no major injury otherwise. Stanley and Chris and a few of the others got to work righting the whale's nose, as parade watchers and participants milled around with a high level of curiosity.

What had been a fairly orderly procession was now a semiparalyzed mob of noise and confusion. Over one shoulder, Jo could hear bits and pieces of a John Philip Sousa melody as some band bravely tried to carry on. The music was accompanied by the shrieks and whinnies of the Centaur Arabian Corps, where ornately dressed riders were hanging on gamely to keep their horses from rearing and bolting. Then there were shouts from forty or fifty Shriners, formerly pedaling an incredibly long bicycle, and now attempting to unwrap their vehicle from around a tree and to retrieve the forty-odd gold-fringed fezzes that were littering the landscape.

This was clearly the most excitement Freedom Lake had seen in a long time.

Abandoning the repair site, Jo wandered back and perched on the fin of the whale to watch Miss Fish Fest's ill-humored efforts to rebend her hair into its former style and to jam herself more completely into her wrinkled, twisted dress.

"Lord," Jo muttered under her breath. "Looks like they're going to have to call out the earth-moving equipment."

Dragging herself away from the slapstick comedy of the too-large girl in the too-small dress, Jo heard a voice call out to the people pounding on the whale's nose, inquiring as to who was in charge there.

If someone was asking for authority figures, it must mean a decision had been made on whether to cancel the parade or try to get it going again. Rising, Jo dusted off the bottom of her cotton skirt, which had a long rip on one seam and a length of lace hanging off the hem. Well, she wasn't going to win any awards for best dressed, now was she? She patted the whale's tail fondly. "Stay put, Junior. I'll be back."

The owner of the loud voice strode forcefully her way, angling through a crowd of parade-goers. Even though the sun was partially in her eyes, she could see he was wearing a dark suit and a blinding white shirt, which seemed to Jo much too formal and too hot for this kind of activity. It also reinforced her belief that he was a parade official.

Except that as he got closer, she saw how beautifully he was dressed. She hadn't expected anyone from Freedom Lake, Minnesota, population 1,452, to wear Perry Ellis suits. Not that she would know a Perry Ellis suit if it fell over her, but she knew she had the right idea, if not the right designer. The tall, slim man in the nice suit was dressed to kill, and he was headed her way.

"Excuse me," he said politely. From at least a foot above her head, he regarded the young woman dubiously. Taking in her generally disreputable appearance, he wondered if he'd made a mistake. But he was sure this was the one the others had said was in charge. And there was no way to infiltrate Water Works without locating the boss, even if said boss was a tiny thing who looked about twelve and had something hanging off her skirt. Best to make sure before he went any further. "Are you in charge of this group, miss?"

No one ever called her "miss." She hadn't the vaguest idea what they *did* call her, but it wasn't that. In response to the unaccustomed formality, she put on her best and most sincere face. "Yes, that's me," she said lightly. Her hand swept the scene, indicating the chaos up and down the street. "Although there isn't much to be in charge of at the moment."

He smiled. "I see your point." After a pause, he offered his hand. "If you have a minute, I'd like to talk to you. I've been reading a piece of your literature."

"Oh." It never occurred to her that someone might actually want to hear about the hazards of water pollution in the midst of a madhouse. "Of course."

Hastily, she stuck her hand into his, and shook it with confidence. His hand covered hers easily, and he held it firmly, warmly, looking right into her eyes. Shading her eyes, she tried to return the stare, determined not to be intimidated. He seemed nice enough, with a forthright, friendly manner, and an absolutely lovely smile that flashed even whiter than his shirt. He wanted to talk about clean water, and she could go on about that for days if necessary. What was there to be intimidated by?

As he leaned forward, he blocked the sun well enough that she recognized him. She should have known immediately. Who else but a politician would wear a suit and tie to a small-town parade? And he really hadn't changed that much since the first time she saw him, when she had been fifteen years old and had dropped a water balloon on his head. He was still tall and slim, still had thick, blond hair without an appreciable part and was still very handsome in a polished, political sort of way. Her lips curved into a smile. "You're Neil Hawthorne, aren't you?" she asked, adding as an afterthought the words that had become inextricably linked to his name in the press. "The heir apparent."

He stiffened, biting off a terse retort. The newspapers were running this "heir apparent" stuff into the ground, intimating that he would be the party's choice to succeed his uncle as governor. And they made it abundantly clear that Neil didn't deserve that kind of preferential treatment. With a governor uncle, an ex-senator father, a grandfather who'd been mayor of Minneapolis and assorted other Hawthornes in other influential positions over the years, the press was sure that all Neil needed was the Hawthorne name to buy himself whatever office he wanted. Hardly flattering.

The very idea of the "heir apparent" label made him seethe, probably because there was a grain of truth in it that he didn't care to think about. But facing Jo, he made a conscious effort not to let it get to him. He had learned at his father's knee that a lazy grin and a manufactured twinkle in the eye could give anyone a Teflon coating.

As Neil scraped up a grin and a twinkle, he noticed the curious look she was giving him. "Have we met before?"

"Well..." Jo paused, turning to face him more fully. "Sort of. You used to date one of my sisters, and I'm afraid the rest of us spied on you. And I—" She faltered as a large party of Shriners hurried by, and then lowered her voice, trying not to embarrass either of them as she explained why she knew him. "I lobbed a water balloon at your head once when you were kissing my sister. I'm Jo Wentworth. Alexandra Wentworth is my oldest sister."

"You're kidding."

His eyes flickered down to hers with a kind of shock. For the first time, he lost a tad of his self-assurance. It was one thing to contemplate deceiving someone you didn't know

and had no connection to. It was quite another to pull one
over on a person whose sister you used to date.

Alexandra Wentworth. Good grief.

It had been a long time since he'd thought about that
particular fiery redhead, who, as he recalled, had dumped
him for a hockey player with a puck scar on his cheek. Alexandra. The very name said it all. She had been the extravagantly beautiful object of his affection for one summer
almost ten years ago, the summer between graduating from
college and starting law school. She was gorgeous, flashy
and came from a crazy family with sisters coming out of the
woodwork. He vaguely remembered the water balloon incident, after which Alex heaved a clump of dirt and grass at
an upstairs window and earned herself a shower of giggles
and taunts of the "naah-naah" variety. He had thought
then that all of the Wentworths were a little batty. And this
was one of them.

He shook his head. Maybe his memories were out of
whack, but he couldn't imagine two more different people
than Alex and Jo Wentworth. He looked more carefully at
the small, delicate woman in front of him. Her shoulder-
length waves were a careless mixture of browns and golds
and reds, barely combed, with long bangs tipping over her
forehead. Freckles dotted her nose. She wore no jewelry and
no makeup to enhance her wide, warm brown eyes. If she
was pretty, it was in a natural sort of way, but nothing ap-
proaching her sister's drop-dead glamour.

"We're very different," Jo remarked tactfully, as if
reading his thoughts. "It works better that way."

"I can understand that. More than one Alex would be a
strain on any family."

She smiled up at him, knowing she shouldn't be enjoying
herself so much. Shouldn't she be outraged, and snapping
at him in Alex's defense? She loved her older sister and the
rest of her family with a ferocity she otherwise reserved for

good causes. Jumping to their defense was something she did fairly often since they tended to be misunderstood on a regular basis. No one ever said it would be easy being the only sanguine member of a rather feisty family.

But in this case, Neil was right. More than one Alex would have been a real pain in the neck. In fact, just one Alex was often a pain in the neck. In all honesty, she couldn't lambaste Neil for telling the truth, could she?

"I suppose I should be flattered," he was saying. "Not many people would remember me from having seen the top of my head once."

"Well, actually, I probably wouldn't have recognized you from that alone. But you do get your picture in the paper quite a bit. And I saw you speak last year at a rally for the homeless." She met his eyes with an admiring look that was in itself a compliment. "You were a last-minute substitute for the governor, but you were awfully good."

He was inordinately pleased that she had liked his speech. As a matter of fact, he'd liked that one himself. "Thank you," he said with genuine warmth. "To tell you the truth, subbing for Uncle John is getting to be a way of life. I was even riding in the parade today as his stand-in."

"Oh, of course. I hadn't considered why you might be here. You were in the parade." Stanley's words came back to her, about a politician in front whose car smashed an ice-cream company float. Startled, she asked, "It wasn't you, was it?"

"What?"

"The crash."

He was definitely confused by the rapid subject change. "Excuse me?"

"I thought you might have whiplash or something. I didn't see the Happy Tyme float, but I imagine any collision can be dangerous."

Light dawned. "Oh, I see what you meant. You wondered if I was in the car that hit the Happy Tyme float. No, that was the mayor of Freedom Lake. I was a few cars behind him, and we got stopped just fine."

"You're lucky. It's a good thing your uncle wasn't in your place, don't you think? I mean, as ill as they say he is." Jo chattered on, oblivious to his reaction. As she would have with any new acquaintance, she asked whatever was on her mind. "Is it true that he's going to resign? And you'll be appointed to replace him?"

Her questions snapped him back to reality. He wasn't supposed to be chatting with this woman, getting chummy and letting his guard down. She was not an old friend; she was a means to a politically expedient end. If he started to like her, he would feel like a real creep using her beloved group for his own purposes.

"No truth whatsoever," he said with precision. He redirected the conversation to more useful turf. "But what about Water Works? Weren't you going to tell me about the group?"

"Oh, right!" Edging over near the whale's nose, she launched into a familiar explanation of the organization she headed, stressing the importance of their mission in the face of government budget cuts and new disasters every day, new rivers and lakes becoming contaminated by carelessness or violation of existing laws.

Jo shook her head sadly. "Right now, the situation is the pits." Gazing up at her fellow volunteers on the float, her expression changed to pride and hope. "As you can see, we're a very young group. In fact, most of the volunteers are still in college. But Fern up there—the one with the gray hair and the Keep it Clean T-shirt—is our senior member. She gives us some class. Don't you, Fern?" she shouted.

"Sure, honey, whatever you say." The older woman waved gaily, although it was obvious she couldn't hear Jo from up on the top of the whale.

"She's our unofficial den mother," Jo said as an aside. "Anyway, what we do is mostly boring stuff like canvassing and petition circulation, but we try to work in a little watchdogging on companies we know have been violators in the past. And we're pushing to increase public awareness of the problem. That's what the float is for."

His eyes held amusement as he surveyed the length of the giant whale. It was bright blue, with a fuzzy appearance attributable to the rough edges of the tissue paper used to make it. They had given it a cheerful smile, a black blob of an eye and a fin that flipped smartly into the air. Like the volunteers who were hammering the blowhole back into place, the Water Works whale exuded a sense of humor and a positive attitude.

Under other circumstances, Neil might have considered joining this group just for the fun of it. Hammering and laughing into the sunshine of an unseasonably warm May day, they seemed to be having a terrific time together. He watched them almost wistfully.

But he had other reasons to get inside Water Works, and they had nothing to do with fun. His father had taken him aside at a recent family gathering and given him strict orders to get close to the Water Works operation. Then the elder Hawthorne had gotten mysterious, telling Neil only that because of the clean-water group's recent flurry of publicity, his involvement would prove to the media there was more to Neil Hawthorne than a famous last name. Details, his father promised, would come later, when the time to proceed drew nearer.

Well, he didn't have details, but the time was here. He took the plunge. "How would you like a new volunteer?"

Jo had been hoping his interest would lead to that question. "Of your caliber, I would love a new volunteer. How many hours can you give us? What would you like to work on? When can you start?"

He shook his head, smiling in spite of himself. He'd have to be careful not to let the rather jaded remnants of his conscience take on new life around Jo. She was so genuine, so enthusiastic about her cause, it was going to be tough to be a spy in her camp without feeling like a real jerk.

"Sorry, Jo, but I don't know any of those answers yet. I mean, I didn't expect to get stuck in a parade and run across a worthy cause I felt like volunteering for."

That much at least was true. It had been a lucky break to discover his target group here at the parade and as much a captive of circumstance as he was. Although it set his father's timetable up by a few weeks and forced him to launch the project without knowing any of the background, the chance to make contact and get inside Water Works under cover of the chaotic parade was too good to pass up.

"Hey, everybody," Jo announced in her loudest voice, which was actually quite loud given her size, "this is Neil Hawthorne, a new volunteer."

Most of the people climbing over the float waved or smiled, and Jo pointed out who was who. Neil quickly lost track of the names she was reeling off. There were bright, enthusiastic people crawling all over the float. He hadn't joined Water Works as much as been engulfed by it.

A tall blonde in red sweats and high-topped sneakers came bounding up, followed closely by a curvy redhead wearing a hot-pink short set and a determined pout.

"Jo," the blonde commanded, "you're in charge of this organization. Do something about Eliza. She was batting her eyelashes at every available man in the crowd, and I am going to be absolutely ill if she doesn't stop."

"Oh, Jo, Kit's being silly. I was bored, and I decided to meet people."

Kit narrowed her eyes. "Eliza, large, ugly, hairy men on motorcycles are not 'people.'"

"Oh, pooh. He wasn't that big or that hairy, and he was kind of cute." Grinning her way around her companion's ill humor, the little redhead flipped long curls over one shoulder and flashed big green eyes at Neil. "Who's this? Where did you find him?"

"Eliza! Stop batting your eyelashes this instant!"

"I'll bat my eyelashes anytime I feel like it!"

As the argument continued, Neil turned to Jo. "More of your volunteers?" he asked dryly.

"More of my sisters," Jo answered with a laugh. "Meet Kit and Eliza."

He wasn't sure he really wanted to know, but curiosity got the best of him. "How many of you are there?"

"Sisters? Five all together. You've met the three of us today plus Alex, and that only leaves Maggie, and she's the sanest one of the bunch." Jo flashed him a quick smile. "See? You're over the worst part."

He wanted to ask if they were really as screwy as they seemed, ranging from small Jo with the large ideals and torn skirt to the one who flirted with hairy men on motorcycles. Instead, he inquired politely if they were all involved with Water Works.

"Eliza's a volunteer, and Kit is our adviser on publicity and advertising. Having a float in the Fish Fest parade was her idea."

"Oh, I see." He nodded at Kit, who would have been lovely without the daggers she was staring at her younger sister. "The whale is great."

"Thank you," Kit responded primly. After one fierce glance at Eliza, she seemed to warm to her topic a bit more. "Actually, I have lots of good ideas for promoting Water

Works. Why, I could generate ten times the publicity Jo's getting now, if she'd let me go all out. We've barely scratched the surface."

"Oh, really?" He eyed Kit more closely. Water Works and its recent publicity were what he had been told to investigate. Mentally, he etched Kit's name on his list of people to look into once he knew more about this undercover scheme.

Eliza crossed her arms over her chest and scowled. "Come on, Kit, quit monopolizing the conversation, will you? I want to know who this gorgeous hunk is, and why I haven't ever seen him before."

Jo's lips curved into a wry smile. "Eliza, meet Neil Hawthorne. I think you were twelve when we threw water balloons at him. You missed. I didn't."

Both Kit and Eliza said "Oh," drawing out the syllable significantly.

Kit recovered first. "Nice to see you again, Neil. You're much better looking from this angle."

"Thanks." He glanced over at her in confusion. "I think."

"Neil, dear," Eliza began in a silky little tone, linking her arm through his, "why don't you join us for the fish fry? I don't think this dumb parade is going anywhere, and we might as well leave, don't you think?"

Carefully, he extricated his arm. "Thank you for the offer, but I'm afraid I'm already spoken for."

"By whom?" As the married sister, Kit had the freedom to pry if she felt like it.

"By Miss Fish Fest. Have you seen her? The governor was supposed to crown her at the fish fry after the parade and be her escort for the evening. I'm afraid she's getting me instead."

"Have fun," Kit said with a malicious grin.

Jo elbowed her sister, but Kit started to laugh out loud, and it was infectious.

"What's wrong with Miss Fish Fest?" Neil asked innocently.

Before Neil knew it, all three sisters were laughing hysterically, pointing weakly down the street to the purple convertible and making no sense whatsoever.

Neil looked from one face to the other, but he remained mystified. Were all the Wentworth women crazy, or was he missing something?

Chapter Two

The time had come to find out the whys and the wherefores.

Early Monday morning, Neil braced himself in front of the dragon lady his father euphemistically called a secretary. He tapped his fingers on an indecently long expanse of mahogany and looked right into her eyes. "Is my father in?"

She raised a painted-on eyebrow. "Do you have an appointment?"

"I'm his son. I don't need one."

From what he'd seen of the Minnesota Corporate Charities Fund Building, he wouldn't have needed an appointment if there were fifteen of him. Except for a lot of thick carpets, potted palms and dark, abstract art, the place was empty. The elder Hawthorne had founded the Minnesota Corporate Charities Fund shortly after his retirement from the U.S. Senate. Neil had visited the opulent MCCF offices a few times, but not in a long while. He hated the dragon lady, and he wasn't that fond of his father, either. He figured it was a classic case of father-son antagonism. Or maybe just a son who disliked bowing and scraping like the rest of the world whenever Byron Hawthorne, still addressed as Senator Hawthorne as a sign of respect, opened his distinguished mouth.

"Tell the old man I'm on my way in."

The dragon lady leaped to her feet to try to block his path, but it was too late, and Neil was too fast for her. He could feel her glare hit him right between the shoulder blades, but he strode on into the inner sanctum.

His father looked like a statesman: tall, impressive, with great teeth. That had always come in handy around election time. As his son entered the room, Byron Hawthorne stood with the sun behind him, casting a halo of omniscience on the top of his smooth gray hair and the shoulders of his impeccably tailored gray suit. "Hello, son," he said heartily, gesturing broadly with one hand. "Please, have a seat."

Neil always felt like turning tail and bolting when his father pulled this elder statesman routine. How unworthy of a Hawthorne son, yet he had never learned to deal with the concrete evidence of his own future. It was a sobering experience to look into his father's eyes and know he was headed on exactly the same path. Without much enthusiasm, he sat as commanded in the upholstered leather chair opposite his father.

"I'm in," he said.

"In?"

"Water Works. The sleepy little clean-water operation you told me to infiltrate. I volunteered on Saturday. So I'm in."

"I see." His father leaned back in his leather chair, balancing his fingertips together. "A bit ahead of schedule, aren't you?"

Neil shrugged. "I had a perfect chance to get in without arousing suspicion. I took it. Any problem with that?"

It was his father's turn to shrug. "I suppose not. What next?"

A small, rather grim smile hovered around Neil's lips. "I was going to ask you that. I want to know why you think spying on Water Works is the answer to my political prayers.''

The ex-senator paused, proffering a box of cigars, waiting until Neil declined and then allowing himself the time to choose one and roll it slowly, carefully between his fingers. It was a routine the two of them had acted out countless times. Always the cigars would be offered, and always refused.

Byron Hawthorne lit his cigar and drew on it with studied detachment. "So you've established a means to get inside. Good. Good. And you already know it involves the publicity they've been getting."

Neil set his jaw with irritation as the first burst of cigar smoke blew across the desk. "Yes. You told me that much, and I checked it out. All the press they've gotten has been positive. They came out sounding like real public avengers. I don't see why you'd want me to investigate that."

"Oh, they sound like heroes all right." Byron Hawthorne shook his silver-gray mane sadly. "The question is whether they are heroes . . ." He paused for emphasis, pursing his lips. "Or liars of the worst kind."

"Liars?" Neil thought of Jo Wentworth's wide, honest eyes. "What do you mean?"

Now his father leaned forward across the desk and got down to business. "Twice in the last month they've stumbled across big environmental messes. They say they caught ChemCo red-handed leaking waste into the Mississippi, and got a tip that Red Metal Manufacturing had dumped toxic waste in half a dozen lakes in the northern part of the state."

"That's what the newspapers said," Neil added.

"ChemCo and Red Metal say different. Fact is they're screaming their heads off that they were set up."

Neil began to get the picture. "And ChemCo and Red Metal happen to be big supporters of the Minnesota Corporate Charities Fund, not to mention Hawthorne candidates, don't they, Dad?''

"You included, my boy, when we manage to convince you to run for something." Flicking ash from his cigar into a cut-glass tray, the ex-senator squinted at his son. "The point is, both ChemCo and Red Metal say toxic waste was diverted from their normal dumping process and purposely left elsewhere for Water Works to find."

After a puff he continued, "It happens that the Minnesota Corporate Charities Fund is the major means of support for this Water Works outfit. We at MCCF feel a certain responsibility to the corporations who provide our monies to screen out groups who commit fraud on the public."

Neil sat up straighter. "I must have missed something. Who said anything about Water Works committing fraud on the public? ChemCo and Red Metal say they were set up, okay, but who says Water Works is the culprit?"

"I'm saying it now," his father declared. "The folks at ChemCo and Red Metal are people I trust. If they say they were set up, I believe them. Now who would have stolen toxic waste and dumped it but Water Works itself, to get the publicity?"

Who indeed? He had to admit, it made sense. "They dump the stuff, then pretend to find it, act all horrified and self-righteous. Lots of good press, lots of contributions..." Neil narrowed his eyes. "Yeah, it fits."

Tilting back in his oversized leather chair, the ex-senator took a long drag on the noxious stogie. "If these people are faking pollution for publicity, I want to know about it. They won't get another dime out of MCCF."

"All right." Neil decided that he wanted all the cards on the table. When ordering him to volunteer at Water Works, his father had said that Neil's political future depended upon it. But why? "What does this all have to do with me?"

"It's perfectly simple, my boy. Your uncle's health is precarious at best. He plans to offer his resignation in two months, and Helen Lindquist will move up to the governor's spot. I want you to replace her as lieutenant governor. Your stint at Water Works will pave the way for that appointment." Puffing away on his cigar, the ex-senator exuded supreme confidence. "Right now, the media has painted you as an inexperienced political hack who is depending on his family name to get ahead. Neither the new governor nor the party can afford to appoint you with that kind of sword hanging over your head. It smacks of nepotism of the worst kind."

"It *is* nepotism."

His father ignored that. "If, however, you uncover a scandal at Water Works, you will shine in the press as a do-gooder, a dragon-slayer, honest Neil Hawthorne who saw a wrong and righted it."

"Enough to make strong men weep," Neil added sardonically.

"Laugh if you will, but it never hurts to be a hero." The elder Hawthorne shook his head. "I know you're not keen on the lieutenant governor position because you don't feel you've earned it. Well then earn it, damn it! Go uproot the place, give us a good scandal and get the damn press off your back for good."

Neil thought again of Jo's open face, and the sprinkle of freckles across her nose. He leaned back and inquired softly, "What if there's no scandal to uncover?" He fixed his father with a level gaze. "What if Water Works is completely clean?"

"They're not. They're a bunch of dirty tricksters. You mark my words."

A glint of humor touched Neil's cynical gaze. "You haven't met Jo Wentworth. Somehow, she doesn't seem like the dirty trickster type."

"Wentworth?" The senator's steely gray eyebrows rose in mild surprise. "Ah, yes. Josephine Wentworth. I hadn't made the connection. She's one of Lilah Wentworth's girls, isn't she? Look anything like Lilah? Damn fine woman."

"I have no idea. But she doesn't resemble her older sister, that I know. I used to date her. The sister, that is. As for Jo, she seems a little goofy, but nice enough."

"Is there a problem?"

Exhaling slowly, Neil mulled over in his mind the morality of investigating Jo Wentworth's group right under her nose. He'd feel a lot better about it if she seemed the type to stage pollution accidents for the publicity. She didn't. He said finally, "I don't know if there's a problem."

"Come on, Neil," his father growled. "Do a little public service. If there's something rotten at Water Works, it deserves to be uncovered."

Neil couldn't argue with that. He didn't much like the idea that one of those friendly volunteers, or even the gray-haired lady, was tossing nasty chemicals in streams and lakes just to get Water Works' name in the papers. It was a lousy way to behave.

On the other hand, if Jo's beloved group wasn't hiding anything, he'd find that out, too, and tell his father that MCCF had better fund Water Works into the twenty-first century as an apology.

One way or the other, Neil would get some answers. And if it garnered him some favorable press for once, who was he to quibble?

COLLISION WAS BECOMING her middle name.

In the week since the parade crash, Jo had been running into things. Especially Neil Hawthorne.

Take last Monday morning for example. Following her usual practice, she had gone barreling backward out the front door of the Water Works office, pushing it open behind her as she said goodbye to the room at large.

Only instead of dashing out the door, she'd crashed—right into the hard, unyielding length of a well-dressed man.

Turning around, she'd looked up into pale green eyes the color of a stormy ocean, and faltered in her litany of apologies. She remembered thinking what a strange and interesting color those eyes were.

Then, thank goodness, he'd said something, and she had realized it was just Neil, so she'd abandoned the "I'm sorry" routine and gushed all over him with welcoming remarks.

If that were the only time, she could cheerfully have forgotten the whole thing and forgiven herself for turning the poor man black and blue.

But yesterday again she'd bashed him with her backpack on the way out of the office. Since she was carrying heavy hiking boots in it at the time, Jo would have bet that she was turning his long, rangy body all sorts of unique colors. Added to that was the fact that these crashes were the only impression he had of her. Colliding at the door seemed to be the only time they were both occupying the same space.

She felt worse that he was so nice about it. Both times he told her it was no problem and she wasn't to worry about it for a second.

Worry? Ha! She had begun to rethink her entire theory of life. She was always in a hurry; that was the way she liked it. She had a theory that leisure time created sloth, that given a normal person's schedule she would end up perpetually in a bikini, sunning in the backyard, as sinfully lazy as a turtle on a rock. So far her theory had not been put to the test because she had never had problems with her hectic life-style. Until now. Now it seemed like living in the fast lane could be injurious to other people's health.

Jo sighed, slid her hands inside the pockets of her overalls, and gave the Water Works door a long, serious look. In less than an hour, she would have to give up the clean-water cause for the day and hightail it across town to a happy hour soirée being given by Grand Affairs, the Wentworth family party-planning company. Recently, she had backed out of a few too many Grand Affairs functions, and her mother especially was not pleased. Because of the time crunch today, her first impulse was to bound right in and get to work, yet here she was, hesitating, wondering if Neil was on the other side of the door.

"Hello."

Wheeling, she exhaled with relief. Thank goodness he was safely behind her. "Hello, Neil."

He took in the faded overalls with rosebuds embroidered across the top pockets, the pink T-shirt underneath, the soft scattered red-gold waves and the bulging backpack slung over her arm. Backing away a step or two, he raised his hands in mock surrender.

"I'm so sorr—" she began.

"No, no, please," he cut in, immediately regretting his little joke. "Don't apologize. I told you, it's—"

"No problem. I know."

She gave him a tentative smile, and he matched it. He put out a hand to shake, and she took it.

"Perhaps it would be the smartest move to go in together," Jo suggested.

Neil laughed and held the door open, neatly sidestepping as Jo and her odious backpack waltzed into what they charitably called the Water Works headquarters. It was really only a big, crowded room, full of overflowing bookcases and old dinosaurs of desks. Taking in the chaos, Neil sighed.

Three floors up in an unfashionable building in Minneapolis, the office shared its neighborhood with students, actors, a Vietnamese restaurant or two and a bookstore where the owner's cats snoozed in the window next to the books. The area held echoes of coffeehouses and vegetarian cafés, of folksingers and flower children hawking handmade jewelry on the streets.

Oh, it fit Jo and her band of volunteers all right, but it made Neil feel like the underhanded interloper he was.

The office itself was stuffy and blazing hot from the sun pouring in at the windows. There were papers everywhere, stacks of them, and a set of filing cabinets the size of a Buick. He'd thought that in all that stuff, he could've found some shred of evidence of wrongdoing. Not yet, anyway.

So far, in a week's time he'd managed to skim a lot of innocent files, chat with several seemingly innocent volunteers, and find out absolutely nothing. Since Jo was the head honcho, he felt sure she would be able to provide some clues on what, if anything, was going on around here. But because she was always in a rush, and usually in when he was out and vice versa, he hadn't been able to pin her down and get a decent conversation started.

It was maddening.

From gossiping with Fern, the sweet, grandmotherly lady who manned the phones, Neil had found out that Jo was a dynamo who got a lot accomplished even on the fly, ate plain yogurt for lunch and preferred to go without shoes whenever possible. From the rest of the staff he picked up vibrations akin to idolization. No one had an unkind word for Jo. Terrific.

Well, today she was here and so was he. Fine time to get his investigation moving. He moseyed over to her desk with calculated nonchalance.

"Got a minute, Jo?" He gazed down at her, giving her his most honeyed politician's smile, guaranteed to knock the socks off recalcitrant voters.

"Sorry," she returned cheerfully without even looking up. "Busy."

He persisted. "Jo, I've been in and out of here all week and I haven't had a chance to talk to you yet."

"Oh, dear." Her face took on the apologetic expression he knew so well. "I'm sorr—"

He sighed. "Don't say it. Please?"

"Well, what is it you need to talk about?"

"Anything." The word came out before he'd had a chance to think about it, but he realized that it was true; Jo and her freckled face intrigued him enough that the topic of conversation didn't seem that important. But, of course, the topic *was* important. He got himself on track quickly. "Actually, about Water Works. About who does what and how it's done." To make it sound like less of an interrogation, he added, "An orientation, I guess."

"Oh, I see." She slid a Sierra Club appointment book out of her top drawer and flipped it open. "Today is an absolute wreck for me, but I'll set aside a block of time for you, I promise. How about tomorrow? Oh, dear, tomorrow's Saturday, and I promised to set up the Tonetti twins' double wedding and then do Muffy Morgan's birthday party at the zoo. Monday, then. Monday for sure." She glanced up. "Monday okay with you?"

Her words passed him by in a blur as he found himself staring at the top of her head, trying to distinguish all the different colors. When she looked up, he held her gaze a beat longer than necessary, taking in for the first time the golden hazel shade of her eyes. Unusual. And very pretty. Why hadn't he noticed before what beautiful eyes Jo had in that small, delicate face? Absently, he mused, "You know, your eyes are a very pretty color."

Heat flooded her cheeks. Honest to a fault, she said softly, "So are yours."

He laughed self-consciously, wondering what in the hell had possessed him to start this inane conversation, and backed away from her desk.

"Monday okay then?" she asked.

"Right."

Watching his retreat, Jo was perplexed. She liked Neil, and she'd known since her water-ballooning days that he was very good-looking. So why did it embarrass her now to compliment him on his eye color, and to accept a compliment in return?

Ever since she was old enough to be socially conscious, she had made it a practice to think of men as people rather than that nemesis, the opposite sex. It made them so much easier to deal with. But each time she'd bumped into Neil, she'd found herself speculating on just where on that very nice body bruises might show up. And in the oddest development of all, she found herself wanting to look more closely into his green eyes, to get a handle on what the color reminded her of.

Propping her chin in her palm, she stole a glance across the room at Neil, only to find that he was staring back at her with the same confused expression she felt on her own face.

Fern called out loudly, "Josephine! One of your sisters just called. She says you're late again and would you haul your body home ASAP."

Happy to take the diversion, Jo began to gather up her things. Cruising toward the door, she tossed "Out for the rest of the day," over her shoulder at Fern.

"Don't forget we're picketing the capitol at six o'clock," the ever-vigilant Stanley shouted from across the room. Dark hair fell into his eyes as he stood up behind his desk.

Hopping on one foot as she slipped her pink tennies on, Jo asked, "Who arranged TV coverage?"

Chris brought his brows together, tipping his wire-rims even farther over to one side. "Why shouldn't we be on TV? We deserve it."

"You are coming, aren't you, Jo?" Stanley pleaded.

"Of course."

Fern contributed, "And remember, punctuality is next to godliness."

"I think that's cleanliness," Jo amended gently. Fern loved to dispense platitudes, whether or not they made a whole lot of sense. No one except Chris, who hadn't seemed to have learned the art of tact, had the heart to fuss about it. After a fond smile for the older woman, Jo made her way out the door. Successfully through, she hoisted her backpack and broke into a grin. She hadn't run into anyone today. A minor victory.

Bemused, Neil watched Jo dance out the door, wondering how one small person could pack that much energy into the space around her. The office seemed flat, as if she'd taken all the zing with her when she sped away. He shook his head, asking no one in particular, "Is she always in that much of a rush?"

"Like a chicken with its legs cut off," Fern supplied sagely.

On that note, Neil decided to get back to the filing cabinet, and to officially cross Fern's name off his list of suspects. It was hard enough to mistrust someone who looked like a grandma in a soup commercial, but it was downright impossible to think that a space cadet like Fern was masterminding a campaign of publicity stunts.

A chicken with its legs cut off? Good grief.

NOT FAR FROM NEIL, a member of the staff smiled with secret satisfaction, savoring the knowledge that Ed's little diversion was planned for tonight. A shiver of excitement and anticipation shook the hand holding the Water Works pen.

Tonight. The surprise on the faces of the other volunteers was going to be something to see. And what would Ed pull? Would he call in a bomb threat? Or something more mundane like shouting obscenities?

Whatever the stunt, it would make Water Works the talk of the town. Tonight.

Chapter Three

Her youngest sister, Eliza, was champing at the bit when Jo finally got home. Eliza threw open the front door of the large, vaguely Victorian, Wentworth house and assaulted Jo with, "Well, it's about time!"

Jo took in her younger sister's appearance, from the floppy white bow in her hair to the white pinafore, to the lace-trimmed anklets and white flats with bows on the toes. "What's all this?"

"It's the white party," Eliza said anxiously, reaching out to bodily pull Jo inside. "You know, the RoRo and the Boats party—everyone's supposed to wear white."

"Oh, good grief." She'd been aware of the afternoon-and-well-into-the-night party Grand Affairs was arranging to celebrate the new hit album of rock sensations RoRo and the Boats. Since RoRo had started out as St. Paul's own Roberta Peterson, and the Boats had been her classmates at the posh Bartholomew Academy in Minneapolis, they were heavy hometown favorites. Jo knew about the party, but she wasn't aware that it had an all-white theme.

"Well, you can't wear that!" Eliza shook her head vehemently, sweeping long strawberry blond curls back with one hand, and turning up her nose at Jo's embroidered overalls. "But don't worry, I set out an outfit for you upstairs.

Just hurry, will you? The others left an hour ago, and they're going to be furious we're not there yet."

"I know. I'm sorry," Jo managed, as her younger sister shoved her up the stairs.

After all, she was a part owner in Grand Affairs and shared in the profits, and it was her duty to be there when they needed her. Stripping and redressing in the white dress on her bed, Jo considered her schedule. There had to be a way to squeeze more time into a day.

It was when she picked the bow up off the bed—one just like Eliza was wearing in her hair—that Jo took a look at the rest of the outfit her sister had provided. "Good heavens," she said aloud.

The dress was white cotton, all pins and tucks, with puffed sleeves, a dropped waist and a round, lace-edged collar. It was a size too big for Jo, but the style was loose enough that it didn't seem to matter. If, however, she wore the silly hair bow and the white shoes and socks lying on the bed, she would look like *Pollyanna, Part Two*.

"Jo, are you coming?" Eliza shouted up the stairs.

Resigned to the fact that it was too late to change now, Jo gathered the shoes and socks, disdained the bow and raced down the stairs to get to the white party.

Within minutes they were off in Grand Affairs' signature lavender van. On the outside of the van, swirling purple script proclaimed, "Make your next affair a Grand Affair."

"We're late, we're late," Eliza grumbled, until Jo told her she was risking being mistaken for the White Rabbit saying those particular words and dressed that particular way. Eliza only scowled at her and whipped around a corner at enough speed to put the lavender van on two wheels.

The entire Wentworth family—with the exception of Kit, who despised everything to do with Grand Affairs—was waiting when Jo and Eliza got to the hotel ballroom where the party was being held.

Oldest sister Alex threw out her lovely arms, fluffed her mane of dazzling red hair, announced, "Jo, darling, thank God you're here at last!" and wrapped her in a heavily perfumed embrace that made her cough.

Their mother, the always impressive Lilah Fitzgerald Wentworth, was not as kind. She wore her fiery hair short and full about the face; right now, it and she were crackling with dramatic energy. "Josephine!" she exclaimed in a rich, ringing tone, "we depend on you to do your part. It's hardly fair to any of us if you refuse to shoulder your share of the burden. What do you have to say for yourself?"

"I'm sorry, Mother," Jo offered meekly.

"That doesn't really ameliorate the situation, now does it?"

Lilah Wentworth was capable of going on like that for hours. Luckily, Maggie, second to Alex in age but second to none in authority, stopped by to put an end to the fuss. Tall, soft-spoken, not flamboyant in the least, Maggie was the de facto boss at all Grand Affairs gatherings, and she didn't put up with squabbles or any other wrinkles in her plans. Somehow she always managed to keep the rest of the family in line without antagonizing or threatening them. No one was quite sure how she did it, but they trusted Maggie to smooth things over and calmly run the show.

Right now, she draped one arm around Jo and the other around their mother. "We can discuss this later," she said quietly. "Mother, would you mind checking on the job they did on the ceiling?"

"Heavens no," Lilah responded grandly. "I'll see to it immediately." With a swirl of white silk, she turned as if to leave them, but then spun back for a parting shot. "You've gotten off easily this time, Josephine, but next time..." Only then, with a majestic shake of her coppery red hair, did she consent to leave, setting off to inspect the ceiling, where yards of pale-colored fabric had been suspended to create an elegant, rippling sky.

Having done her penance, Jo was just glad it hadn't gone on any longer. "I'm really sorry I'm so late," she told Maggie. "I just lost track of time this morning."

"Don't worry about it, kiddo. Everything is right on schedule, and no harm was done." Twisting the end of her auburn ponytail in one hand, Maggie checked her clipboard quickly. "We still need tablecloths and centerpieces set up. Do you want to do that?"

"Sure."

As she swung out thick white tablecloths and arranged wicker baskets of baby's breath and white roses, Jo hummed to herself, happy to be useful and glad her tardy arrival hadn't caused more of a controversy. She dearly loved her family, and it hurt to feel that she was letting them down.

From behind her, Maggie asked, "Are you finished, Jo? It's almost time to start letting people in. Here's the guest list. You and Eliza are on guard duty. And remember to keep out anybody who isn't wearing white. RoRo said not Prince, not Nancy Reagan, not even the pope if he isn't on the list and dressed in white."

Jo finished up her last basket of flowers quickly, scooping extra buds and bits of baby's breath into a box. She responded dryly, "I think the pope always wears white, so he shouldn't be a problem."

Maggie laughed. "And I'm sure he'll be coming to a RoRo and the Boats party."

"Who knows? Maybe he's a Boats fan." She lowered her voice to a scandalized whisper. "But you'd better get out of sight, Mags. Looking like this, you won't do at all."

Indeed, Maggie was defiantly dressed in gray jeans and a red rugby shirt. "Ah, but I'm in charge. That's why I get to hide in the kitchen with ear plugs, and you get to be on the front line. Have fun," Maggie said airily. With a quick wink, she turned and took off for the kitchen, her ponytail swinging gaily behind her.

"Coward," Jo called out.

From then on, a steady stream of party-goers kept Jo and Eliza hopping at the front doors. The guests themselves were somewhat surprising. Jo recognized several influential society matrons and company presidents, plus a hefty percentage of the Twin Cities' wealthy, young, hip crowd.

RoRo and the Boats had obviously decided to celebrate the release of their album with the jet set rather than the new wave.

Jo had only one gate-crasher to deal with: a surly teen with an orange mohawk who stuck out like a sore thumb amid the generally wealthy, well-heeled crowd. She figured if he didn't leave quietly, she could always tell him his hair didn't fit the color code. But he departed with only a few grumbles.

She was watching his orange hair recede down the hall when she heard Eliza testily inform a couple that their names were not on the list.

A cool, patrician voice responded, just as testily, "Check again, young lady. Not only are we most certainly on your list, but so are our son and daughter. We have lived on the estate next door to Roberta Peterson's parents for twenty years. Why, my husband was instrumental in getting RoRo her first job!"

Jo glanced over at the owner of the voice, a tall, elegant woman with a classic pageboy and a clenched jaw. The distinguished gentleman holding her arm asked coldly, "Do you know whom you're addressing, my dear child?"

Uh-oh. An unfortunate choice of words. Eliza hated the word "child" coming within twenty miles of her. A stubborn pout and a dark pink flush stole over her pretty face.

Jo interceded just as she sensed something ugly was about to burst from Eliza's lips. "Maybe I can help," she offered, brandishing her own copy of the list. "What was the name?"

"They're not there," Eliza hissed, and Jo elbowed her out of the way neatly.

"Hawthorne," the woman snapped. "Senator and Mrs. Byron Hawthorne."

"You must be Neil's parents," Jo said brightly. "How nice to meet you." Shifting her pen and clipboard to the other side, she offered her hand to shake. It was ignored.

Hearing that these were the parents of that dynamite Neil Hawthorne, Eliza muscled around to get in front of Jo. "We saw Neil at a parade recently. Did you know he used to date our sister?"

Senator Hawthorne looked from one face to the other without a trace of humor. In a tone that brought to mind the dressing down of an impertinent servant, he added, "Are we permitted to go in now?"

Quickly, Jo scanned the list. "Yes, please, go right in. Sorry about the mistake." She shot Eliza a disparaging look for creating a fuss when the names were there all along, as clear as day. Normally, she didn't believe in criticizing Eliza in public, but this was egregious.

"Look, Eliza—Senator and Mrs. Byron Hawthorne, right here on page two, right before Diana Hawthorne and then Neil. How could you miss all four?"

"Neil's coming?" Eliza inquired hopefully.

Jo glanced back at the list of names, finding the confirmation right there in black and white. "Oh, no," she moaned, "Neil's coming here, tonight." She looked down at the fussy little dress she was wearing and then raised doleful eyes to her sister. "And I look like Pollyanna!"

Eliza regarded her with suspicion. "Since when do you care what you look like?"

Their sister Alex, the very soul of fashion vigilance, chose that moment to make an appearance, looking smashing in a slinky white jumpsuit with gold braid epaulets. "Heavens, children," she drawled. "Why are you glowering at each other?"

"Jo is fussing about her outfit," Eliza announced indignantly, as if that were akin to changing one's name to Tanya and joining a revolutionary brigade. "And Neil Hawthorne is coming to the party."

Alex murmured, "Neil Hawthorne..." in a low, lazy voice. Her exotic emerald eyes narrowed as she tapped a sparkly gold fingernail against her lips. "Good lord, it's been ten years. How utterly appalling. But what a guy—gorgeous, tons of money—I think he even has a yacht. I wonder if he's still single?"

"Yes." Jo realized she had never considered that he might be married. "At least I think he's single."

"Hmm. Now that's something to think about. You know," Alex said suddenly, "I thought I recognized the people snarfing the chicken puffs. Now I know why. They're his parents and his snooty sister. Mommy, Daddy and what is the sister's name? Diana, I think." She sighed extravagantly. "Dull, dull, dull. And with their aristocratic noses ever so high in the air. North Oaks snobs, every last one."

It was Alex's business to know those sorts of things. If she said they lived in North Oaks, then it was a cinch they did. It wasn't so surprising that the Hawthornes would choose a prestigious area like that, no doubt living in the most palatial of its wooded estates, where deer munched calmly on the lawns.

Jo sent a quick glance over to the chicken puffs, where the Hawthornes were holding court. An elegant blonde who must be Neil's sister Diana had joined them. As Jo watched, her own flamboyant mother charged up to them, earning herself a kiss on the hand from the ex-senator and stiff, frigid glares from the two women. Both cool, blond heads turned ever so subtly to the right, cutting Jo's mother without saying a word. That sort of thing didn't bother Lilah, who was still cooing at Byron Hawthorne for kissing her hand, but the unfairness of the women's reaction offended Jo's sense of justice.

It appeared that Alex was right. They did act like snobs, with polished smiles that didn't waver and polite disinterest in everything but themselves. *Jo*, she chastised herself immediately, *you don't even know them*. "Maybe they're shy," she said aloud.

Her sisters exchanged pitying glances and shook their lovely red heads.

"Sure, sweetheart, you keep looking for the silver lining. Meanwhile," Alex purred, "I'll look for Neil Hawthorne."

Squealing, Eliza demanded, "Who said you got first dibs? Jo and I saw him first."

Alex paid no attention, pooh-poohing Eliza with a careless wave of one hand. "I saw him ten years ago, darling Lizzie. So keep your charming paws off."

"Dibs? Paws? That's disgusting!" Hands on hips, Jo faced her sisters angrily. "I happen to think he's a nice person. He's one of my Water Works volunteers, for goodness sake. If you're going to talk about him like he's a piece of, of, ground round, well, I just don't know!"

With that, Jo stalked across the ballroom, deciding to put a little distance between her and her sisters before she smacked one of them.

Not too far from the Hawthornes, heaps of white-chocolate-dipped strawberries were displayed on tiers of cut glass. Thinking the display looked a bit bare, Jo arranged to have more strawberries brought out, and she even sneaked one off the tray, which was strictly against the rules at Grand Affairs affairs. Cheering herself up with the small gesture of defiance, she licked the chocolate carefully and scanned the room.

There were a lot of faces rustling around the fabulous white ballroom, but none of them was Neil's. Stealing another strawberry, she kept her eyes on the door. Was he coming or wasn't he? If he did, would Alex snap him up like one more hors d'oeuvre?

Jo wished the RoRo and the Boats performance would get moving, so the lights would go out and she could legitimately escape to the picket march at the capitol. She had been looking forward to seeing Neil, even given her goofy clothes, but now she was just as happy to miss him. Let Alex run rampant out of Jo's eyesight.

In a very few moments, the room went black except for the candles. An expectant hush fell, followed by the first strident chords from the round stage in the center of the room. Blue spotlights clicked on as a curtain swirled and parted, revealing RoRo and the Boats, bright, electric, shocking blue against the completely white backdrop of their audience. Tonight, even RoRo's hair was blue.

Jo gasped, as did many of the people around her. Blue hair? Blue spiked hair? Apparently RoRo would stop at nothing to be the center of attention tonight. It was a cinch that the wealthy in-crowd wouldn't try to rival blue hair.

Ducking into the kitchen, mumbling about blue stegosauruses, Jo asked Maggie for a spare set of keys to the van.

"Jo—" Maggie began sternly.

"I know, I know," Jo returned before her sister could lecture her. "But I'm needed at a very important picket march. I promise I'll come back to help clean up, okay? This party could go on all night, maybe all weekend, and I should make it back in plenty of time. Believe me, Mags, it's for a really good cause."

"It's always for a good cause." Maggie gazed at her younger sister indulgently, with just a hint of exasperation.

They both knew that Jo would go anyway; the only question was how much of a fight Maggie planned to put up before letting her sister off the hook. "Just go," the elder redhead said with a sigh. She shook her head and dug the keys out of her jeans pocket, fixing Jo with a firm stare. "But you'd better be back here for the cleanup. I'm saving a garbage bag just for you."

"Promise." Catching the keys in midair, Jo sent her sister a smile and ducked out the back door.

Within minutes she was sitting behind the big wheel of the lavender Grand Affairs van in her pinafore and lace anklets. It made her feel strange, as if she were a child driving a grown-up's car. But there was no time for worries like that. The others were probably already at the capitol, and with any luck, they'd be too busy marching to notice that their leader was dressed like Sweet Polly Purebread.

As she parked the van, she saw them, dutifully circling at the bottom of the capitol building's huge stone steps. Jo hurried to join them, picking up a large sign that read, "Keep Our Water Clean" and cutting into the line of marchers behind Fern, Chris and Stanley.

Chris had taped his glasses to even out their previous imbalance, but Jo could see his ominous glare around the obstruction. "It's about time," he grumbled.

"Better late than never!" Fern shouted happily. Obviously excited by the protesting process, she reached around her sign to give Jo an encouraging pat on the shoulder.

Jo smiled. "Nice to see you, too."

She was saying hello to the people around her, reading the signs and getting into the spirit of things, when Neil appeared out of nowhere and squeezed in beside her. He was, as usual, beautifully dressed. Somehow, the "Stop Dumping Now" sign didn't really go with the outfit. She stared at him, wondering what he was doing at a picket march on a

Friday night when he had been expected at the hottest party in town.

Actually, he was feeling very relieved that she'd finally shown up. Earlier in the day, he'd told himself he would keep an eye on the march and press the other volunteers for information. Missing RoRo Peterson's party hadn't been much of a hardship, since he'd thought RoRo was a brat when she was growing up next door and she seemed to have gotten worse since becoming a star. Besides, he resented being told what to wear.

Now he smiled to himself, admitting that walking around in a circle carrying a sign was not exactly stimulating stuff. For some reason, seeing Jo was. He prompted, "Are you going to say hello?"

"Of course. I'm sorry. I'm just surprised. I didn't expect to see you here." She didn't add that she was glad he was here instead of at the white party getting devoured by her sisters.

"Why are you surprised?" he asked good-naturedly. "Don't you think I'm the protestor type?"

"Now that you mention it, no." She saw the hurt look he adopted, and she laughed, patting his arm. "But you can be a protester if you want to." Surveying him up and down, she offered, "Next time, maybe you should dress down. It tends to make you seem more sincere if you're scruffy."

"Scruffy?" He dropped his jaw in feigned shock and switched his sign to the other shoulder to get a better look at her clothes.

"Don't say anything," she warned. "It was a last-minute choice and it isn't even mine."

"I like the bows on your toes."

"I'm glad someone does." She gazed up at him with a soft smile curving her lips, thinking that Neil was really a very nice person, and nothing like his snooty family. Even more than being pleased he'd stayed out of her sister's clutches, she was glad to have him here just to get to know him better.

"All right," he said, "I give up. Why are you dressed like that? I wouldn't have picked you as the white anklets type."

"I'm not. But I was at a party with an all-white dress code, and I had to borrow clothes or risk getting kicked out."

He raised an eyebrow, quite frankly surprised. "RoRo's white party? You were at RoRo's white party?"

"I'm afraid so."

Shaking his head, he moved her protest sign to one side so he could catch her eyes. "You're the RoRo type even less than the white anklets type, Jo. Do you have a secret life I don't know about?"

Her eyes danced as she maintained the teasing mood he'd started. "It wasn't that weird a party. I mean, your parents were there. How strange could it be?"

"You met my parents?" He sighed. "How bad was it?"

"I didn't say I met them exactly. It was more like I saw them and they saw me."

"Hmm. That sounds ominous. What did they do, snub you?"

"No, of course not," she assured him. It wouldn't have been nice to tell him what she really thought of his parents. "Besides, I wasn't there as a guest. Hired help only—my family owns the catering company that was giving the party."

"Ahh. So you do have a secret life."

She smiled, crinkling her nose and bringing some of her freckles closer together. "Mata Hari had a secret life. I just have an extra job."

"No wonder you're so busy all the time."

"'Fraid so."

Tipping his sign against hers in a toast of sorts, he said in a mocking tone, "But you managed to tear yourself away from RoRo's scintillating party to show up here and do your duty for clean water.''

"Well, of course."

Suddenly, out of the corner of her eye, she caught a glimpse of a burly man in a plaid shirt stalking toward them. When she turned, she realized that he was coming rather quickly considering the size of the metal bucket he was carrying.

"Who in the world is that?"

The Water Works staffers scattered in and out of his path, demanding to know who he was, but he ignored them, racing toward Jo. With barely enough time to turn and take in the fact of his existence, she recoiled and heard herself scream as slimy, greenish water splashed out of the man's bucket and all over her.

"What? Why?" she shouted, as the swampy water ran in rivulets down her hair and all over Eliza's pristine white dress.

A cameraman dashed up to Jo, determined to capture the now newsworthy incident.

Out in front of her, the man with the bucket knew he had the spotlight. Squinting small, piggish eyes, he jumped back, shouting insults at the marchers, swinging his bucket around in a wide arc and egging on all comers.

Oblivious to the man's threats and the erratically swinging bucket, Neil threw himself at him, trying to keep out of reach of the bucket and yet manage to throttle the man at the same time.

Standing there dripping, still half in shock, Jo watched Neil race past her. There was a savage light in his eyes and his jaw was clenched into a murderously hard line. He looked like a different person than the one she'd just been chatting with. The transformation of charming Neil into Rambo was almost more shocking than the initial attack of the crazy man with the water.

Then she saw the bucket land a sharp blow to Neil's ribs, and panic rose through her stupor and pressed against her chest so that she couldn't breathe.

At her side, Chris, the volunteer with the bent glasses, decided to join in. He handed Jo his glasses for safe-keeping, and she accepted them in a daze, gripping and twisting the frail wire rims between her hands. Then he, too, jumped into the melee. He pulled another one of the volunteers into action, and the two of them edged behind the area of the scuffle to try to dislodge the bucket while Neil kept the man occupied from the front.

Meanwhile, the cameraman, now joined by friends from other channels, kept cranking. Jo sent them a few desperate glances, wishing they were anywhere but here, recording the chaos that her demonstration had become.

As Neil lunged for the man's throat from the front, Chris knocked the guy off balance from behind, and they all tumbled to the ground in an unruly, writhing heap.

Without thinking, Jo passed off Chris's glasses and dashed into the wrestling match to pull Neil out of it. Just as he brought back his hand to smash the slime-wielding thug in the face, Jo grabbed him.

"No more," she pleaded, dragging him away. "Look, they're sitting on him. He's not going anywhere."

He nodded, breathing so heavily he was unable to speak, and leaned down to rest his forehead on the top of Jo's head for a moment.

She stood very still, aware suddenly of every breath she took, of every ragged movement of Neil's rib cage. She found herself wanting to put her arms around him, to soothe away the horrible image of violence and blood letting, to touch her fingers to the scratch on his cheek and the bruise on his jaw and magically make them disappear.

She wanted to close her eyes and block out everything but the two of them, to somehow safeguard a niche of good feelings in this maelstrom of bad. Instead, she held herself absolutely motionless, wondering what this could mean.

"Are you okay?" he asked finally, raising his head as he bracketed her face with his hands and carefully took stock.

"I'm fine." She took a deep breath. "Just sort of in shock and kind of wet. But you, are you all right? He hit you with the bucket..." Tears sprang to her eyes, born of outrage and anger. "You must be hurt."

"No, I'm okay, really." He extracted a handkerchief from his pocket and gingerly dabbed at the moisture on her face, tilting it up with a hand cupped lightly under her chin. "Poor Jo," he said softly, "slimed on television. Now you'll make the news for sure."

He didn't mention the fact that he, too, would make the news—bloodied, messed up and brawling, with all the self-control of a raging bull. His father would no doubt have a few choice words to offer on the effect of this little escapade on the Hawthorne public image. The elder statesman would never understand that it was simply something that had to be done.

The main group of picketers crowded around them, chattering excitedly and rehashing these amazing events, and Neil released Jo to welcome the others.

"Wow, Neil, you were like a wild man," Stanley declared, slapping him on the back. A broad grin broke through his dark beard. "Better get home so you can see yourself on TV."

"Yeah," someone else chimed in, "Water Works is big-time news now!"

Although Neil accepted the hearty congratulations of the group, there was something about this little drama that didn't feel right. The words "Water Works is big-time now" reverberated in his brain. Once again, the clean water group would find itself the apparently unwitting beneficiary of a publicity bonanza. How convenient.

He realized now that the timing of the man with the bucket was awfully good. The guy had started his mean and ugly routine at the same moment the cameraman arrived. And if the thug really wanted to harm Water Works, he'd done a terrible job. When TV viewers turned in, they'd see poor, tiny, defenseless Jo, dripping with slime and looking about as pitiful as they came. Water Works couldn't have asked for better publicity if they'd staged it that way.

The question was, did they?

If only he could remember who'd been where before it began, or think of any suspicious behavior he might have seen. But he'd been too busy exchanging pleasantries with Jo to pay any attention to anyone else. Damn it all to hell. He had gotten inside Water Works for one reason only. Now he'd blown his best opportunity to see one of their dirty tricks in operation, and for what? So he could become pals with a woman who, for all he knew, was the very dirty trickster he was looking for.

No, he told himself, that was ludicrous. It was not Jo.

At that moment contemplating her unkempt attire and the odor emanating from it, Jo wrinkled her nose and lifted her hands away from her body. She knew it was partly from shock, but she began to giggle. "I smell like old tuna. I'm surprised every cat within ten blocks isn't howling at my skirt."

There was no return laugh or even a chuckle from Neil. He was still berating himself for missing his opportunity to break the case. "Sorry, Jo," he said absently. "I didn't hear what you said."

"It was nothing important." She hesitated now that she had his attention. "But I would like to say thank you. Thanks for..." For what? She didn't want to thank him for committing acts of violence on her behalf. But she was touched that he had immediately jumped to her defense, that he had used his handkerchief to wipe the muck off her face and most of all, that he had acted like a friend. Holding his gaze steadily, she stretched up and gently kissed his cheek, right under the nasty scratch he'd gotten in the fight. She said simply, "Thanks for being here."

Neil's eyes softened and a tiny smile lifted one corner of his mouth. "You're welcome."

She backed off a step, wiping already-dry hands on her wet dress self-consciously. "Well, I'd better get going. I have the company van and I have to take it back to the party."

His smile widened. "You're going to be a real hit at the party smelling like that."

"That's not the worst of it." Mischief flickered in her eyes. "Wait until Eliza sees what I did to her dress."

Chapter Four

Jo could address a crowd of one hundred protestors or stare down an angry opponent without a twinge, but giving blood was making her woozy. Leaning back against the pillow, she rearranged the folds of her skirt—anything to keep her eyes away from the needle in her arm, and away from the blood slowly draining out of her body.

"It's for a good cause," she muttered, prompting the nurse who was extracting the blood to ask if Jo was okay.

She smiled weakly. "I'm fine."

The nurse happened to be a friend from college, and she was the very one who'd begged Jo to show up and lend her blood to this No More Military Madness sit-in. Protesting American involvement in Central America, the group had dragged half a blood mobile unit into the middle of their U.S. Representative's office. They intended to send the blood to help supply hospitals in beleaguered nations. This kind of demonstration was virtually arrestproof, since the congressman's staff couldn't very well call the police to throw out people engaged in the humanitarian act of giving blood. Although the congressman's receptionist looked as if she might like to try.

Actually, Jo thought, the poor woman was probably upset that her routine for the day was shot, her office was a zoo and the protestors showed no signs of leaving. Beginning to feel guilty for the stress inflicted on the receptionist, Jo rose on an elbow and asked her friend, "Are we almost done?"

"No." The nurse pushed her back onto the pillow unceremoniously. "It isn't my fault if you have slow blood. Just relax, will you?"

A telephone rang in the background as Jo tried to lie still. After the obligatory opening remarks, the receptionist covered the receiver and demanded, "Is there a Josephine Wentworth here? There's a call for her on my phone, and whoever it is will not take no for an answer."

Jo raised her hand politely. "That's me."

Sighing, the woman reluctantly toted the receiver around her desk, uncurling the long cord as she came. She set her lips primly as she thrust the receiver at Jo's available hand. Grumbling, "I'm not doing anything more for you people," she spun smartly and returned to her desk. "And don't stay on the line all day, either."

"Sorry," Jo offered, and then said hello into the receiver.

"Jo, is that you? Thank goodness I found you! That creature who answered was positively iceberg city, and I wasn't at all sure she'd let me talk to you, even though I told her it was simply crucial. I need a favor, Josie dear, and if you even think of turning me down, I swear I'll perish in a puddle of misery."

Alex. Even without the hyperbole, Jo would've recognized her oldest sister's dramatic drawl immediately.

"Alex," she hissed, "what are you doing calling me here? I'm in the middle of giving blood, for goodness sake. And how did you find me?"

"Oh, la-de-da! That Fern person knew where you were. And you know I wouldn't have tried to reach you except in case of absolute emergency. That's what this is. Truly."

"Okay, okay. But make it fast, will you?" Jo was starting to sweat under the evil eye of the receptionist, who obviously wanted her phone back. Not to mention the fact that she felt silly talking on the telephone lying flat on her back with her blood draining away.

"If I speak any more quickly," Alex retorted, sounding peeved, "I won't make a particle of sense. Do you want to help me or not?"

Jo sighed. "Of course I'll help you, Alex. Tell me what you need."

"All right, then." Mollified, Alex said delicately, "Here's the thing—I need you to fix up the teeny-weeniest date for me."

"Date?" Since when did Alex, also known as the Siren of St. Paul, need Jo to get dates for her? "With whom?"

"With Neil Hawthorne, of course."

"What?" Shouting into the phone, Jo bolted upright, only to be severely pushed back down again by her friend the nurse.

"You said he hangs out at that dreary Water Works place of yours, didn't you?" Innocence and charm dripped from Alex's voice. "So all you have to do is hop right over there and persuade darling Neil to treat the woman of his dreams to lunch today."

"You?"

"Of course me," Alex snapped. "Who else is the woman of his dreams?"

"Oh, Alex..." Jo balanced the phone between her shoulder and her ear and dropped her free hand over her eyes. Unfortunately, she couldn't think of a single rational reason to give Alex that would explain why this scheme sounded so repugnant.

Generally, she'd do anything short of cutting off her arms if it meant helping out a family member. But the prospect of setting up a date for her sister and Neil struck her as simply disgusting. She avoided the issue by not saying anything for a long pause.

"What gives?" Alex demanded. "Do I surmise you are less than happy to do this one small favor for your beloved sister?"

She could feel defensiveness raise her hackles. "Of course not. But why does it have to be Neil? And why do I have to participate?"

Alex let out a long "Ahhh," as if she'd suddenly discovered the theory of relativity.

"What is that supposed to mean?"

"It means you don't want to set me up with Neil because you've got the hots for him yourself."

Jo blasted up like a shot. "It does not!"

The nurse glared at her and shook her head in disgust, but she pulled out the needle anyway, then briskly stuck a cotton ball over the hole and bent Jo's arm up over the cotton. "Happy now?" she muttered. "Like taking blood from a jack-in-the-box."

Jo paid no attention. "I do not have the hots for anybody," she said fiercely.

"Well, it's not like I'm blaming you. He's perfect if you like them blond, good-looking and rich. Which *I* do. But I didn't think you did."

"I don't." Logically, Jo knew that her type ran to honest but poor—the kind of man who'd never consider buying you a fur coat or eating lettuce picked by downtrodden workers. Even if Neil seemed nice enough, she had no idea where he stood on these or other issues. In her mind, physical attraction was an outgrowth of a meeting of minds. "Getting the hots" for someone she barely knew was an impossibility. "Definitely not."

"Good. Then there should be no problem. Get me Neil Hawthorne."

"Or perhaps just his head on a silver platter?"

Alex was oblivious to the snippy tone Jo had adopted. "Heavens, no. That would be leaving out all the good parts.

But, you know, Jo, if you did happen to be harboring some mysterious attraction to Neil—''

"I'm not.''

"But if you were,'' Alex persisted, "even in theory, I think you'd be better off trashing the notion. Neil isn't your kettle of fish, sweet sis—trust me. I can assure you he isn't going to grow up and join the Peace Corps like the heroes of your modest fantasies.''

"Fine,'' Jo returned. Why did her sister's theory make her feel so cranky, when she wasn't interested in Neil in the first place? "Why can't you bag him without me? Surely your deathless charm can do the trick all by itself.''

"Jo! I can't believe I'm hearing correctly! Is this the Jo I know and love, flinging barbs at her own sister, when that sister arranged for the Minnesota Vikings to do a video for hunger? When that sister wheedled thousand of dollars in pledges for clean water?''

"Stop, please, Alex.'' It was all true; Alex had come through for her again and again. And snooty remarks were not Jo's style at all. Her temper began to wilt and she twisted her fingers in the loose folds of her flowered skirt. "Why is this so important to you?''

An exaggerated sigh came wafting over the line. "In case you've forgotten, one month from today is my birthday. I am going to be *thirty*, Jo: the big three-oh. In one lousy month. And I haven't had a date in two weeks.'' She began to sound a little hysterical. "Can you imagine the fragile state of my psyche?''

Actually, Jo could well imagine. She had realized long ago that men and social engagements were the cornerstones of Alex's self-image. Of course, Jo didn't like encouraging that state of affairs, but she had given up any hope of steering Alex into more meaningful interests.

Nonetheless, she gave it a shot. "I don't suppose you'd consider filling your life with good works instead of men?''

"It's easy for you to talk," Alex said with a miserable little catch in her voice, "sitting there on the sunny side of twenty-six. But *I'm* knocking on thirty's door. If I don't get something started immediately, I will be over the hill. And the only decent prospect I have is a ten-year-old connection to Neil Hawthorne. I tell you, Jo, I've sunk into deep depression, and you're the only one who can help me out."

"But, Alex, this is all so silly."

"Ah, Jo, how little you know of the real world…" Alex's voice dropped. "I'm already starting to fade."

A picture of Alex popped into Jo's mind. There she was, pale and without makeup, dressed all in black. Her hair, now a dull brown, hung unkempt around her face. This imagined Alex sat next to the phone, lifelessly leafing through photo albums of past glories. In Jo's imagination, a teardrop slid slowly down Alex's wan cheek, to splash on an old picture in the album.

Jo felt herself begin to waver under the combined pressure of her sister's tale of woe and her own exaggerated conscience. "And you're sure you haven't gone out in two weeks?"

"Would I make up something that demeaning?"

Jo reflected. Alex was not one to dwell on her own flaws, and a lack of admirers would seem to her like the end of the world. Desperation time, indeed. Jo bit her lip, already giving in, knowing she couldn't let her sister down even though she didn't like it one bit.

"You will do it, won't you?" Alex pleaded. She rushed on, not giving Jo a chance to say no. "You fix it up, and I'll meet him at your Water Works place at one, all right? See you then. Oh, and thanks again, Jo. 'Bye!"

And Alex was gone, leaving Jo holding the congressman's phone and the dubious honor of roping Neil into lunch with her sister. Not that it would require much roping. Grimly, Jo decided that Neil, like every other red-blooded male in the universe, would no doubt jump at the chance to escort the lovely, exciting Alexandra Wentworth anywhere, anytime.

And, given her deep sense of family loyalty, Jo should have been jumping at the chance to brighten her sister's mood during this time of gloom.

So why was Jo the one feeling gloomy? And why did suggesting one lousy date make her feel like she was being disloyal to *him*?

Neil was a casual acquaintance, maybe even a friend if you counted the moments they'd shared at the capitol, but that was it. She didn't know how he felt or what he thought or even what kind of person he was deep down. If Alex wanted him, what difference did that make to Jo?

Must be loss of blood, she decided, still holding her arm bent over the cotton ball as she got to her feet for the first time in twenty minutes. Clutching the receiver in her other hand, she put on her best and nicest smile and faced the congressman's receptionist.

"Would it be okay if I used your phone one more time? It's for a good cause."

IT WAS ALL SET UP. All she could do now was wait. And mope and worry and bite her nails and feel like a pimp. A pimp? She told herself that was a bit extreme.

Neither Neil nor Alex had arrived at the office yet and Jo considered ducking out before they showed. But, no, this fix-up date was proceeding under her auspices, and she would have to see it through.

It was really dumb to let it bother her this much. She loved her sister; she liked Neil Hawthorne a lot. So where was the problem? And why did it give her a headache every time she thought of their sharing a cozy tête-à-tête?

Be strong. Alex needs you.

As Jo wrapped up the pep talk in her mind, Alex made her entrance. Loaded with a ton of gold jewelry, she was beautifully decked out in a clingy turquoise summer dress with a flippy skirt and a big bow on the derrière. Far from the bleak, pathetic creature of Jo's imagination, Alex was as flashy and spectacular as ever.

"He's not here y—" Jo began, but Alex cut her off, sashaying up to Jo's desk and inquiring in a stage whisper, "Who's that?"

Jo's gaze jumped from one innocuous face to another around the office. "Who?"

Alex gave her a slow predator's smile. "Tall, dark, beard. With the great hands."

Heavens. Who noticed the hands of the Water Works volunteers? But tall, dark and bearded could only mean Stanley. Jo sent a quick glance to his hands. They looked normal enough to her.

"Who is he?" Alex persisted, sizzling a dazzled Stanley with her hottest come-hither stare.

Jo gazed on in amazement as Stanley rose from his desk like a zombie and slid across the room toward Alex.

"H-hello," he managed. He wiped a hand on his No Nukes T-shirt and extended it to Alex. "I'm Stanley Hoffmeyer."

"You're adorable," Alex whispered. "Alexandra Wentworth. So pleased to make your acquaintance."

Tossing a thick cascade of red hair over one shoulder, Alex slipped her elegant hand into his and Stanley brought her fingers to his lips.

Kissing her hand? Jo smiled. Alex in action was truly something to behold. And poor Stanley—sweet, industrious boy that he was—never had a chance. He was now hopelessly, irrevocably lost in Alex's spell. Murmuring softly in his ear, Alex linked her arm through his and led him to the door.

With a tiny frown, she paused, and turned back to her sister.

"Tell Neil— Oh, I don't know." Alex waved a hand in dismissal, jangling several bracelets. "Say there was an unexpected hitch in the proceedings. That sounds good."

"No problem." Jo dashed to the door to close it behind her sister and her new escort. Once it was safely shut, she clapped her hands together and whooped out loud.

"What are you so happy about?" Chris grumbled. He was perched on Fern's desk while the two of them carried on an M&M poker game. Chris must have been losing, if the black look on his face and the pile of M&Ms in front of Fern were to be believed.

"Stanley and my sister Alex!" Jo enthused. "Love at first sight!"

"Well, my goodness." Fern's gray eyebrows rose dubiously. "They're not exactly two peas on the head of a pin, now are they?"

"Well . . . no." Peas on a pin or in a pod, they weren't. In fact, they were a very curious mismatch. Stanley was good-looking, she supposed, in a shy and inconspicuous way, but she'd never thought of him as a man, just as a pal, another Water Worker. And the moment you took in his faded jeans, T-shirt and grubby sneakers standing right next to Alex's sensational slinky dress and pounds of gold, you knew they didn't belong together. Nevertheless, Jo kept an open mind. "They saw past the obvious, that's all. There's more to an attraction than a superficial thing like appearance."

Chris sneered and threw down his cards. "Yeah, they're a real match made in heaven."

"Okay, okay—so they're an odd couple." To herself, she said, *Better than Alex and Neil. Probably better than Neil and me.* She dismissed that. "Anyway, all in all, I think it's sweet."

"I think it's gross." Chris's contributions were succinct, if unpleasant. "Unless there's a lot more to our pal Stan than he's been showing us, that woman will eat him alive."

"Now wait just a minute. 'That woman' is my sister, you know."

"What's going on around here?" someone asked from the doorway.

Jo recognized the smooth, cultured voice, and she wheeled back in that direction, sending her long, full skirt swishing around her calves. "Hi, Neil!" She realized she was beaming and she quickly adjusted her face to a more suitable expression for the bearer of bad tidings. "I'm sorry, but—"

"Wait a second here," he interrupted, raising a hand. "Didn't you call me less than two hours ago and beg me to take your sister to lunch? I could swear I just saw her leaving, draped all over Stanley Hoffmeyer."

"I know." Jo tried to look sorry. "The truth is, something came up and Alex can't make it. I hope you'll accept my apologies."

"I have a feeling it's Alex who should be apologizing." A mischievous smile turned up his lips. "Can you imagine? Me, rejected."

Jo was instantly contrite. "Oh, dear. You don't feel rejected, do you? It really has nothing to do with you, I promise. It's just Alex being Alex. She doesn't mean anything by it."

He wondered what to make of this situation. When he got the call asking him if he would please, please take her sister to lunch, it made him mad, pure and simple. It wasn't something he could exactly put into words, but he'd thought he and Jo were hitting it off nicely after the mess at the capitol, that they had begun to be friends. He had no interest in sticking Alex into the middle of that. Alex was ancient and not particularly memorable history as far as he was concerned, and lunches with *that* Wentworth would only be a waste of time. But Jo had asked it as a personal favor, and so he'd gone along, figuring it couldn't hurt his mission to get into Jo's good graces.

So here he was, delivered on the hoof for a lunch date, only to find that his presence was no longer required. He didn't know whether to be miffed or relieved.

But Jo now owed him one, and he could see from the woeful expression on her face that she felt bad about the whole thing. Might as well be practical, and take the advantage fate was throwing his way. He told himself that an hour with Jo might yield valuable information, and he shouldn't pass up the chance. It didn't hurt that he might actually enjoy the time spent in her company.

"I'm not sure how you can make this up to me," he said lightly. "I came all the way down here just to do you a favor, and I got stood up. It doesn't seem fair to me."

"Oh, dear." And fairness was practically sacred to Jo. She considered her options. Although this fiasco was Alex's idea, Jo was the one who'd dragged Neil down to Water Works to carry it out. Therefore it was her responsibility to put things right. Resolutely, she offered, "How about if I take you to lunch? I know I'm not Alex, but I'll try to be entertaining." She smiled as she imagined herself juggling or standing on her head as part of the lunch table entertainment. "I'll even treat. What do you say?"

"I say I'll let you assuage your guilt."

A playful spark lit his eyes as he held open the door, and she wondered if he, too, were envisioning Jo the Juggler. After hastily slipping into her shoes, she led the way.

They hit the street before she thought about where to go. It was a lovely summer day, so she preferred to pick a place within walking distance.

"The Wienery," she said aloud. "Perfect."

"Excuse me?"

"I've decided to take you to the Wienery, which is just what it sounds like. Great hot dogs."

"I thought you said the Winery."

"And you thought I was taking you to San Francisco for lunch?" She grinned up at him. "I hope you won't be disappointed. This isn't dinner at the Ritz."

Lunch with Alex would no doubt have required something continental and expensive, and Neil thanked his lucky stars he hadn't had to endure it. That was too much like business. Dashing out for hot dogs with Jo was more like playing hookey. He matched her smile. "Sounds great to me."

"Good. I'm starving."

She grabbed his hand and hurried him along the sidewalk, stopping to check on the cat sleeping in the bookstore window, and then pulling him down the street and into the restaurant of her choice.

The Wienery was a very small place, with a maximum occupancy of around ten. It had a black-and-white linoleum floor and revolving stools in front of a stainless steel counter, with pastel cups and plates and scattered plants as the main decor. It had an ambiance all its own.

And Jo loved it. After dumping Neil at one of the three tables—the red one—she ordered Chicago-style hot dogs with all the trimmings for both of them. When she settled down at the table, she wasted no time on niceties. She bit off a big hunk of her hot dog and grinned at Neil.

"Well, Neil," she said in an encouraging tone. "Tell me about yourself."

"I think you know all there is to tell," he returned quickly. "And besides, it's not very interesting."

Having sidestepped her question with practiced ease, Neil watched the enthusiasm she put into her eating with amazement. Why had he assumed that a meal with Jo would include green leaves and sprouts? He shook his head. She was more intriguing than he liked, leading him far away from the path of his supposed investigation. If he expected to get the facts his father wanted, he'd have to remember to look at Jo as a representative for Water Works, nothing more and nothing less. It was time to get down to brass tacks. But subtly.

"So," he led off, "how long have you been with Water Works?"

Flicking a few chunks of onion off her hot dog, she considered the question. "Since before the beginning."

"Okay." He laughed. "Do you want to explain that?"

"Sure." She took a big bite of hot dog and chewed it with gusto before getting on with her answer. "There was an informal group before I came along, but they didn't do much more than put on a one-day clean-up festival on the Mississippi. I got involved in that, and then I sort of pushed them into organizing."

He gave her a curious look. "You know, Jo, it's hard to imagine you as a bully, pushing people around. You're so—"

"Small?" she supplied, with a naughty light in her eyes. "It has been suggested that I have a Napoleon complex."

He smiled. "I'd buy that."

"Pooh." After swallowing the last bit of her hot dog, she began to cast covetous eyes at his.

"Here," he said with a sigh, sliding his basket over to her side of the table. "Take it."

"Thanks." She squirted a generous amount of mustard onto it, and then glanced up. "What were we talking about?"

"Water Works," he prompted. What else was there? But he knew he had to keep digging. "I've been impressed with your staff. Nice bunch of folks, don't you think?"

"They're great."

"Really involved in clean water, aren't they?"

"Of course. Why else would they work there?"

Good question. He needed to know if anyone seemed more interested than the others, if one of the volunteers was enough of a fanatic to make up his or her own rules. But how could he frame an inquiry like that?

He tried, "Have you known them long?"

"Only a few of them." Delicately licking mustard off her index finger, she remarked absently, "Chris was around before I was, and he brought Fern and Stanley along later. I think they're the only ones left from the original group. They're all from the same neighborhood, isn't that funny?"

"Funny? Yeah, sure," he muttered. He couldn't keep his eyes off that little pink tongue, darting out to dab at the yellow spot on her finger. He barely heard what she was saying.

"It turns out that all three of them lived in Westlake Heights. Do you remember when it was in the news?"

That penetrated, and he sat up, pulling his attention away from her finger and her tongue. "Minnesota's mini Love Canal. Some company contaminated their water and everybody had to drink bottled water for a couple of years. Property values died over night."

"Right." The discussion of contamination didn't inhibit Jo's appetite any, and she started in on Neil's French fries. "So I guess Fern and Chris and Stanley have good reasons to work for clean water."

He nodded, digesting the information.

"The other volunteers come and go. I guess they all have their own reasons. Then there are my sisters, of course." She rolled her eyes. "Much as I'd like to think they're around out of social conscience, I know they only volunteer because I ask them to. That's one of the nicest things about family loyalty—my sisters and I would do anything for one another."

Including a few dirty tricks to advance a sister's favorite cause? The Wentworth women were willful enough to try just about anything. Alex's ride off into the sunset with Stanley Hoffmeyer was evidence of that.

"This has turned into quite a different lunch than I'd anticipated," he mused.

"Different how?"

"You," he said, "instead of Alex."

"Oh, Alex." She had forgotten about Alex. Jo shook her head and pushed wayward hair away from her face at the temples.

It was all so confusing.

A few short hours ago, she had arranged to offer Neil to her sister like a virgin sacrifice. Not that she imagined Neil was a virgin, of course. Warmth suffused her face at the idiotic direction of her thoughts, and she ignored it and Neil's inquisitive gaze as she poked around in the basket of French fries.

Now that she'd shared lunch with him, she liked him even better than she had before, and she felt even worse that she had tried to foist him off on her sister. Was Alex done with him? Or would the Siren of St. Paul put Neil back on her hit list when she was finished with Stanley? Given Alex's mercurial mind, it was entirely possible.

These were truly rotten things to be thinking about one's own sister, and Jo chided herself for small-mindedness. If Alex decided, in good faith, that she wanted to pursue Neil, then Jo would, as a good and loyal sister, do her best to help out, providing that nothing dishonest or manipulative was involved. That had been her way of dealing with Alex in the past, and it had always worked out.

She reminded herself that the arrival of Neil Hawthorne on the scene was no excuse to ignore the rules of family solidarity.

Jo frowned. Did she really believe that? Did she care? Did she know if she cared or not?

She swore at herself. This kind of self-analysis was going nowhere in a hurry.

Concluding from Jo's annoyed expression that he had goofed by bringing up Alex, Neil changed the subject immediately, announcing, "I think you've killed that French fry, Jo. Maybe you ought to go to work on a new one."

She hadn't even noticed that she'd been crushing a French fry into the plastic basket, stubbing it out like a cigarette. "Good grief," she said brightly, sticking a phony smile on her face. Phony anything was against her principles, but it was the best she could come up with on short notice. Wiping her fingers on an extra napkin, she pushed up the sleeves of her baggy white cotton sweater and stood up abruptly. "We'd better get back to the office."

With a more amiable mood forcibly restored, Jo guided Neil along Cedar Street, the West Bank's main drag. They were within a block of the office when a long, battered blue car came screeching to a halt at the curb. It made a great show of honking, and the passenger door was vigorously pitched open as the two of them gingerly approached it.

"Friends of yours?" Neil inquired, surveying the sidewalk hopefully to see if the wreck of a car could possibly be honking at someone else. "I don't think anyone I know drives a car with that much rust."

Jo ignored him. That old Ford had been around so long it was almost a member of the family. "It's Gerald."

"Gerald?"

"Gerald Ford. Or I suppose it should be Gerald *the* Ford. He's my sister Maggie's car."

"He?" He didn't know why he bothered to ask. If they named their cars, why wouldn't they assign them genders in the process?

"He has to be a he if his name is Gerald," Jo pointed out logically. "Come on. Let's see who's driving. It can't be Maggie. She doesn't drive like a bat out of hell."

A perky redhead with pink flamingo sunglasses waved back at her from the driver's side.

"Hello, Eliza," Jo said calmly. "Were you looking for me? What am I late for this time?"

"A family emergency." Eliza sat up straight with self-importance. "I'm supposed to bring you home immediately."

But Jo was suspicious. "Is this something to do with Alex? I don't consider her social calendar an emergency, even if she does."

She heard Neil chuckle behind her, as Eliza said petulantly, "It's nothing to do with Alex. Get in, will you? And you have to bring him with you."

Now Jo was very suspicious. "What's he got to do with it?"

"I'm not telling. But his presence is absolutely required." Eliza fixed her older sister with a brilliant smile, and enunciated clearly, "Drop everything."

The magic words. Since the time they were old enough to fake their mother's voice and get one another out of classes, they had used those words as a code. "Drop everything" meant that a surprise was in the offing, and if you knew what was good for you, you'd go along meekly.

In a louder voice, Eliza demanded, "Will you hurry up and get in, Josie? But go in the back. Neil can sit up here next to me and keep me occupied." Sliding her sunglasses halfway down her nose, Eliza attempted to wink at Neil very slowly and provocatively.

"Is there something stuck in your eye, Eliza?" Jo asked dryly.

Always mature, Eliza responded by sticking out her tongue.

Nonetheless, Jo hopped in the back seat without another word. She'd lived with the other Wentworth women for over twenty-five years, plenty long enough to know that the spontaneous adventures they cooked up were well worth the price of admission.

When Neil didn't follow Jo into the Ford, Eliza said pointedly, "Him, too."

Jo poked her head out the window. "Your presence has been requested. Do you want to come?"

"What exactly am I letting myself in for?"

"I don't know. But not knowing is half the fun."

Noting the spark of mischief in Jo's eyes, he had definite qualms about this. But what the hell? What could a couple of batty redheads do to him? Gingerly, he folded himself into the car and shut the door.

"And you get to sit right next to me!" Eliza squealed, pinching his cheek and then whipping the big old car out into traffic. The pink flamingo sunglasses hovered on the tip of her nose, and she peeked over the top of them, focusing on Neil instead of the road. "Aren't you excited, Neil dear?"

The question hung in the air inside Gerald the Ford.

Chapter Five

They arrived at the Wentworth house to find strange things in progress. As Eliza slammed the car into the driveway, Jo caught a glimpse of her mother balanced up inside the large silver maple in the front yard, winding pastel streamers in and around the tree's branches.

"Good heavens. Mother's up a tree."

Eliza giggled and Neil's expression became even more doubtful. Jo leaned foward and patted his shoulder reassuringly, even as she tipped her head toward her sister.

"Is this the emergency, Ellie? Mother's stuck up a tree?"

"No, silly." A sneaky chuckle wafted behind the youngest Wentworth as she exited the car and bounded up the front walk toward the tree.

"I'm back, Mother dear," she sang out. "Is it all right to go ahead into the house?"

The Wentworth house was a peaceful, lazy-looking place, even if its occupants could hardly be described that way. Wondering why it was suddenly necessary to ask permission to go inside, Jo gazed up at the house where she'd grown up.

It was big and white, haphazardly built in the first place and added onto in the same casual spirit over the years, with a roomy front porch and an eccentric conical tower on one corner. Nothing matched, not the gingerbread trim around some of the windows, or the bricks in the crumbling foundation. Yet the house managed to hold itself together with a cheerful dignity that Jo found endearing.

Reminding herself for the umpteenth time to tell Maggie the place needed a paint job, Jo abruptly switched her focus to the silver maple in the front yard, where a big branch about halfway up was emitting an ominous cracking noise.

The overgrown maple had been there for years, brushing up against the window to Jo's room on the second floor. When the girls were young, they'd carved their initials in its bark and used it as a ladder to climb down from upstairs without their mother's knowledge.

"The tree's gotten a lot bigger," Jo murmured absently. Her mind slipped back to the time Neil and Alex had stood underneath it, entwined and all primed to kiss good-night. The other Wentworth girls disrupted Alex's dates as a matter of course, and they had concocted a great plan that night. When Alex paused under the maple for her customary good-night kiss, they were going to bean her with water balloons.

Jo had been leaning dizzily out the window, laughing breathlessly with her sisters. There she'd hung, desperately clinging to a slippery balloon and squinting as she aimed for the top of Alex's blazingly beautiful head. She was never sure she really meant to let go, but one of the others had jostled her and it was bombs away, whether she wanted to or not. Only she hadn't hit Alex; the airborne missile had veered from its target and blasted Alex's unfortunate date instead. Who was, of course, a handsome man named Neil Hawthorne.

Conjuring up the memory, Jo covered her mouth before she burst into raucous laughter all over again. Now that she knew Neil better, it was even funnier.

"You're thinking about the water balloon thing, aren't you?" he guessed.

Her eyes flashed back to his, reflecting guilt.

"And you still think it's funny, don't you?"

She nodded, fully aware that her eyes were dancing and her lips were curving upward into a malicious smile.

"Someday you'll get yours, Josephine Wentworth," he whispered.

As he spoke, a commanding voice from above rang out with "Josephine!" and they all craned their necks to peer into the tree.

"Mother?" Jo called. "I can't see you anymore. Where are you?"

"In the tree, of course!" her mother shouted. "Unfortunately, I find myself unable to get down gracefully. Send your young man up closer, will you?"

Earning Jo's eternal gratitude, Neil didn't bat an eyelash at being called her "young man." "Coming, Mrs. Wentworth," he said politely, and stepped forward like a good little soldier.

Suddenly, her mother came tumbling out of the tree. Lilah Fitzgerald Wentworth was a blur of thick perfume and green jersey knit—and then she was sitting on top of Neil.

"Oh, my goodness." Jo rushed forward to help her mother to her feet so that she could attend to Neil underneath. Never any good in a crisis, Eliza stood off to the side, howling with laughter and gasping for breath.

Jo gave her younger sister a disgusted look as she poked at Neil, praying that he hadn't broken anything. Lilah wasn't stout exactly, but she wasn't light as a feather, either. Fortunately, except for a glazed look in his eyes and rumpled clothing, he appeared to be in one piece.

As her mother rearranged her dress and patted her glorious red hair back into place, Jo tried to dust off the jacket of Neil's suit. "Mother, really! You might have killed him."

Lilah dismissed Jo's concern with a careless wave. "He was supposed to catch me. And look at him—why, he's so handsome he must feel dandy. Isn't that right, dear?"

Neil was so surprised by the whole sequence of events, he didn't know what to say.

"Your suit is a mess," Jo lamented, bashing at a few blades of clingy grass with a vengeance.

He caught her hands. "Thanks for helping, Jo, but I think I can manage. You're liable to do more damage than the fall did."

Instantly contrite, she mumbled "Oh, dear" and backed away.

"Don't worry." He managed a smile. "As weird as it sounds, I'm getting used to physical violence when I'm around you. It seems to follow in your wake."

"Who is this nice young man, Josephine?" her mother trilled, looking Neil up and down with coy glances.

He got to his feet and put out a hand. "I'm Neil Hawthorne."

His smile was unconcerned and charming, the one she remembered seeing on more than one occasion, and Jo breathed a sigh of relief. Rather than injured or even embarrassed, he seemed amused that her mother had dropped out of a tree and flattened him like a pancake.

"I'm very happy to meet you, Mrs. Wentworth. Now I know why your daughters are so...beautiful."

Jo felt sure his first choice was more on the order of "birdbrained" or maybe "bananas" instead of "beautiful," but she had to give him brownie points for having the presence of mind to come up with something positive. Smiling, she wondered what he thought of his unorthodox introduction to the Wentworth clan. Oh well, at least now he knew what to expect.

Meanwhile, her mother hadn't noticed anything wrong, and was purring all over him as she pulled him into the house, with Eliza not far behind.

Watching them, Jo couldn't help a shaky laugh. The members of her family were what they were, and she didn't make excuses for them. Nonetheless, she did feel a certain sense of foreboding about Neil's visit; so far, she'd been very unlucky as far as he was concerned. Putting her rather strange family into the equation was bound to make the problem worse.

She stripped off her shoes and wiggled her toes in the cool grass under the tree, expelling a long breath of contentment. Pushing up the sleeves of her loose white sweater, she bent over to pick up the rolls of crepe paper streamers her mother had discarded on the ground near the tree. There was a partial roll of pink and another in pale blue.

"Pink and blue?" Jo said aloud. Did this mean what it seemed like it ought to mean? What else could a drop-everything family surprise with pink and blue streamers mean? Her other concerns vanished as she pondered the mystery of the streamers. "Pink and blue," she whispered, shaking her head. Catching up the crepe paper, she raced inside after the others.

There was the normal jumble of Dresden shepherdesses and china cups on tea tables, of sprigged wallpaper and lace doilies and faded family portraits. But a few new items had been added to the decorating scheme.

In the front hall, big pink and blue balloons bumped and scattered, vying for space above Jo's head. Streamers in the same colors were looped along the stair railing, and a papier-mâché stork drooped from the bottom of the entryway chandelier.

The nature of the surprise had become crystal clear.

"Where is she?" Jo demanded, cutting around the door into the living room.

The person she was looking for was right in Jo's line of vision, sitting serenely on the Chesterfield sofa that had been sent west by Great-grandmother Fitzgerald in Queen Victoria's time. Seeing the beatific expression on her sister's face, Jo broke into a smile. At this moment, her sister Kit resembled an angel, with pale blond hair spilling around the shoulders of a bright red sweat suit.

"Kit, you sly dog!" Jo exclaimed. "You're pregnant!"

Kit nodded, looking rather tentative about all the fuss, and Jo dashed around three tables of knickknacks, expertly avoiding collisions, to hug her sister thoroughly.

"How are you feeling? How far along are you? When is it due? Our first baby!" Barely waiting long enough for answers, Jo launched into a few more questions. "Where's Riley? Is he dying?"

"Here," her brother-in-law announced as he slid in from the kitchen with a glass of water in his hand. He looked a little stunned, and his light brown hair was a mess, as if he'd just run his hands through it several times in a row.

Kit's expression changed from angelic to saucy as she winked at her husband. She whispered loudly to Jo, "I think he's still in shock."

Without waiting for Riley to comment, Jo hurried over to wrap him in the best hug she could muster. Kit's husband or not, Riley was a special friend, and Jo knew exactly how he must feel about this news. He had been in love with her sister for most of his life, but had had quite a struggle pinning down stubborn, hot-headed Kit long enough to propose. Now, married and sharing a baby, Riley was seeing all of his dreams pay off. This happy ending was almost enough to make Jo cry. Misty-eyed, she squeezed Riley. "I hope you know how lucky you are."

Riley's blue eyes crinkled at the corners as he ruffled his small sister-in-law's hair. "Yeah, but can you imagine Kit with a baby? This ought to be pretty funny."

Jo burst out laughing, Kit pretended to glower at her, and Riley laughed, too, in the process jiggling the glass of water he was holding in his outside hand.

From across the room, Neil took it all in, amazed. He'd never seen a family like this. It was a scene washed in love and affection, tempered by the slightly screwy outlook they all seemed to share.

First, there was Jo, as usual without shoes, arm in arm with her brother-in-law, bubbling over with laughter, and Eliza, balancing her silly pink sunglasses on the top of her head while she cooed and babbled on one side of Kit. The matriarch of the clan had taken the other side, and was midway through an impromptu lecture on proper prenatal diet.

There was chatter everywhere, mixed in with bobbing helium balloons and the rustle of wrapping paper as Kit gamely pulled bright-colored toys out of boxes, paying no attention to the people shouting in her ears.

Edging away slightly, Neil leaned against the door frame and tried to make himself inconspicuous. He contemplated slipping away to leave them to their private family celebration, but remembered he didn't have a car there, since he'd arrived in Gerald the Ford. Just as he considered cabs and how to find a phone in this madhouse, Mrs. Wentworth came floating by and pinched his cheek.

"Isn't this lovely, dear? Nothing like babies to bring a tear to one's eye. Of course, engagements are almost as much fun as babies, don't you think?" She waggled her eyebrows meaningfully at Jo, who was still standing over by Riley. "Now then, tell me, dear boy, how long have you known our Josephine? I can say with complete honesty that she has the best temperament of all my daughters, and is such a lovely child, don't you think?"

He recognized a predatory mother when he saw one, and he relaxed and smiled. *This* he knew how to handle.

Jo caught the gist of her mother's words from across the room and choked on the glass of water she'd appropriated from Riley. Had her mother mentioned engagements? Lord, what next? Stifling giggles, Jo made a move to get across to rescue Neil, but Eliza interrupted, all in a dither because Kit was thinking of naming the baby something Eliza didn't approve of.

"Rudyard, can you imagine? Rudyard! Have you ever heard anything more hideous in your entire life?"

"She's probably only teasing you, Eliza," Jo returned with less than complete attention. "Excuse me, but I have to discuss something with Mother."

"Wait! Look at these! Have you ever seen anything more adorable in your entire life?"

Before Jo could even see what had gotten Eliza so excited, her younger sister had swooped down on one of the gift boxes, snatched up two rattles shaped like tiny marimbas, and started to shake them in a Latin rhythm. She pulled Kit off the couch and into a makeshift conga line around the coffee table, and they hauled Riley in to join them. Their mother couldn't resist something that wild, and she took over the front of the line, shouting out instructions.

At first, Jo refused to participate. Neil was all by himself in the doorway, and she ought to at least talk to him, if not help him escape. She met his eyes hopefully, trying to gesture that she was coming over there as soon as she could make it without risking life or limb. He only smiled and shook his head, and then Riley grabbed her around the waist and shoved her into the conga line, and what could she do?

Soon she was laughing and kicking as enthusiastically as anyone, snaking around the furniture with this group of inmates let out for Latin dance lessons.

"Neil, come on! Get on the end!" she invited cheerfully, narrowly missing his shin as the wobbly line came kicking past.

He backed more securely into the door frame. "Looking good," he yelled out, trying to sound encouraging. What the hell was he doing here? He didn't even know these people.

"Excuse me."

Someone tapped on his shoulder and he turned to accommodate another body in the narrow doorway between the living room and the hall.

"What's going on?" the newcomer asked, in a calm, but seriously puzzled voice,

He knew immediately that she was related to the rest of them. The deep red hair and green eyes were his first clue, but it was mostly something indefinable, a sense of presence, that told him she was a Wentworth. This one was a good six inches taller than Jo, and her coloring was darker, but she had the same small, delicate features that stamped them from Alex down to Eliza. She seemed a good deal more reserved than the others, however.

"We haven't met," he shouted over the din. "You must be the fifth sister. Maggie, right? The one with the car."

Her expression became even more confused. "No," she said carefully, loudly, "I'm Maggie. The second sister."

"Excuse me?"

"Second—I'm second. Eliza is fifth. Who are you?"

It was obvious to Jo that Neil and her sister Maggie were having some sort of difficulty over by the door, because they were shouting at each other. Forcefully, Jo twisted the conga line and headed it over in that direction. If she'd had any sense, she would've dropped out the last time they passed Neil.

"Maggie!" someone cheered as they neared the doorway. "Have you heard the news?"

Then they were all hugging and smiling and congratulating each other, and Neil found himself grinning like a fool and nodding along with the others, even if he did feel like a party crasher. In his experience, the golden rule of family life was to smile politely and never create a fuss because a reporter might see you. But these people seemed to thrive on the fuss itself. Their mother, who might have been expected to be the most mature, was perhaps the worst offender. He certainly couldn't imagine his own elegant mother jumping out of a tree on top of a perfect stranger or kicking up her heels in a makeshift conga line.

He must have let his eyes light on Jo's mother while he was thinking about her, because she appeared next to him all of a sudden with avid curiosity stamped on her lovely face.

"You naughty boy," she said cheerfully. Completely ignoring the fact that she had abandoned him while she danced with her daughters, she chided him with, "You got away from me before I got answers to any of my questions!"

Just as Jo was about to corner Neil, she saw him get swept away by her mother. She put her hand to her forehead and heard her mother call him a naughty boy. If she wasn't concerned about how Neil was taking all of this, Jo would've laughed out loud at her mother's idea of social niceties in the eighties.

But at least Maggie had arrived. That sister could always be counted on to fix things.

"Maggie," Jo hissed, "I need help."

"Oh, no, not me." Raising her hands, Maggie started to back away. "I haven't got an extra minute for picket lines or sit-down strikes. Really. If I hear the words 'good cause,' I'll break out in a cold sweat."

With a hand on Maggie's elbow, Jo nudged her sister over into the corner behind a chintz wing chair. "It's nothing like that. Promise."

"Who was the guy in the doorway?" Maggie whispered. "Alex's latest?"

"He's with me."

"With you?" She glanced back and forth between Neil and Jo. "He doesn't look like your type."

"Who says I have a type?"

Jo's tone was a tad sharp, and her sister looked up in surprise. "Well, well," she said softly.

Jo paid no attention. "I need you to help me, Maggie—this is important. You see, I brought him with me, kind of by accident, and Mother's giving him the third degree. It's gotten very..." She stopped. It wasn't easy to say this about her own mother. "It would be funny, but I don't think Neil is used to this sort of thing. He hasn't known me that long, and, well, it's embarrassing, Maggie."

Maggie's calm green eyes regarded Jo for a long moment, as if she were digesting the information that the fabric of Jo's unquestioning loyalty to her family had suddenly developed a hole. Finally, she serenely said, "No problem. I'll just refocus Mother's attention. You can get to your friend and rescue him before Mother even notices. Follow my lead, okay?"

Jo nodded, grateful that Maggie understood such things without the need for eight hundred verifiable reasons. They arrived as their mother was kneedeep in a lecture on the virtues of wedded bliss. Jo groaned.

"Mother, dear," Maggie interrupted. "Did I hear Kit say that she and Riley were moving to Alaska as soon as the baby was born?"

"What?" Lilah Wentworth shrieked, slapping a hand to her heart. "With my first grandchild? We'll just see about that!"

Maggie winked broadly at Jo as she steered their mother away, and Jo took the opportunity to grab Neil.

Before he knew what hit him, they'd dashed through a swinging door and emerged onto the overtly feminine tuft of a lavender-flowered kitchen.

"Well," he said, straightening his tie. "You certainly have an unusual family."

Jo stuffed her hands into the pockets of her wide, gathered skirt and gazed up at him. "They're really very nice, Neil—they really are. They're the kindest people you can possibly imagine, and they just get a little overwhelming sometimes. My mother didn't mean any harm, I can assure you."

"Whoa, there. I believe you, okay? Anyway, I think they're terrific. I've never seen people who enjoy themselves so much." His voice was light, but it was difficult for her to know if he was telling the truth. "But I have to admit I'm a little confused as to what I'm doing here."

"Eliza," Jo said. "It's because of Eliza. I'm guessing she decided on the spur of the moment to drag you along. She tends to latch on to pretty faces on any old pretext."

"That's me?" he asked doubtfully. "A pretty face?"

Jo colored. "Well, sort of. To Eliza, anyway. She has this thing about older men, especially when they're attached to one of her sisters." Her face grew warmer. "Not that you're attached to *me*, of course, but Eliza isn't one for details. If she has the slightest reason to think you belong to a member of the family, she'll decide she's madly in love. It's a basic character flaw."

"I guess." His suspicions were confirmed; these people were out of their minds. But they were also entertaining, and he found himself enjoying the mayhem against his better judgment. It was tempting to jump right in and join the fun, to become one of these laughing, dancing, happy fools.

The hubbub from the other room intensified, with Kit's voice steaming above the rest, and Jo could only guess that an argument had broken out over the imaginary move to Alaska. Guilt descended upon her. "Listen to that. And it's all my fault."

Neil lifted an eyebrow. "Excuse me?"

"I thought you understood."

"Understood what?"

"It was all a ploy," she explained with exasperation. "Maggie made it up—about Kit moving to Alaska—to help me get Mother off your trail long enough to stage an escape. And Kit and Mother never have gotten along very well, and now they're screaming at each other because of me." Jo sped over the words, barely stopping for breath. "I really don't approve of lying, you know, even for the best motives, and now Maggie's lied for me, and it got poor Kit in trouble, who had absolutely nothing to do with any of this! You see now, don't you?"

Actually, most of it was a blur. But he nodded sympathetically. He said soothingly, "They seem rather temperamental anyway. I don't think you should blame yourself."

"You're only being diplomatic."

"No, really." He held up a hand. "Honest."

"You're a politician," she said with a laugh. "Everyone knows that politicians and honesty are mutually exclusive."

More accurate than she knew, he thought cynically. He had learned at an early age that diplomacy could easily cloak outright lying. To Jo, truth was an absolute. To him, there were always shades of gray.

A loud crash rocked the wall the kitchen shared with the living room, and Jo jumped back. "Someone's thrown something!" she said with horror.

At that moment, the door to the living room swung open a sliver. Maggie sneaked around the edge.

She whispered rapidly, "The battle is escalating. I told them it was a misunderstanding, but Mother and Kit are furious with each other anyway. Riley's trying to calm them down, but it isn't going too well."

"I think I should help," Jo said softly. "We can talk this out like mature adults."

Maggie sighed. "Jo, talking doesn't do any good when no one's listening. If you value your life, you will not get between those two right now." Shaking her head grimly, Maggie crossed to unlatch the back door. "What you should do is smuggle this guy out of here before his opinion of us gets any lower than it already is."

"Maggie—" Jo protested.

"Good idea." With his hands lightly on her shoulders, Neil pushed Jo ahead of him out the door. "Nice to meet you, Maggie."

"Nice to meet you, too," she yelled after them.

Chapter Six

Neil started to go around the house, back toward the front.

"Where are you going?"

"Minneapolis, I guess, if you'll give me a ride back."

Jo smiled. "With what?" Holding out her hands, she showed him they were empty. "No keys, no car. Unless I go back in the house, of course. If I can find anyone with keys, I can beg."

"Don't beg," he said, appalled.

"Don't worry." She hadn't really wanted to go back inside anyway, even if she should want to, to straighten out the fight she'd started. "How about a tour of my garden?" she suggested. "We can hide out there till things cool down inside."

Taking his agreement for granted, Jo led the way, pulling Neil behind her. Lilac bushes, their blossoms long since gone but their foliage still thick and green, bordered both sides of the long lawn, giving the birds a place to sit while they sang. Passing those, Jo slipped around behind a colorful, undisciplined flower garden at the end of the yard.

"Sit," she commanded, pointing to a cracked stone bench partially obscured by scruffy flowers and weeds. When he did as he was told, she followed, leaving a respectable space between them on the bench. She was content not to speak for a few seconds, letting the rustle of flowers and leaves and the call of a nearby blue jay replace the frantic pace of the indoors.

"I don't like it," Jo said after a moment, frowning and shaking her head.

"What?" Neil scanned their surroundings. What wasn't to like?

"Sitting out here while they're in there screaming at one another. As a matter of principle, I mean."

"Oh." He preferred to ignore such things rather than analyze them. "I think I understand." Even though, of course, he didn't.

"No, you don't." Jo smiled and played with the stem of a big blue iris that was poking her in the leg. "What I'm trying to say is that I'm normally a very loyal person, and now I feel disloyal because I engineered a fight in my family just to make things more comfortable for myself." She considered. "And more comfortable for you, too, of course."

"So it's kind of a conflict of loyalties, is that it?"

"Maybe." She stood up and surprised him by kneeling in the grass next to the bench and yanking spindly weeds out from between tiny bunches of violets. "But I'm not going to worry about it, because they fight all the time, anyway, and no matter how many times I try to intercede, it doesn't do a bit of good. Of course, I still truly believe that Mother and Kit would get along better if they could just get through to each other, but I don't think that's likely, do you?"

"I, uh, haven't got a lot of experience in these things."

"Oh." Jerking hard, she uprooted a weed down to the roots and knocked herself back onto her bottom with a thud.

She sat there for a moment, stunned, staring at the clump of dirt and roots dangling in her hand, and at the layer of rich soil dusting the front of her white sweater. Looking down at it, she started to laugh at herself.

"Come on," Neil said, helping her to her feet and disposing of the dirt lump. "Even weeding the garden turns into an adventure for you, doesn't it?"

Jo pushed her bangs off her forehead, leaving a smudge. She said pensively, "Things have been weird ever since that parade in Freedom Lake. I swear I never had these problems before."

Tugging on her hand, he brought her back to the bench. As he tried to help her brush the dirt off the front of her sweater, he faltered where the line of soil streaked across her breast.

"You'd better get that yourself."

Her gaze flashed down to the small curve he was focusing on, and her eyes widened. Feeling heat tinge her cheeks, she said, "Of course." She wiped ineffectually at the streak of dirt, but she could still feel his warm gaze touching her. Deciding the subject needed changing, she went back to the safe topic of her family and the fight they'd just witnessed.

"I hope my family hasn't given you a bad impression. They're sweet and fun, even if they are a little crazy."

"Oh, no," he assured her, casting about in his mind for a way to put a positive light on the things he'd witnessed. "I thought they were great. Very...lively."

She smiled. "I'd imagine your family is a little more on the sedate side."

His eyes narrowed. "My family?" There was a long pause, and Jo could almost see barriers come down in the wary expression in his eyes, and the careful tone of his voice.

"Of course it would be hard not to be more sedate than us," she ventured with a laugh, trying to put him back at ease. His jaw was still tense, a sign that she had not succeeded.

This was her first glimpse that there was more to Neil than the calm, collected public servant he portrayed. To know that he had anxieties and problems like any normal person made her want to reach out, to help him. And besides, she was curious. Why would mentioning his family make him so guarded? She prodded him, saying sympathetically, "It must be hard to be a part of a family as public as yours."

He shrugged. "I've had a lot of practice." And he turned away.

Realizing that she had been told, very subtly, to pry no further, that no matter what he really thought of being a Hawthorne, he wasn't sharing it with her, Jo gazed down at the scattered buttercups and violets dusting her garden. She played with a purple sweet rocket that was threatening to overpower the bench, and she decided that if her garden and her life were disorderly, she liked things that way. How annoying it would be to watch her step at every turn like Neil must have to do, deciding what was and was not off limits, what was and was not appropriate behavior.

Neil watched the gentle way she stroked the tall purple flower, and he felt almost sorry he couldn't tell her the things she seemed to want to know. But it was simply too ingrained to keep Hawthorne family matters private from anyone but Hawthornes. He wouldn't have known how to open up if he'd wanted to. What would he say? *I don't much like them, and they don't much like me, and that's the only life I know? How pitiful.*

Instead of the sorry state of the Hawthorne dynasty, he chose to contemplate the picture that Jo made against the backdrop of her garden. Her hair was tossed around by the breeze, and it glinted with touches of red and gold in the summer sun. It, and she, were as untamed and as naturally beautiful as the collection of flowers. Even her skirt echoed the deep bursts of color found in her garden.

"I've never seen a garden that looks like this," he said, meaning, *I've never met a woman like you.*

"I'll take that as a compliment," Jo said with a wry smile. "My mother thinks I should have a few neatly pruned rosebushes and some scraggly petunias like the rest of the world. But that would be cheating, don't you think?''

He wasn't really paying attention. "Excuse me?''

"Okay, unnatural then.'' She was getting more involved in this impromptu defense of her garden. He could see the spirit in her eyes as she gestured to the mass of unruly blooms behind them. "Every flower here came up because it wanted to. I just closed my eyes and tossed out a bunch of wildflower seeds. Whatever was here, was here. No hybrids, no fussing around with cuttings and strains. These flowers are all wild, did you know that?''

He could well imagine Jo flinging seeds over her shoulder with her eyes shut. "Why do I get the feeling you identify with your wildflowers, Jo?''

She laughed self-consciously. "There's a fine line between wildflowers and plain old weeds, you know. It's all in the eye of the beholder.''

"As the beholder,'' he offered gallantly, "I think you're a flower, not a weed.''

"Thank you.'' Turning back, she picked a violet and held it between two fingers. "If I identify with anything, I'd say it's the weeds. Like a dandelion, maybe. Definitely a weed.''

"And what does that make me?''

"You?'' She pondered the question earnestly, considering and rejecting possibilities. "Maybe an orchid, or an American Beauty rose, or how about a Boston fern? You'd have to be in a hothouse,'' she said absently. "The best dirt, a big brass pot, showy, expensive—''

He lifted an eyebrow ruefully. "I never thought of myself as showy and expensive.''

"I didn't mean it as an insult.''

"I didn't take it that way.'' He grinned at her, finding it amusing that he was developing a definite attraction to a woman who thought of herself as a weed.

She warmed to his smile. "I'm really glad you came to Water Works, Neil. Sometimes I think accidents like that parade crash are meant to be, no matter how cranky they make us at the time." She pounded a fist on her knee decisively. "The parade had to crash so you could discover Water Works and we could become friends. It's as simple as that."

Neil's grin faded. Things were always so black and white to Jo. But he would have come to Water Works with or without a parade, and with or without Jo, because of his undercover assignment to get the scoop on their activities.

He sighed. He liked Jo. And suddenly he didn't want to poke into her group any more than he wanted her poking into his relationship with his parents. He wasn't a man who put much stock in blind faith, but how could you look at Jo and not trust her? Even he—as jaded and cynical as they came—believed her. "Jo," he ventured slowly, "what do you think of all the publicity Water Works has been getting lately? I mean, first there was ChemCo and then Red Metal and then the guy at the capitol. Does that strike you as odd?"

"I don't know." She glanced up at him with frank surprise, thinking this was a strange topic to bring up out of the blue. "Why do you ask?"

"I just wondered how you felt."

He waited for Jo's reaction, pinning all of his plans for the investigation on this one toss of the dice. If he got the right response, he would drop the whole damned thing. Jo deserved no less.

"Well..." She hesitated. Why did Neil have this sudden interest in Water Works publicity? But then again, did it matter? She had nothing to hide. "To tell you the truth, I'd rather avoid the pollution in the first place, and do without the publicity." She watched relief wash over his face. Now she was even more confused. "Well, is that it? Did I pass the test?"

"There was no test to pass, Jo." But he was smiling. He knew now what he had to do. He would go to his father and tell the old man his theory about Water Works was nothing but hot air.

"Look, Jo," he began quickly. "I have something I have to take care of right now."

"What's going on?"

"Nothing." He grinned. "Not a thing."

"I don't understand."

"I'll explain later, okay?"

He reached out and squeezed her hand before hustling away from the bench and the garden. Wheeling back to wave, he took in the bewildered look on Jo's face and couldn't resist coming back to reassure her.

"I really enjoyed today—your flowers and your family. I'd like us to get to know each other better."

And then he bent down and Jo's senses came alive. Her awareness of him multiplied with each extra second of his nearness. He was so close she could smell the earthy, sunny fragrance of his skin, and distinguish the long, light lashes around his stormy green eyes. He was watching her intently, and she felt hot and lazy, as if she'd been out in the sun too long.

"Neil, I—I—" she began, but her throat was dry.

"Shhh."

She let her eyelids flutter closed and her lips part slightly, caring not a bit if he favored supply-side economics and cutting off welfare mothers. This was different. She just wanted him to kiss her. Now.

But all she felt was the gentle pressure of one finger stroking the curve of her cheek. And then it and he were gone.

Her hand to her cheek, she watched him leave. She swallowed and stood mute for a long moment, letting her body and her mind return to more reasonable states.

So what if he was an expensive Boston fern while she languished down with the weeds, she thought defiantly. She liked him. A lot. And obviously, he liked her, too.

"Wait!" she shouted across the lawn. "Neil, where are you going? You don't have a car here!"

AFTER FINAGLING the keys to the old blue Ford from Maggie, Jo insisted on driving Neil back to Minneapolis to get his own car. To her surprise, he asked her instead to take him to his parents' house in North Oaks, which was, as its name implied, on the north edge of St. Paul.

"The return engagement?" she teased. "You had to endure meeting my family so now you're paying me back by making me endure..." She broke off as she drove up to the North Oaks gates, realizing that once again her mouth was working faster than her brain. He was sensitive enough about his family without her calling them unendurable. She backtracked quickly. "Of course, I didn't mean that meeting your family would be unpleasant. They're very charming, I'm sure."

Next to her, Neil smiled wanly. "Don't worry. You can just drop me off without going in."

"Oh. Of course."

After some serious scrutiny, due no doubt to the rusty, disreputable appearance of Gerald the Ford, the guard waved them in, and Jo concentrated on navigating past the winding cul-de-sacs according to Neil's instructions.

She tried to avoid the thought that kept popping into her mind, but there it was again. The fact that Neil wanted to be rid of her. He wanted her to dump him at the door and then hightail it out of there. Why? That was easy. Because he didn't want her to meet his parents.

Remembering Neil's hesitation to discuss them even casually, Jo could understand a reticence on his part to bring a new friend in for introductions. Pulling up in between a fountain and a huge stucco mansion, which could've housed the entire Environmental Protection Agency in grand style, Jo understood even better. No one in his right mind would bring a woman with a dirty sweater and wayward hair into a place that looked like *that*.

The servants would never allow it.

Grand Affairs had done parties at houses as impressive as this one, but Jo had never really hobnobbed with the owners. Now, here she was, escorting the fair-haired son, schlepping him straight from a madhouse to a solemnly beautiful museum. Talk about culture shock.

She turned off the motor and gave him a wobbly smile. "Quite a place you've got here. I never knew anyone with a fountain in his front yard before."

"Thanks, but I don't live here." He tried to make light of the situation. "All those marble floors are murder when you have to get out of bed in the winter."

"Ahh . . . I see."

He wondered what she thought she saw. Damn it. He didn't like feeling this way, like he owed Jo explanations. Maybe she would understand without explanations if she saw the inside of this mausoleum. "Would you like to come in, Jo?"

Her lips parted slightly. Now that was a nice surprise. Neil wasn't ashamed of her in the least, even given the car she'd brought him in, and the smudge on her face. How very illuminating. And if he could look past superficial appearances, she certainly could. She lifted her chin and tossed her unruly hair back from her face.

"I'd love to."

He took her small, pale hand in his and led her up the steps to the massive front doors. Half expecting a butler to swing open the door with a haughty "You rang?" Jo was just as happy that Neil simply let himself in. They were in a large, open hall decorated in tasteful whites and grays. It was all very chic, with discreet marble busts of dead Hawthornes and subdued, pale paintings of things like the Washington Monument. Jo's first impression of a museum was turning out to be depressingly accurate.

"Did you grow up here?" Jo asked in a hushed, careful tone. She couldn't imagine being a child in these beautiful, bleak surroundings.

"You don't have to whisper."

But his words echoed in the cavernous hall, and Jo decided she'd just as soon keep her voice down after all.

"What's this?" a woman asked from the side, and Jo unconsciously grabbed Neil's arm for protection as they both wheeled in the direction of the voice.

He patted her hand, keeping it between his. "Hello, Barbara." It was the same patrician blonde with the sleek page boy who'd been at the white party. Wearing a beige linen suit and small, square gold earrings, she looked as if she'd just come from a meeting of the Junior League.

Barbara, Jo thought. *He calls his mother Barbara?* They resembled each other more than she would've thought, sharing the same gray-green eyes under pale, arched brows, the same decisive jaw. His mother, too, was tall and slim, and she held herself as Neil did, with grace and dignity.

"How nice to see you at home, Neil. If you'll excuse me, I should let Cook know you'll be here for dinner."

"No, that's all right. Please don't bother." His voice was as cool and distant as his mother's, and his lips shifted into a vague, rather insincere smile. "Perhaps some other time."

"Of course."

But Jo noticed a flicker of something—something that looked a great deal like unhappiness—behind Barbara Hawthorne's eyes as she looked at Neil, as if the woman were troubled by the awkward gulf of politeness between her and her son. The impression disappeared as soon as Mrs. Hawthorne's gaze passed to Jo.

"You haven't introduced your friend, dear."

Neil quickly remedied his lapse and made the introductions. Thank goodness he let it go at Jo. It would've felt like false pretenses to enter the world of the Hawthornes as a Josephine instead of plain old Jo.

Neil continued, "I left my car in Minneapolis, and Jo was kind enough to chauffeur me here. I need to talk to Dad."

"I'm not sure he's available."

"He can make himself available."

Barbara Hawthorne smiled faintly. "I'll tell him you're here."

As the older woman swept away, Neil jammed his hands into his pockets and glowered at no one in particular.

Jo felt herself soften with sympathy. "You know, my sister Kit swears she'll suffocate if she's in my house for more than three minutes at a time. I've actually seen her start to wheeze if Mother makes her stay when she doesn't want to."

"Really? I find that difficult to believe."

"That's what everyone says except Kit," Jo continued with a laugh. "Do you know what bothers her the most? The pastel colors. She insists the color scheme makes her physically ill."

"Ah—I see what you're doing. You've figured out that this place makes me uncomfortable, and you're trying to reassure me that I'm not alone in disliking the house where I grew up. Is that it?"

"I guess." Jo lifted her hands palms up, admitting to the ploy. "It's a perfectly normal way to feel, you know."

Neil reached out to gently touch his finger to the tip of Jo's freckled nose. He was touched. "Thanks."

"Neil."

A curt, clipped voice packed disapproval into the one syllable. It was the distinguished, gray-haired man Jo had seen at the door to RoRo's party. It was Neil's father.

The elder Hawthorne's jaw was clenched tight, and he looked distinctly displeased. "I knew you'd show up sooner or later. I need to speak with you."

"And I need to speak with you. But first I'd like to introduce someone. Dad, this is Jo Wentworth. My father, Jo."

A curt nod was the only indication Mr. Hawthorne gave that he had heard the introduction at all. Then he turned smartly on his heel and went back the way he'd come.

Neil indicated that Jo should wait for him on an upholstered gray couch along the wall, and then he followed his father down a long hall. With mounting apprehension, Jo watched him disappear. The tension in this place was so thick she could have used a machete to hack her way out.

She tapped her fingers on the arm of the couch and pretended to study the nearby bust of Jedidiah Hawthorne, mayor of Minneapolis seventy years ago.

Neil's father had been positively rude, and it didn't fit. He was a quintessential politician, wasn't he? Everyone knew that politicians were supposed to be smooth and oily, so friendly they made your teeth ache. So why had Senator Hawthorne purposely snubbed her?

Something was very wrong here. Jo could only wonder how much it had to do with her. She didn't want to get Neil in trouble with his father, but she wasn't going to sit there and be squashed like a bug by some pompous old windbag of a politician, either. Crossing her arms over her chest, she stuck her tongue out at Jedidiah Hawthorne for the sins of his descendants.

Down the hall, in the dark-paneled office of the ex-senator, Byron Hawthorne was glaring at his son. "You'd better have a damned good explanation," he said tersely.

Neil narrowed his eyes. "For what?"

"For that disaster at the capitol." The former senator pursed his lips. "You're supposed to be exposing their scams, not participating in them, remember?"

"Oh, I remember, all right. But I got some good press, didn't I?" His tone was soft and mocking. "Isn't that the important thing?"

"No, damn it!" The elder statesman glowered as he pounded his fist on the desk. "The important thing is for you to figure out who's responsible and turn the evidence over to me. You should be investigating them, not playing footsie with that little Girl Scout out there."

Neil shook his head in disgust.

His father paid no heed, continuing to berate him. "Do you have any idea what it looks like for you to be in fist fights on the evening news? It looks like hell—like you're a crazy man who can't control himself, let alone the state government."

"It was your idea that I ally myself with Water Works," Neil reminded his father curtly.

"Oh, no," the old man retorted. "You ally yourself with that sinking ship and your political future is sunk, too. I wanted you to *use* them, not join them."

"And I've done that—I am doing it."

"What you've done is get yourself on TV, brawling one minute and cuddling with political undesirables the next."

Neil's lips compressed to a thin line. "What in the hell is that supposed to mean?"

"It means that your touching scene with Miss Wentworth during the picket march did not go unnoticed. Very sweet, but hardly smart. The gossip columnist from the *Times* was bothering your mother again this morning, demanding to hear all the dirt on what exactly is going on between, as he put it, 'the heir apparent and the bedraggled girl whose face he was washing.' Next you show up in my home with grass on your clothing, dragging along the self-same girl, who is even more disheveled than you are! It looks for all the world like the two of you have come straight from an assignation in the back of a barn.''

Neil was halfway to the door. "I'm not going to sit here and listen to this."

His father waved his hand. "It doesn't matter. Sit down, sit down. All I want is your assurance that you will stop brawling in front of television cameras."

"And you would've preferred, for the sake of the gossip columns, that I had stood by and done nothing, is that it?"

"I would've preferred that you had given some thought to your public image before conducting yourself in that manner," his father returned stiffly.

Firmly reining in his temper, Neil kept his voice calm. "Look, she happens to be a very nice lady. When a person I like is physically assaulted, I tend to let my precious public image fend for itself. You see—" The reasonable approach was going nowhere with his father. Neil shook his head. "The hell with it," he said wearily.

"I'm not finished with you yet."

"Well, I'm finished with you and your lousy investigation. There is not one damned thing going on at Water Works. They're clean. And I quit." He headed for the door again.

Byron Hawthorne gave a short, derisive laugh. "So you've decided they're clean, have you? I might have expected as much."

Neil flexed his hand against the door knob.

"You dig around that penny-ante place for over a week and come up with absolutely nothing," his father continued. "I make one phone call and establish a concrete link between Water Works and the dirty tricks. Are you lazy or just incompetent, Neil?"

He let his hand drop from the knob. "What link?"

"You didn't answer my question."

"You didn't answer mine."

The ex-senator shrugged. He offered smugly, "I asked the police chief for some information, and he was kind enough to look into it for me. The thug who did all the damage at the capitol is..." He paused and picked up a half sheet of paper. "Ed Bergstrom is the name. He has a record of petty misdemeanors."

"So?" Turning back to look his father in the eye, he knew he was practically shouting. "What's the damned link?"

"Mr. Bergstrom is no longer in custody, although he was charged with a few things. It seems that someone came in and posted bail for him."

"And?"

"And that someone is a member of the Water Works staff."

If it were Jo, he swore he'd go out in the hall and wring her miserable little neck personally. It was just the sort of do-gooder, turn-the-other-cheek mentality that appealed to her. "Who?" he demanded.

The ex-senator fingered the half sheet of paper he'd been holding. Patiently, drawing out the drama for all it was worth, he squinted at the paper and then read aloud, "Fern Richardson. Anyone you know?"

"Of course it's someone I know," Neil snapped. Relief filtered through his veins, but it was mixed with disbelief. Fern? How could it be Fern? She was the first one he'd crossed off the list. "There must be some mistake."

Byron Hawthorne shook his impressive head from side to side, as if it pained him to witness his son's thick-headedness. "There's no mistake. Now you get back to work, all right? You pin down exactly what this Richardson woman has done and who else is involved, and we'll forget the mess you've made so far. Once we blow the whistle on this scheme, the media will forget everything else. We'll be sitting pretty," he concluded with satisfaction.

"I don't like this."

"If you pull it off, everything will be fine," his father said soothingly. "But no more fist fights, you hear? No more nuzzling sweet young things on the capitol lawn." He eyed his son shrewdly. "Stay away from the Wentworth girl if she's a distraction. But get this mess cleaned up pronto. I can't stall them forever on the lieutenant governor appointment, you know." He paused. "Are you in?"

Neil sighed. "I'm in." He thought of Jo waiting for him in the hallway, and he felt pretty low. But he couldn't deny it any longer; Water Works was *not* clean. If Fern had bailed out the guy with the bucket of water, then there was an obvious connection between the group and the "lucky" publicity they were getting.

Back there in the garden, he had started to buy into Jo's fairy-tale world of nice, warm-hearted people, of trust for its own sake, of ignoring the bad and focusing on the good. But no more.

His inability to see the forest for the trees so far only made him more determined to get at the truth. He would not be made a fool of by a ditsy old woman and a bunch of clean-water nuts. The door slammed behind him as he exited his father's study.

"You look awful," Jo announced when he rejoined her. In fact, he looked worse than that, like he'd been through the wringer. His hands were crammed into his pockets, ruining the line of his suit, and his tie was partially undone. His eyebrows were drawn together, and he was wearing the blackest look she'd ever seen on Neil. Good heavens. What kind of father did that to his child in the space of a ten-minute conversation? For the first time, Jo was almost glad her own father had bowed out when she was very young. If this was the way fathers behaved, who needed them? She began to feel indignant on Neil's behalf.

"Was he mean to you?" she asked outright. "I think I should go in there and tell him a few things about treating other people with dignity and respect. There's just no excuse for making you look so unhappy."

Neil felt a smile threaten his dark mood. Jo was so damned appealing when she took up a cause. But his father's words echoed in his mind: *Stay away from the Wentworth girl. She's a distraction.* And, much as he hated to agree with his father, so far she had been a distraction. Otherwise he wouldn't have bungled things so badly.

But how was he going to stay away from Jo?

Adopting a cool, polite tone, he said, "I don't need any help dealing with my father, Jo. I'm sorry you waited so long out here. I shouldn't have asked you to."

She knew a dismissal when she heard one. It seemed that Neil was telling her to keep her paws off his family problems. If only it weren't so tempting to interfere, to champion his cause. Back off, she told herself, if he wanted your help, he would ask. But she couldn't help thinking that he needed her help, whether he realized it or not. His family was mean and rude, and Neil needed a little trust and support in his life for a change.

"I'll see you later, Neil," she said quietly.

Her eyes were huge and warm, but he steeled himself against noticing. "I'll see you at the office, I'm sure."

At the office? But before he went in to see his father, he'd talked about them getting to know each other better. Why this abrupt change of heart? Her vision of possible camaraderie evaporated into the polished gray hallway.

"Sure," she said softly. "I'll see you around. And, Neil?"

He looked up. "Yes."

"You take care."

And then she smiled at him and backed out of the oppressive Hawthorne house, hoping he understood she wasn't giving up on him yet.

Chapter Seven

She could tell from across the room that he was not in a good mood. He hadn't been in a good mood for days.

Jo shuffled the papers on her desk and tried to figure out what to do about this morale problem in her little group. Everyone else in the office was excited to get the rest of the day off for a free trip to the racetrack, but not Neil. Nope. He was grumpy and he had acquired the habit of following Fern around.

That was the weird thing.

Jo hadn't really expected him to turn up at Water Works acting like her best pal after the abrupt dismissal from his parents' house. Well, maybe secretly she'd hoped for something like that, but she wasn't surprised when it didn't turn out. But she could never have anticipated him avoiding her like the plague, looking all deep and gloomy, and then coming up with the most transparent excuses to hang around Fern. *Fern*, of all people.

Since when was Fern so fascinating?

Jo reshuffled her papers.

"Jo?" Stanley asked, appearing at her shoulder. He flipped hair out of his dark eyes anxiously.

"Yes, what is it?"

"I thought we were leaving for the racetrack a half hour ago."

Trust Stanley to be precise about the time for their group outing. "You're right, of course. Get everyone together, will you? And start loading the bus. I'll be right out."

Acting with more authority than she would've expected, Stanley rounded up the volunteers quickly, clapping his hands and shouting orders at them. It appeared that Alex's overbearing attitude was rubbing off.

Neil lagged behind, not filing out with the others.

"Aren't you coming with us?" Jo asked sweetly.

"I'm not sure the racetrack is good for my image. Or yours."

Whew. He was cranky. The best she could do was explain the impetus for the trip. "Neil, I can assure you it's all aboveboard. Mr. Bredon used to be one of our biggest contributors until profits at Sunset Park took a dip. This year he felt terrible because profits have gotten so low he couldn't make a donation at all, so instead he offered us all a trip to the track, on the house. Most of us are looking forward to a day at the races," she tried in a patient and extremely nice tone, "and a day to relax away from our normal problems. I'm sure you'd enjoy it, too. Why don't you come with us?"

"I don't think so."

She rolled her eyes. "*Fern* will be there," she said snidely.

There was a pause. "Well then I'd better come, hadn't I?"

The way he looked at her, as if he were speculating on what she knew and when she knew it, she was sure she was right. There *was* something funny going on with his mysterious attachment to Fern.

"Mr. Bredon sent the Sunset Park bus for us. We'd better hurry or we'll miss it." Her words tumbled out as she watched him carefully. He hadn't denied the fact that he was pursuing Fern. What was going on?

He left her to lock up the offices and jogged down the stairs to the bus. He wanted to get on and get a seat before the only one left was next to Jo. Damn, but he must have been obvious trying to interrogate Fern, or Jo never would've noticed. And the worst part was that Fern refused to cooperate. She said she didn't know a thing about publicity, and she didn't drop so much as a clue or look even a little bit guilty. If Fern was masterminding illegal publicity scams, she was doing a great job of feigning innocence. And he couldn't exactly apply thumbscrews to someone who looked like his grandmother.

Which meant he was bested at the art of interrogation by Grandma Moses and, in the process, seen right through by Jo, who was about the equivalent of Pollyanna. Maybe he should hang up his trench coat now and get it over with.

Jo wasn't giving up; he could see that. She scooted over him to take the seat next to the window and gave him an encouraging pat on his knee. He looked up into warm, golden eyes that were full of concern.

"Would you like to talk about it?" she asked gravely.

"About what?"

She sighed. "All right then, have it your way. Pretend nothing's wrong. But if you want to talk about…well, about you and Fern, or anything else, I'm here." Vaulting back over him to get to the aisle, she patted his knee again, and then lurched down the center of the moving bus to share Fern's row.

He could feel both pairs of eyes on him, and he knew they were whispering about him. He could just imagine the theory those two fertile minds would come up with to explain his behavior. A cynical smile twitched at his lips and he looked out the window. Some spy he was turning out to be.

The Sunset Park racetrack was well outside the metropolitan area, and it was a long, quiet ride through the country before they got there. Finally, big orange flags marked with yellow half circles, apparently some artist's conception of a sunset, let them know they had reached the outside gates.

Jo waited for him to get off the bus, and then she fell into step beside him as they entered the park. "How are you feeling?"

"Fine, thank you. How about you?"

"Fine." Glancing up at him, she caught the glimmer of suppressed laughter in his eyes and around the corners of his mouth. "What's so funny?"

"You."

"Why?"

"I get the idea you think I have some strange and unnatural attraction to Fern. I find the concept pretty amusing."

"Oh, Neil," she said compassionately, "it's nothing to be ashamed of. I understand. Really. It's like a mother complex, right?"

He bit his lip to keep from laughing. Jo and the misplaced concern shining from her face were as endearing a sight as he could imagine. "No, Jo, it isn't. And I promise that there is nothing the least bit strange about my interest in Fern, okay?"

"I guess so." Shaking her head, she put her hands in the pockets of her jean skirt and stared at the ground. She glanced up quickly. "As long as you're sure you don't have an Oedipus complex."

"I'm sure. Trust me on this one." And then he did laugh; he couldn't hold it back.

"Okay," Jo said doubtfully, "but leave Fern alone for a while, will you? She's feeling a little uncomfortable about your sudden interest in her."

"Fine," he returned, and he took her hand as they entered the gates of the Sunset Park racetrack, just to prove he wasn't suffering from any deadly attraction to Fern. Since he was being ordered to stay away from his quarry for the day, he might as well enjoy himself with Jo.

All of the Water Works were sitting together, not too far up in the stands. Their number included Chris, grousing about the fact that his new glasses didn't fit right and how he almost preferred the bent ones; Fern, huddling between two college kids and purposely avoiding Neil's eyes; the unlikely duo of Stanley and Alex, looking quite pleased to be in each other's company; and even Eliza, there by virtue of her status as a sometime volunteer.

If Sunset Park was doing poor business, it didn't show at the track today. In the bright June sunshine, the colors of the horses' and jockeys' bright silks flashed gaily past the crowd, and people were shouting for their favorites, jostling at the fence for a better look, spending money hand over fist from the look of things. Everyone seemed to get into the spirit of the day, placing bets wildly and running back and forth for refreshments from the concession stands.

Jo couldn't even pretend to understand what was going on. When Alex and Stanley told her that the Pick Six hadn't been won in several days, and that the pot was piling up, she gave them a blank stare.

"You pick the winners in six consecutive races," Stanley explained carefully.

"Oh. Why would anyone want to do that? I mean, I'm enjoying it here, really I am. But just between us, don't you think betting on horses is a waste of money?"

Alex put her arm around her younger sister. "The point, dear Jo, isn't betting. It's winning." Smiling wickedly, she sidled up to Stanley. "And I do feel lucky today, Stan darling, don't you?" She winked. "Want to go for it?"

He blushed, and the two of them wandered off together. Jo only shook her head.

"Did you see that?" she murmured. "Poor Stanley. She'll bankrupt him."

"He can afford it," Chris sneered, while Neil came up behind her with hot dogs.

"What was that?" Neil asked.

"Nothing." But she smiled to herself at the phenomenon of opposites attracting. Against all odds, Alex and Stanley seemed to be hitting it off famously. Alex had already confided to Jo on several occasions that Stanley was a refreshing change of pace and just what the doctor ordered. Dating the same man for a whole week straight was probably a new record for Alex.

"Come on," Neil coaxed, "let's sit down. There's a horse named Water Witch in the next race, and I put twenty bucks on her." He grinned. "I need you to sit by me for luck."

She was more than happy to oblige. She even borrowed binoculars to keep an eye on Neil's horse close up. As she was focusing the binoculars, she turned them on the crowd farther down, near the fence. She fanned past an overweight woman in a Hawaiian print shirt, and drifted over a man with a cigar who was filling out a racing form while he rocked a stroller with twins in it. Deciding that coming to the racetrack could be lots of fun without placing a bet, Jo moved her binoculars on to a new clump of people.

Her fingers froze on the outside of the glasses.

She put them down for a few seconds, and then picked them up again, going through the whole routine of focusing just to be sure.

Yes, it was him. Her stomach turned over just looking at him. He wasn't wearing plaid today, but his thick lips and nasty, piggish squint looked just the same.

"Jo? What is it?"

Wordlessly, she handed Neil the binoculars and pointed to the section she'd been scanning.

"I don't see anything." Removing the glasses from his eyes, Neil gave her a worried look. "What was it?"

"Not what—who. It was that horrible man who threw water at me." Jo reached for the glasses. A long horn blast sounded the beginning of the race, and she found the starting gate through the lens, determined to forget the creep with the piggy eyes. "I'm okay now," she said, with a great show of sunny good humor. "It was just the shock of seeing him here. I sort of panicked for a second."

Neil didn't like the sound of this "coincidence." There were already a few too many of those. "You're sure it was him?"

"Oh, yes, I'm sure." She wrinkled her nose, remembering the smell of the fishy water and the smirk on the face of the man who'd thrown it. "Believe me, I'll never forget what he looked like."

Standing up, Neil snatched the binoculars from her hands. Jo could see that he was tracking through the same section of the stands where she'd seen the man, going face by face until he found him.

"Got him," he announced with grim satisfaction. He grabbed for her hand. "Let's go."

Jo didn't want to go anywhere near that awful person and she tried to pull her hand away as Neil raced up the stairs with her in tow. "Go where? Why?"

"I want to talk to that guy." Maybe Fern was keeping her mouth shut, but if he got his hands around the throat of the menace from the capitol, Neil guaranteed he'd find out why Fern bailed him out and who the jerk was working for.

Jo wasn't thrilled with the prospect. "Neil," she begged, dragging backward on his arm to curb his progress, "Why are we doing this? That man's a nut case, a sicko. We don't need to talk to crazy people! We should stay away from him, not antagonize him even more."

"I'm not going to antagonize him. I just want to find out who he's working for."

The severity of his expression and the power in his grip as he hauled her along the outer rim of the concession area belied his words. In another minute, they'd be up to the section where Ed was sitting. Jo knew she had to act now, before it was too late.

"Neil, think for a minute!" Exerting all the strength she had, she pulled him to a stop. Her hands rested on his forearms, and she shook him gently as she spoke in a persuasive, passionate tone. "Did you see his eyes when he ran up to me with the bucket? He's crazy, Neil, certifiable! People like him sit at home and write in little notebooks that the demons in their Rice Krispies are ordering them to shoot the president or throw dirty water on demonstrators. People like that don't work for anyone."

"Sometimes they do."

"Neil, Neil, Neil…" She pushed her bangs out of the way with the heel of her hand. "You're not listening to a word I'm saying. First it was the thing with Fern, following her around and pestering her with all sorts of questions, and now you want to take on a madman, just for the fun of it. If you don't watch it," she declared, pointing her index finger at him meaningfully, "*you're* going to be hearing demons in your Rice Krispies."

"I don't eat Rice Krispies."

"Well, in your Cheerios then!"

"Cap'n Crunch."

In spite of the gravity of her mission to dissuade him, she was taken aback. "You don't really eat Cap'n Crunch?"

"Jo," he returned swiftly, "Ed Bergstrom is going to get away. I don't think my breakfast cereal matters that much, do you?"

"Ed Bergstrom?"

"The guy with the bucket," he said impatiently, without thinking.

Confusion flickered in Jo's eyes. "How do you know his name?"

"It was in the paper."

She accepted the explanation so readily he almost felt guilty, but the momentary twinge passed. After all, he thought cynically, lying had always come easily to him.

"You can't—" she started, but he shushed her quickly, putting his hand over her mouth when he saw a burly, unkempt man lumbering out the exit from the spectator area and into the concourse where he and Jo were standing.

It was Ed all right. Wearing tan work pants, slung low to accommodate a large gut, and a nylon windbreaker over a knit shirt, he had the face Neil remembered wanting to smash in. Neil's jaw tightened as he shoved Jo behind him for protection.

"What do you think you're doing?" she demanded, and stomped on his foot, hard. She didn't appreciate being pushed around by a man with what appeared to be a wobbly grasp on his sanity.

Neil yelped and hopped on one foot while he promised himself never to consider Jo defenseless again. Luckily, there were enough noisy people bashing around the concourse to mask the noise and to hide them both from Ed's line of vision.

"I was protecting you!" Neil moaned, still hopping.

"Well, I don't need protecting. I didn't even want to come over here if you recall."

"Be quiet, will you? Ed will hear you and know we've seen him."

"I can't believe you call him by his first name," she grumbled. Although she believed with all her heart in settling disputes through discussion and negotiation, she felt like kicking Neil again. How dare he manhandle her that way and then tell her to be quiet when all this racing around to find Ed was *his* idea? "You're the one who wanted to confront him. How can we do that without him seeing us? Or did you plan to smuggle messages into his refreshments?"

"I changed my mind," Neil snapped. "He looks suspicious. I want to follow him."

She had to admit that Ed looked suspicious. He was holding himself stiffly, wearing a creepy little smile, and glancing down at his feet a lot, as if he felt conspicuous and was working hard to act cool.

She dismissed that. "He's a crazy person. Of course he looks suspicious."

"There he goes, around the corner." Excitement threaded Neil's words. "Keep your voice down, and we'll just tail him, nice and easy."

"And what, pray tell, do we expect to find by tailing him?"

"Not what, my dear, but who. I think he's going to meet someone." The idea that Ed might be at the racetrack to meet his Water Works contact had just occurred to Neil. If his hunch was right, he would know for sure which of the Water Workers was in league with Ed, and even Jo, with all of her faith and loyalty, would be convinced that something was rotten in her group.

"He probably already knows we're here, and he's looking for another bucket," Jo reflected. Her gaze swept today's outfit—a soft, full jean skirt with a dropped yoke, and an embroidered T-shirt. "At least this time I'm machine-washable."

"Damn."

She glanced up quickly, trying to ascertain the reason for the muttered curse. Neil's eyes were directed over her head and away from Ed, who was waiting in line at a beer counter.

"Frank Colfax," Neil said tersely. "And he's definitely seen me."

"Who's that?"

"Damn." Although his mouth adopted the smooth, careful smile she'd seen before, his eyes were still calculating. To her, he whispered, "Friend of my father's: big bucks. He'll know something's up if I ignore him, so you're going to have to follow Ed, okay? Above all, be careful. But don't lose him. Just find out who he meets and then come right back and tell me. If he sees you, get back here immediately. Be careful."

"No way." Now she really wanted to kick him. "This *Magnum P.I.* thing is *your* baby, not mine. I don't sneak around behind people. It isn't right," she insisted.

Neil tore his gaze away from the distinguished man advancing on him. With his hands on Jo's shoulders, he focused straight into her eyes. "Please, Jo, I wouldn't ask you if it weren't important. Will you do this for me? Can you trust me that far?"

His eyes were such a pretty, soft green, and he really did sound sincere. This was Neil, she reminded herself, the man who wiped her cheek when she got slimed and was nice to her mother even after she tried to squash him. He was one of her people, one of her Water Workers, and she would defend any of them to the death. How could she not give him the leap of faith he was asking for?

Meeting his steady gaze, she murmured, "Is he still in the beer line?" and Neil responded with a "Good girl" and a quick hug with one arm.

It caught her off guard. Even that small embrace was enough to shock her, to send little jolts of electricity racing up and down her nervous system. Her eyes went wide as she checked to see if Neil was similarly affected, but he was gazing over her head, keeping an eye on the progress of Frank Colfax. She wondered how unaffected Neil would be if she played it by instinct, threw her arms around his neck, and pulled him down a lot closer.

Blast it anyway. Sometimes maintaining her own ethical standards was a real pain. But she'd said she'd go follow Ed, and she would, regardless of funny twinges in remote regions of her body, and a lack of oxygen in her brain.

Pulling free of his arm, she turned to go, but Neil nudged her back. "Thank you," he said quietly, and he dropped a kiss on her cheek before sending her off after Ed. "Be careful," he commanded, and then his smile was back in place and she heard him call out a hearty "Frank Colfax! Great to see you, buddy!"

The words faded behind her as Jo wove in and around the racetrack crowd while maintaining a respectable distance between her and Ed. Even though she could still feel the imprint of Neil's kiss on her cheek, or maybe because of it, she felt immoral and sneaky following another human being like this. She hoped Neil had a good reason for all this subterfuge.

Sliding behind an orange Sunset Park banner, Jo watched Ed slurp down a beer and stuff a Polish sausage in after it. Not a pretty picture. At least she had to give him credit for properly disposing of his garbage. It just went to show there was some good in everyone.

As Ed trundled back into traffic, Jo left the shelter behind the banner and trailed after him. When his destination became clear, she leaned back against a pillar and frantically tried to figure out what she should do.

Ed had ducked inside the men's room.

Well, she wasn't going in after him, that was for sure. Finally, Ed reappeared, carrying himself as if he were wearing an invisible back brace. His spooky smile was spookier than ever, and he hesitated, sending shifty little glances right and left before edging into the crowd.

His path brought him painfully close to Jo, and she shrunk back around her friendly pillar, still watching him. His left hand was stuck in the pocket of his nylon windbreaker, and it was accompanied by a rather significant bulge that hadn't been there when he went into the men's room.

Good God, he had a gun. He was going to shoot someone.

She thought about screaming for help, but he ducked around behind the opposite side of the same pillar she was using and all she could do was freeze where she was and pray she wasn't the target of his gun.

Peeking around the corner, she saw that he was facing away from her, making it probable he hadn't seen her.

Whew. Time to disappear and dump all this in Neil's lap, since it was his idea, anyway.

But wait a minute. Ed was reaching into that left pocket, and pulling out...

An envelope.

An envelope? Jo quickly chastised herself for imagining anything so ludicrous as a gun. A lump in a pocket, and she was ready to call the FBI.

As she watched, Ed opened the thick envelope, licking his lips. Jo's eyes widened as he removed a stack of bills—all crisp, new twenties—and started to count them.

Heavens to Betsy. Had Ed found four hundred dollars in the bathroom? Jo's heart was beating like a bongo drum, and she thought she might throw up from all the excitement.

Or maybe it was from watching Ed down another beer and Polish sausage in one gulp, breaking one of the twenties from the envelope to pay for it.

Then he sauntered back around the concourse to his original gate, and Jo caught sight of Neil, leaning up against the side of a betting window, with his hands in his pockets.

He ran to meet her.

"Well? Who did he meet?"

"No one," Jo retorted. "But he went to the bathroom and came out with a big bulge in his pocket and I thought he had a gun. Neil, I was petrified! Here I am, following around a maniac!''

"He came of out the bathroom with a gun? Are you okay?''

"Of course I'm okay. It wasn't really a gun—I just thought it was at first.''

"Oh.'' He glanced down at her, obviously confused. "But he didn't meet anyone?''

"No, I told you he didn't. But wait—you didn't let me tell you about the money.''

"What money?''

"The bulge that I thought was a gun was money. He counted it not two feet away from me. Four hundred dollars, Neil!''

"What?'' Hands on her narrow shoulders, he held her steadily. "Tell me the whole thing again, slowly this time.''

And so she did, right up to the second Polish sausage and the brand new twenty Ed used to pay for it.

"Damn.'' Neil twisted away, furious with himself. "They were too smart for me. Instead of a face-to-face meeting, the person paying Ed left the money in the men's room.''

"How do you know where he got the money? This is a racetrack. Lots of people win money and carry it around. Maybe Ed picked six or whatever.''

"You tell me, Jo—did Ed ever go near a pay window?''
She shook her head.

"And he didn't have the money before he went in to the bathroom, did he?''

Biting her lip, she shook her head again.

"Unless they've added pay windows to the men's room, somebody dropped that money for Ed to pick up, and I'll bet you anything it was Ed's payoff for busting up the picket march.''

"But who would pay him to do a thing like that?''

Neil sighed loudly. "You're not going to like it, but I think it was Fern."

"Fern?" Jo's mouth dropped open. "Is this a joke?"

"I told you you wouldn't like it."

"And I'm supposed to believe that Fern left an envelope full of money in the *men's* room?"

"So she had an accomplice."

"Neil," Jo murmured, her eyes full of pity. "You've been working too hard, you don't get along with your mother and father, and your grip on reality is slipping. I understand."

"No, you don't understand." With one quick grab, he caught her hand and swung off in the direction of the Water Works crowd. "We're going to call her bluff."

He came up short with Jo only inches behind. "We know about the money, Fern," he said contemptuously.

The older woman blinked. "What money, dear?"

"You paid Ed Bergstrom to throw that slimy water at Jo, didn't you?"

At the mention of the name Ed Berstrom, Fern's face went as white as a pearl onion. Her mouth puckered up and then she sat down, hard, on her plastic seat.

"I only did it for my sister," she wailed. "She's married to him. She wanted him out of jail, so I bailed him out. Blood's thicker than woodwork, you know."

"Woodwork?" Neil asked, while Jo shrieked, "He's your brother-in-law? Why didn't you tell us?"

"I thought you'd all hate me," Fern whimpered. "It isn't my fault if my sister married a skunk."

Neil interjected, "Hold on a second here. We know you bailed him out. But what about the money in the bathroom?"

Fern blinked again, fastening round gray eyes on Neil. "I don't know anything about any money in any bathroom."

"The men's room," Neil prompted. "Four hundred dollars."

"No, I'm sorry." Fern pursed her lips, stating with conviction, "I've never been in a men's washroom, and I don't plan to start now."

It was Jo's turn to flash Neil an I-told-you-so look before she parked herself in the next seat and put her arm around Fern. "It's all right, Fern. We believe you."

"And you know," Fern began, "I can't imagine why he'd do something like that to our lovely picket march. But he's always getting into scrapes with the law, so I don't know why I'm surprised. Why, everyone at Water Works has heard me rant and rave about that louse. Anyone can tell you."

The others chimed in with "That's right" and "I've heard her talk about her brother-in-law the troublemaker."

"We all have." Jo's face was a study in sympathy. "Poor Fern."

"It's—it's terrible," Fern sniffled, and her eyes began to well up with tears. "I told my sister not to marry him, and now he's made my name mud, too."

"Does anyone have a tissue?" Jo asked hopefully. With no response, she dashed off to get some.

"Who ever would've known the creep at the capitol was the same guy Fern was always complaining about?" Stanley asked, shaking his head.

Fern fastened hopeful eyes on Neil. "You do believe me, don't you? It isn't my fault. Really! I'd just as soon never see him again as long as I live. Why, I still haven't gotten over the time my sister made me go get him out of the drunk tank."

She burst into a new flood of tears, and Neil looked around in vain for Jo and the tissues she was supposed to be bringing. "It was horrible," Fern managed. "And one of my friends at Water Works had to drive me down to the station. I was so humiliated." Her gaze jumped from face to face. "Who was it? I can't seem to remember. Oh, dear! Did any of you drive me?"

No one volunteered the information, and Fern grew even more confused. Nonetheless, everyone backed up her story that she had a no-good brother-in-law, and Neil knew he'd have to be content with the story that it was all one big coincidence.

"See, Neil?" As she returned with the long-awaited tissues, Jo faced him triumphantly. "It doesn't mean anything that that creep was here today. Of course Fern had nothing to do with the four hundred dollars, and however Ed got that money, it has nothing to do with us."

"Right as rain. Just a coincidence," Fern trilled. "By the way, Neil dear, how did you know I posted his bail?"

Neil wasn't as convinced of Fern's innocence as Jo was, but this wasn't the time or place to press the point, with the whole world looking on. "Another coincidence," he mumbled. Of which there were too damn many, as far as he was concerned.

ONE OF THE VOLUNTEERS listened to the interchange with more than a little apprehension. It had been risky, arranging the payoff here, but who knew Neil and Jo would stumble across it? At least they appeared to be satisfied that it didn't concern them. For the time being, anyway.

But some precautions would now have to be taken. No more using that oaf Ed, for one thing, meaning that the "accidents" on the agenda would have to be handled personally. Dangerous, but unavoidable.

It also meant the the nosy Ms. Wentworth and Mr. Hawthorne were going to have to be occupied while these important matters were taken care of, to make sure they didn't get any more bright ideas about how the pieces of the puzzle fit together. A nice wild-goose chase couldn't hurt anything. Better get to a phone and get the ball rolling.

After all, better safe than sorry....

Chapter Eight

Although Jo had come out in the bus with the rest of the group, Alex and Eliza had not. Instead, they had driven the Grand Affairs van and met them at the racetrack. For the return trip, Stanley now offered to drive them all in the van.

It seemed silly for Jo not to go back with them, since they were going directly to the Wentworth house. So Stanley and Alex took the front seat, while Jo and Eliza camped out on the floor in the back of the lavender van. Eliza promptly went to sleep, tucking herself into a fetal position and conking out as soon as the motor kicked in.

"Jo," Alex demanded, "what was all that about Fern and money hidden in the bathroom?"

Jo chewed her lip. "From what I can figure out, Neil's got a bee in his bonnet about what happened during the picket march, when that man threw that gunk at me. He thought Fern paid the man to do it."

Letting her voice trail off, Jo rubbed her temples. All this emotional upheaval was exhausting and she didn't want to think about it anymore. None of it made sense, and if Neil could've enlightened her, he wasn't talking.

"If only Neil would open up to me," she murmured. "I wish he'd think of me as a person he could talk to."

"Jo," Stanley offered gently, "if Neil would talk to anyone, I'm sure it would be you." He darted a glance into the back. "How did he find out about Fern bailing that guy out? Her brother-in-law, wasn't it? What a shocker."

"You're not kidding it was a shocker." Jo tucked her knees under the denim folds of her skirt. "Neil said it was a coincidence, that he saw the guy's name in the paper and then the name jumped off the page of some police records of another case he was working on."

Stanley stroked his beard thoughtfully, driving with one hand. "That *is* a coincidence. I didn't even know he practiced law. I thought he was a politician."

Jo hadn't known, either. It was only part of the enigma known as Neil. People learned her whole life history within five minutes of meeting her, even if she didn't mean to be effusive. It all just sort of tumbled out. But with Neil, every tiny bit of information had to be pried out with a crowbar.

"He told me he's a nominal junior partner at some posh firm in Minneapolis, but I don't think he's there much." Dry humor flashed in her smile. "I guess he has to do something to occupy himself in off-election years."

"So he decided, out of the blue, that little old Fern hated your guts enough to get her brother-in-law to throw stuff at you, and that she was going to pay him for his efforts in the silliest and most convoluted way possible?" Rich, tickled laughter spilled from Alex. "Can't you just imagine Fernie-poo sneaking into the men's john and salting some money away behind the urinal? Get real!"

"It does sound pretty farfetched," Jo agreed. "But Neil was really convinced."

"Hie that boy to a psychiatrist, Josie, dear."

"Oh, Alex, there's nothing wrong with Neil." Gazing down at Eliza, still dozing peacefully, Jo smiled and leaned over to brush a strawberry-blond curl away from her sister's face. "You know, Neil didn't have the advantages we did," she said softly, "of growing up with people to love and trust him. You should see his parents and his house!" She paused. "Actually, I suppose you have seen his parents and his house, back when the two of you dated. But it doesn't matter, anyway, because they're cold and rude and they treat him terribly. I'm not surprised if his thinking is a little negative."

"Negative? Fern in the men's room is preposterous."

"He hasn't had an easy life," Jo said in staunch defense. "He just needs to learn to trust people, that's all."

"Oh, dear Lord, spare us." Ever dramatic, Alex lifted a limp wrist to her forehead. "Our darling Josie has tripped over yet another reclamation project." She shook her fabulous hair, fixing Jo with dancing eyes. "And I'll bet you're already casting about for a way to turn the poor, mistreated man and his ice-cube family into little puddles of warmth and affection, just by opening them all up to the goodness in the world—am I right?"

Stanley chuckled, and Jo ignored the sarcasm. It wasn't her fault if she thought other people's happiness was a worthwhile goal. She was phrasing a suitable reply to chide Alex for her selfish, uncharitable attitude when Eliza woke up, yawning prettily and wiggling in a exaggerated stretch.

"What did I miss?" she asked.

"Not a thing," Alex declared. She winked at Jo. "We've determined that Jo's new beau is nuttier than a fruitcake, which means he'll fit in perfectly *chez* Wentworth, *n'est-ce pas*?"

"No, I don't *n'est-ce pas*." Eliza narrowed her eyes at Jo. "Is she talking about Neil? What's wrong with him, and since when is he your beau? *I* thought the field was clear."

"Tut, tut, dear Lizzie, any dimwit can see the two are smitten with each other. A man would have to be crazier than Neil not to fall for our Jo when she's in a redeeming mood, with that feverish little gleam in her eye. And since we all know that nothing makes Jo gaga faster than a lost cause, I'd say she's a goner, too. Love makes the world go 'round.'' Alex blew a kiss across the seat at Stanley. "Just like *moi* and Stan the Man."

"Oooh!" Eliza cooed. "Isn't that sweet?"

The lavender van pulled to a stop and Jo sang out, "We're here." And just in time to avoid further discussions she didn't want to take part in. She wrenched open the doors of the van, hopping out hastily.

Within a few moments, Alex and Stanley were parked at the kitchen table, dithering over where to go to dinner to celebrate the new emerald bracelet Stanley had given her, while Jo dialed in to Water Works' answering service to see if anything significant had transpired while the staff was out having a good time.

There were a few messages from possible donors, one from someone who wanted to volunteer, and one of a more disturbing nature.

"The person wouldn't leave a name," the woman from the answering service reported. "To tell you the truth, the voice was so low, I couldn't even tell if it was a man or a woman. Here's what they said: 'Markham Industries is dumping in Loon Lake, about fifteen miles from Creosote, Minnesota, and somebody from Water Works better get up there right away to check it out.' That's the exact message."

"Okay. Thanks." Jo replaced the phone on the wall with a troubled expression.

Stanley jumped to his feet, immediately attentive. "Problem?"

"Oh, no, you don't." Alex yanked him back into his chair. "If there's a problem, Josephine will handle it so that her dear sister Alex and the object of said sister's affection may keep their dinner date. Right, Jo?"

No answer.

"I said, '*Right*, Jo?'"

"Sure, sure." Jo bit her lip. How was she going to handle this? Everyone was scattered for the weekend, and even if she could run them down, how could she ask them to make a long drive to check out what might be nothing more than a joke? Delegation of unpleasant tasks not being her strong suit, she already knew she would end up undertaking this mission herself.

She brought her head up slowly. "Has either of you ever heard of Creosote, Minnesota?"

"They were in the high school hockey tournament last year," Stanley offered. "Way up by International Falls, I think."

"That's almost Canada," Jo lamented. "It'll take forever to get there, which means an overnight trip for sure. Who can I get to trek all the way up there?"

Alex said protectively, "Not Stanley," while the man himself was dying to know why in the world anyone needed to go to Creosote.

"A tip came in that Markham Industries is illegally dumping up there. It may be a hoax, but we really can't ignore it completely," Jo finally revealed.

"Sure you can. Send the police." Alex always had a solution.

Stanley disagreed. "We can't send the police, Alex. They may already know about it, and be looking the other way on purpose. Jobs are scarce up on the Iron Range, and Markham Industries is a big employer. I think we better send someone of our own—someone impartial."

"I agree." Jo shook her head. "But who? I'd go, but I don't feel very comfortable about doing the field testing. I know what happens in theory, but I've never done it myself. It's always you or Chris."

"I would if I could, Jo. You know that." Stanley spared an anxious look in Alex's direction.

Patting his arm, Jo returned, "I know, Stanley."

4 FREE!

SILHOUETTE DESIRE NOVELS

PLUS! 2 Glass Oyster Dishes **AND** a Surprise Mystery Gift

Silhouette Desire romances bring you all the heartbreak and ecstasy of fulfilling and contemporary relationships as they are lived today.

And to introduce you to this powerful, highly-charged series, we'll send you 4 Silhouette Desire titles, a beautiful pair of Oyster Dishes <u>plus</u> a Surprise Mystery Gift, absolutely FREE when you complete and return this card.

We also reserve a subscription for you to our Reader Service, which means you could enjoy:

◆ **6 wonderful novels-** sent direct to you every month.
◆ **Free postage & package-** we pay all the extras.
◆ **Free regular newsletter-** packed with competitions, author news, horoscopes and much, much more.
◆ **Special offers-** selected exclusively for our readers.

JUST FILL IN THE COUPON OVERLEAF ▶
FOR YOUR **FREE** BOOKS & GIFTS

Reader Sevice
FREEPOST
P.O. Box 236
Croydon
CR9 9EL

FREE BOOKS CERTIFICATE

Yes! Please send me my **4 Free Silhouette Desires** together with my **Free Gifts**. Please also reserve a special Reader Service Subscription for me. If I decide to subscribe, I shall receive 6 Superb new titles every month for just £7.80 post and packing free. If I decide not to subscribe I shall write to you within 10 days. The **free** books and gifts will be mine to keep in any case. I understand that I am under no obligation whatsoever – I can cancel or suspend my subscription at any time simply by writing to you. I **am over 18 years of age.**

9S9SD

NAME _____

ADDRESS _____

_____ POSTCODE _____

SIGNATURE _____

FREE GIFT

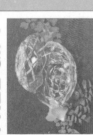

Return this card now and we'll also send you this beautiful set of 2 Glass Oyster Dishes absolutely FREE together with...

A SURPRISE MYSTERY GIFT

We all love surprises so as well as the free books and glass dishes, there's an intriguing mystery gift especially for you.

POST TODAY!

"Besides, you don't have to do the tests on site. You could just collect the samples and bring them back for lab testing."

Alex's exotic green eyes danced with mischief. "And, to spice things up a bit, why not take Neil with you?"

"Why would I take Neil?"

Offhand, Stanley said, "Well, he *would* be able to tell you if going in is legal, being a lawyer and all."

"Right. *And* he'd be able to extricate the two of you from jail if you should be so unlucky as to land there."

"Alex! We're not going to get arrested."

"Stranger things have happened, dear," Alex tossed out, picking up the phone and handing it to Jo. "Now call the boy right this minute and see if he'll go."

"I don't know—"

"What's not to know? It will be divine, Jo, just think— some dishy little lake, moonlight, just the two of you, completely and irrevocably alone." Alex produced a theatrical shiver. "You may go out there a girl, but you'll come back"—she dipped her voice low—"a woman."

Jo laughed out loud and swatted at her sister, but it didn't faze Alex.

"I'm absolutely serious, Jo. You said you wanted him to open up to you. What better place to…talk…than all alone under the stars?"

"I just want him to trust me, Alex." A vague recollection surfaced, of her feelings rising to something a bit more provocative than friendship on several occasions. But dealing with the heavy breathing of a co-worker was not what he needed right now. "I think he needs a friend."

"Well then, what are you waiting for? This is the perfect opportunity to get chummy. Grab it, little sis!"

Jo looked up suspiciously, but Alex's eyes were wide and innocent. "Do you really think so?"

"I really think so."

And Stanley chimed in with his hearty agreement, so what could Jo do? She reached for the phone.

AFTER A GOOD NIGHT'S SLEEP and the time to scrounge up some supplies, including topographical maps of the area and everything else she thought they might possibly need, Jo was anxious to get underway. When Neil pulled up outside in his dark green BMW, she practically leaped into the passenger seat. Then, of course, she had to get out so they could rearrange the supplies in the trunk, plus she thought it was worthwhile to advise Neil on the utility of the things he'd brought, which necessitated unpacking everything he'd already packed.

Finally underway, Jo was happy to engage in a little friendly chitchat, hoping to make the miles pass and get a better handle on Neil at the same time.

But his replies to her conversational efforts kept getting shorter and less informative, even as she tried to draw him out. She asked about his childhood, his sister, his college career, his hobbies and his taste in literature. She got back a few polite smiles and several hems and haws about not knowing much about this or that topic. He also changed the subject quite a bit, deftly steering her into talking about herself instead of digging into his psyche.

Gritting her teeth, she persevered. After all, Jo didn't believe in giving up.

She said pleasantly, "Thanks again for coming with me. I'm sure you had better things to do with your weekend than drive me to Creosote to get water samples." The hint was definitely there: *what did you otherwise have planned for this weekend?*

Neil shrugged, keeping his eyes on the road, and avoiding the hint. "I told you I didn't mind coming with you."

As a matter of fact, he would've paid for the privilege. The anonymous phone tip sounded a lot like the ones that had signaled the ChemCo and Red Metal publicity bonanzas. He couldn't help but wonder if this trip to the northland was cut from the same cloth. His time and a few extra miles on his BMW were a small price to pay for the opportunity to walk into a full-fledged scam with his eyes open.

If only he could've gotten a different camping partner. He glanced over at Jo, who looked younger than usual in shorts and a Talking Heads T-shirt, with her hair pulled back in a scruffy ponytail. After rolling down the window of the BMW, she'd hitched her leg up and stuck her bare foot out the window to catch the breeze. He couldn't help smiling to himself, noting the diminutive size of her foot as she wiggled her toes in the wind.

Oh, being in Jo's company was entertaining enough; that wasn't the problem. Or maybe that *was* the problem. He enjoyed her company so much, his plots and schemes went up in smoke, and he came off looking like an idiot. He was going to have to keep his mind off her tiny feet and the pattern of freckles on her nose, and stick to business.

Deftly quashing Jo's attempts to chat, he forced himself to consider the possibilities as the miles dragged by. First scenario: Fern was the ringleader of the whole thing, maybe even with an accomplice. Next: someone else was the ringleader and Fern was the accomplice. Or what about someone else as the ringleader and Fern as the unwitting dupe?

That last struck him as most likely, especially given Fern's revelation that one of the Water Workers had driven her to get Ed out of the drunk tank. At first that seemed like a minor and meaningless bit of information, but Neil was beginning to wonder.

Because the person who drove her to the drunk tank would have had the perfect opportunity to meet Fern's lowlife brother-in-law and decide he was just the man for a nasty job. And that conclusion put Neil back to square one, with the entire group under suspicion. If only Fern remembered who drove her to the drunk tank.

"You're awfully quiet," Jo ventured, coming right out with it. "Are you mad that I repacked everything?"

He gave her an amused glance. "I told you it didn't bother me. If you feel the need to inspect my toothbrush, so be it. But I still can't imagine we'll use all the junk you brought."

"I'm not a very experienced camper. I wanted to be sure I had everything, just in case of emergency."

"*You're* not much of a camper?" Dangling his right hand over the steering wheel, Neil grinned in spite of himself and ran his left hand through his hair. "We're in big trouble, Jo. I've never done this before in my life. I figured you for the expert."

"Sorry." Jo considered the possibilities. "Aw, come on. What are we worried about? How bad can one night be?"

They both had plenty of time to ponder that question as they drove on and on toward Creosote. Finally, they arrived in the general vicinity of the lake and the alleged illegal dumping.

A friendly taxidermist in Creosote who rented canoes on the side gave them directions, telling them that Loon Lake was a pretty little spot and they should enjoy themselves. He hadn't heard any report of any dumping, and hooted at the very idea.

"Naah," he said cheerfully. "You shouldn't have any problems. 'Cept bears and moose, maybe. And bugs, of course, though they haven't been too bad this year." He smiled hopefully. "You catch a bear, you bring it back to me to stuff for you, eh?"

"You bet." But Jo's smile was weak at best, and Neil looked a little green around the gills.

Back in the BMW, he demanded, "Bears? You didn't tell me there were bears up here."

"Neil," she pointed out calmly, "you have lived your entire life in Minnesota. How could you not know there are bears in the wilderness?"

"Jo," he responded, just as calmly, "I have been to every town in this state big enough to have a parade or fundraiser. That includes everything from the Donnelly Threshing Bee to Bean Hole Days in Pequot Lakes. But nothing in Creosote, and nothing with bears."

"Okay, okay. Don't worry, I'll protect you. Turn right at the two spindly pines."

The rest of the taxidermist's directions were easy to follow, and they parked the car off to the side of the gravel road that came as close as they could get to the lake.

Watching Neil haul things out of the trunk against a rustic, rugged backdrop of tall trees, Jo decided he made an incongruous picture. Standing there so tall and polished, with sunlight lending a golden glow to his beautifully cut hair, he belonged at a golf or tennis resort, not in the middle of the woods. He was dressed casually for him, wearing fashionably loose khaki trousers and a dark red polo shirt with a designer trademark on the chest. Somehow, even after seven-plus hours in the car, he managed to come out looking together. The stylish man's version of back-to-nature, she thought, complemented by the sleek green yuppie-mobile behind him.

And then she chastised herself for the criticism her attitude implied. He was here, wasn't he? None of the other free spirits would've made the trip without a lot of moaning and groaning, including reliable old shoe Stanley. Even looking like the politician that he was, Neil had come because she needed him, and she had to give him credit for that.

Joining him at the trunk, she grabbed her backpack for the first trip, lugging personal items, her sleeping bag and the tent in a pack marginally smaller than Jo herself.

Entering the path to the lake was like opening a door on a different world, and she ignored the straps biting into her shoulders as she drank in the serenity. There was still plenty of late-afternoon sunlight trickling through the high canopy of towering pines and aspens, painting big splotches of gold into the deep greens and dusty browns of the trail. Around them there were trees and more trees, perhaps the rustle of a few bird wings, but otherwise, complete silence.

Jo breathed in deeply of the damp, woodsy air, feeling coolness and calm descend around her, sweeping away the stickiness she'd brought with her from the hot car and the bright summer day. It was too early to tell if all this nature and solitude would prove a tonic to Neil's unwillingness to open up, but Jo knew she felt better already. The pack strapped to her back was heavy and cumbersome, but she felt healthy and woodsy and strong in spite of it. Amazing how a few gulps of pine-scented air could do all that.

Luckily, it proved to be a short, level path from the road to the lake, so the task of fetching supplies wasn't all that arduous. The fifteen-foot aluminum canoe they'd rented in Creosote was the worst, and Jo wisely let Neil handle that, bowing to the difference in height as a bar to a joint effort.

Rounding the last curve in the path, she decided the lake would've been worth it, even with double the hassle. It wasn't big, but it was lovely—a clear, dark expanse of water, with tall pines marking its edges in every direction.

They discovered that they were on a ridge, ending in a rocky, sun-splashed ledge some twenty feet above the lake. A pile of blackened rocks not far from the ledge had obviously been used as a fireplace many times before, and Jo thought it would be a great idea to build a fire, sit on the log that had been dragged up to it, and watch the sun set over the lake in a few hours.

Dragging herself away from the spectacular view, she picked a level spot under some pines farther back on the ridge to set up their borrowed tent. Although they had to read the instructions to figure out all the cords and poles, they managed nicely in the end.

Neil scrutinized the tent and then raised an eyebrow at Jo, as if questioning the lack of separate sleeping quarters, but Jo refused to answer for it.

Heavens, it was a four-man tent, fully eight feet across, and she wasn't going to suggest toting along a whole extra tent just to avoid a few moments of awkwardness. They were adults, weren't they? They could sleep in the same tent without any problems if they were mature about it.

So she ignored him and roped the bag with their food in it securely up a tree, away from the noses of prying bears.

"You don't exactly seem like a novice at this," Neil remarked, as she threw him air mattresses to blow up and put under their sleeping bags.

"I never said I was a novice." Jo grinned at him as she pulled out the water sampling kit. "I just said I wasn't much of a camper. But I have done it before. And I follow instructions well."

She clasped her thumb and little finger, intending to bring the other three fingers up in a salute, but before she got them near her eyebrow, Neil said, "Aaah, that explains it. You were a Girl Scout."

"How did you know?"

He lifted an eyebrow rakishly. "I've bought a lot of cookies in my time."

She laughed, as she knew he'd intended, and took her bottles around the side of the ledge and down the path to the water. As she knelt next to it, she ran through the checklist in her mind. First, it looked and smelled clean and clear. Second, there was evidence of algae, but not too much, which might have indicated trouble. And there were none of the other telltale signs, like discoloration of the water from chemicals, or dead birds or fish. The ones playing in and around the lake looked hale and hearty enough.

In fact, it seemed like an idyllic spot. Shaking her head, Jo did simple litmus tests that came out perfectly normal, and then filled two more bottles to take back to the Twin Cities for lab tests.

So far, so good.

By the time she climbed up the path to Neil, Jo had decided there was nothing wrong with this lake.

"Do you think we could have the wrong place?"

He shook his head. "Loon Lake is what the map calls it, and what the taxidermist in Creosote called it. I think the anonymous tip was either a joke or a mistake." Zipping the tent closed, he brushed his khaki pants and looked up thoughtfully. "Unless the dumping hasn't happened yet." If it was being staged for their benefit, it might even occur while they were there.

Taking in the lush greens and browns of trees and rock, and the deep, savage blue of the water, Jo felt a sense of outrage. "How could anyone knowingly destroy all of this?"

Neil was wondering the same thing. But someone he knew, someone he had met, might be toying with the idea, just for the sake of a few lines of copy in tomorrow's newspaper.

As they put together a quick dinner of sandwiches and fruit, with instant lemonade made from bottled water they'd brought in, Neil realized he wasn't hating the camping experience as much as he'd expected to.

"You know, it's kind of nice out here. A little hot and sticky, maybe, and I could do without the bug spray, but otherwise, nice."

Jo smiled indulgently. He was relaxing in spite of himself. "If you help me with the canoe, we can go for a ride before it gets dark. Stanley said that we should get samples from deep and shallow water, and from different sides of the lake. I'd just as soon do it tonight, so we can leave first thing in the morning. Is that okay with you?''

He shrugged. "Sure. Why not?"

The aluminum canoe slid smoothly in the calm water, even if their paddling strokes didn't match very well. It was a hot, still night, muggier and buggier close to the water, and the sun was just beginning to dip. Intent on paddling, neither spoke much as they got far enough for Jo to gather her deep water specimens. But when Neil spun them around cleanly to skim past a thick patch of lily pads along the shore, Jo found it necessary to comment on his obvious skill.

"Let me guess—Boy Scout? Junior voyageur six years running? Or counselor at Camp Wikiwatchee?" Gingerly, so as not to rock the boat, she twisted around enough to catch his grin through a haze of humidity.

"None of the above. I rowed sculls in college. It's been a while, though."

"You know," she said pensively, wiping sweat from her brow and swatting at a mosquito at the same time, "I have this vision of you in a fishing boat. It's the weirdest thing, as if I've seen a picture of a very young you, in a rowboat, wearing a dumb fishing hat with lures hanging on it. Where would I have gotten that?"

"*Newsweek*."

"You're kidding. When?"

"Years ago."

"Okay." As usual, he wasn't talking. But he seemed to be in good spirits, anyway, not clamming up with a noncommittal remark or charmingly changing the subject. She asked nonchalantly, "Why were you in *Newsweek*?"

Watching her scoop up another water sample, Neil answered almost without thinking. "It was when they were talking about my father as a possible vice-presidential candidate, back in the late sixties. He made a big deal of going out fishing rather than talking to reporters while he was waiting for the call. *Newsweek* ran a full-page photo with the caption, 'Hawthorne wants to be alone.'"

"Yeah, I remember now. That was a famous picture, wasn't it?"

"I suppose."

Jo nodded sagely, thinking that perhaps she had misjudged Neil's father. Instead of making his family wait on pins and needles, the busy senator had gone fishing with his teenage son. It was a homey, comfortable image. "I suppose that must be a pretty special memory, going fishing with your father while he waited for a call from the president." Very carefully, she tucked in her legs and shifted all the way around in her seat. "It's really too bad the photographers intruded on your private moment."

Neil rubbed his thumb along the grain of his wooden paddle. He said softly, "No, Jo, you don't understand. We weren't really going fishing—it was just supposed to look that way."

Poking his paddle between the thick white cups of the adjacent water lilies, he was surprised at himself. He had never told anyone about the sham fishing trip that put him in *Newsweek*. But for some reason, he didn't mind talking about it now. There was something about the unquestioning acceptance in Jo's eyes, something about the heavy stillness in the air and the complete privacy of the wilderness setting, that made keeping secrets seem so meaningless. He found himself wanting to let his thoughts trip off his tongue without censoring them first.

"It was all posed for the photographers' benefit," he offered after a long pause. "My dad wanted to look like a real guy with a real kid, goin' fishin'. I rowed us out to the middle of the lake, and we stuck our poles in, and then we sat there long enough for plenty of photo opportunities."

"How awful."

He glanced away, across the water. "Yeah, it was pretty awful now that I think of it. I was so damned proud to get my picture in *Newsweek*, but at the same time I felt like a phony." He shrugged. "Funny the things that bother you when you're a kid."

"Oh, Neil, that's terrible." Smashing a mosquito who was chewing on her leg right through the thick layer of bug spray, Jo leaned toward Neil sharply and felt the canoe wobble beneath her. "I can't believe your own father used you to perpetrate a lie."

He gazed into dark golden eyes shooting sparks of outrage, and one corner of his mouth lifted in a sardonic smile. "It's the way of the world."

"Not my world."

"No." His voice was dry, amused. "I suppose not."

"My way's better."

Mindful of her sincerity, his smile lost its cynical edge. "You won't get any argument from me."

And then he stretched down and plucked a fat white blossom off its stalk to present to her. He tipped forward, holding out the lily, but when she reached out to take it, he edged it safely away, out of her grasp.

Her voice came out husky in the thick evening air. "Tease."

"Come and get it."

Even in the fading light, she could make out the twinkle in his eye. *Why, he's flirting with me.* And she suddenly became excruciatingly aware that she was a woman and he was a man. And they were very much alone in the middle of nowhere.

The heat and humidity pressed down around her, making her feel breathless and light-headed as she edged toward the back of the canoe, going painstakingly slow to keep the boat on an even keel. Soon they would be knee to knee; after that there was nowhere to go but in his lap.

It struck her suddenly that no matter what she'd told Alex about wanting to be Neil's friend, she wouldn't have minded tumbling into his lap and holding on tight. Could it be that there was a time and a place for friendship and a time and a place for... whatever this was?

Whether she had admitted it or not, the attraction had been there for a long time, at the racetrack and in the garden, at the capitol and even during the parade. Neil was so closemouthed she still didn't know where he stood on a lot of things. But it didn't seem to matter anymore. She wanted him anyway.

Jo Wentworth, true believer, was on fire for a man, not just a mind. She wanted to feel his eyelashes brush against her cheek, his long, elegant fingers tangle in her hair, and his narrow, clever mouth glide over her neck and her throat and the backs of her knees.

The air was thick and sticky; Jo's mouth was dry even as her hair was damp at the temples and on the back of her neck.

Leaning forward as far as she could, cushioning herself against the sway of the boat, she took his hand, still cupping the lily, and curled her hot fingers around his. Slowly, she drew his hand and the flower up to her nose. Fragrance wafted up to her; it was unbearably sweet. Her fingers trembled as she held his hand inside hers and breathed his lily.

And then, feeling his gaze on her, she blinked and looked up directly into his enigmatic green eyes.

There was only the slighest hesitation before he asked, in a gruff and uneven tone, "What would you do if I kissed you right now?"

Chapter Nine

Her mouth was dry. "Are you asking permission?"

Shrugging, he wiped at the drops of perspiration drizzling down his brow. "Are you giving it?"

"Okay," she said with a small smile. "Permission granted."

He smiled, too, and laughed as she tried to lean into him. Her movements weren't as careful as they'd been before, and the canoe tipped dangerously to one side.

"Steady." Neil's voice was also steady as he attempted to pull her into his lap.

But the boat was having none of it. If they were too close to each other, or both near the back seat, the weight was apparently not distributed properly and the canoe threatened to dump them both in the lake. The best they could do was a chaste face-to-face kiss if they stretched toward each other as far as they could go across their knees.

With a growled curse, Neil grabbed the lily and threw it back in the water. "This is ridiculous."

Jo couldn't help laughing. It was certainly not the most romantic situation she'd ever been in, with a rocking boat and contortions required to produce one rather unsatisfactory kiss.

"Doomed to failure," Neil concluded with a sigh. The hands she had been dying to feel on her body settled on her shoulder blades, nudging her to turn around and go back to the front of the canoe. Neil rattled around for a few seconds and then silently handed over her paddle.

"We'll just have to try again under better conditions," Jo said hopefully.

"We really ought to get back, anyway. It's getting dark." He wondered if he should be thankful that the canoe was as unaccommodating as it was. Otherwise, they might very well have started something neither one would want to finish. For his part, he told himself he certainly didn't need to get embroiled in that kind of emotional maelstrom.

As he spun the boat around to head across the lake to their campsite, four or five birds laughed over their heads.

Jo's voice reflected an ironic conclusion. "Loons," she said. "Why am I not surprised they think we're hilarious?"

Clutching her precious water samples, Jo waited as he secured the canoe, and then they hiked up the path to the ledge, careful of their footing in the dwindling light.

She packed away all the bottles as he stood watching her progress. She sensed he felt a bit uncomfortable about the awkward interchange in the boat; she knew she did.

Finally, he asked politely, "Do you still want a fire to watch the end of the sunset?"

"Too hot for a fire, I think."

"You're probably right."

Her tone verged on the testy when she said, "I'm not *probably* right. I *am* right. It's too hot for a fire."

"Okay, okay. Take it easy."

She was immediately sorry she'd snapped at him, and she would've apologized, but the loons were laughing at them again, circling over the lake and sending down a shower of deep-throated cries. The flapping wings drew Jo's eyes, and she watched as a few of them zoomed in for a landing on the flat mirror of the water. With eerie, mocking calls, the birds dipped lower, then skidded and skated across the water as if it were a landing strip.

Neil's eyes were wide and he glanced quickly at Jo. "Have you ever seen anything like that?"

She shook her head.

"Wow."

He took her hand, and they moved up to the log on the ledge for a better view of the show the black and white loons were giving. After some noisy arguing and playing around, three of the birds formed a line, toeing up on top of the water.

Neil murmured, "What can this be? It looks like they're lining up for the hundred-yard dash."

They were. After the equivalent of a starter's pistol, the loons took off, running upright across the lake, as if the surface were as solid as concrete. Excitedly flapping their wings, they began to lift off near the end of their runway, until all three were flying smoothly, circling once in a farewell, and then winging away, leaving only a trace of a melancholy hoot.

"Do you think that's a normal thing for them to do?" Jo squinted at the other birds, none of whom seemed predisposed toward foot races. "Running on the water?"

Neil patted her hand and said kindly, "I'd be surprised if they developed this trick just for us."

"Well, you never know."

He smiled as he eased a little closer on the log bench. They were both sticky with bug spray and perspiration, and neither minded in the least. Together, in companionable silence, they sat on their log and watched the last pink embers of the sun fade in the western sky. It wasn't a spectacular sunset, but perfect nonetheless, with streaks of gold and orange and glowing pink playing against the dusk and reflecting in ripples on the water.

"I'm sorry I bit your head off about the fire," Jo offered after a while.

"And I'm sorry I threw the lily back in the water."

Jo shifted to look in his eyes. "It was sweet that you picked it for me, even if you did throw it back."

"In a fit of pique."

"It wasn't your fault."

"Sorry."

"It's okay."

And so they sat there, barely touching, but very aware of a few small patches of skin—his finger brushing her arm, her hand skating past the smooth fabric on his knee, a lock of her hair ruffling back against his shoulder.

"Wouldn't it be nice to live in a place like this?" Jo ventured. "You could sit out here every night and watch the sunset."

"And the loon races."

"Who needs the horses at the track? We could bet on loons."

"Tough on the jockeys, though."

Laughing, Jo poked him in the ribs. "Forget it—I'm banning gambling here. I guess we'll have to find another place to watch the sunset."

"It's a nice place, though, even without loon races." He paused and then said casually, "My parents have a house on a lake near Brainerd. I haven't been there in a long time."

"Not your style?" she guessed, catching his expression when he mentioned it. "Okay, then, if you could live anywhere in the world, where would you go?"

"The White House?"

She drew back and stared at him. "Do you really mean that?"

"I don't know. I've never really thought about it."

She had gotten that answer a few too many times. Jo sighed with exasperation. "Do you mean to tell me you really don't know? That you never sat back and pondered the mysteries of the universe or what you wanted to do with your life or where you'd live and what you'd do if you could wave a magic wand?''

''No,'' he said truthfully. ''I've never done that.''

Jo was sitting there, staring at him, with a stunned and astonished expression.

Stifling the urge to laugh, Neil asked, ''Why do I get the idea you've considered these questions more than once?''

''Well, of course I have! I thought everyone had.''

''I'm glad one of us is prepared.'' Humoring her, he handed over a small, bent stick. ''Okay, Jo, here's your magic wand. I believe you said this gives you the right to choose any place in the world to live. So, where are you going?''

''Do you really want to know?''

He tapped the end of her freckled nose. ''Of course I want to know. I asked, didn't I?''

''All right then.'' She rocked back on the log and gazed into space, collecting her thoughts. ''If I could live anywhere, I guess I'd take a big house in the country. Nothing fancy, just a big white house with peeling paint and a huge front porch facing west.''

''Sounds like the house you've already got.''

''Ah, but that's not mine. It's my mother's, and I share it with Eliza and Maggie and a thousand other Wentworths who drop by whenever they feel like it.'' Chewing her lip, Jo continued to formulate her fantasy. ''This house would be all mine, and people would have to ask before they visited. It'd be in the country, and I'd want some land attached. I'd cram it full of kids, dogs, cats, rabbits and squirrels and make all my own quilts, and plant wildflowers instead of grass. What do you think?''

''Oh, it's you all right.''

"And what about you, Neil? I really don't believe you about the White House, you know. You don't seem ambitious enough."

"I can be if the occasion calls for it."

"Okay," she said, "if you say so. This is your fantasy, not mine. So politics is your life's work. But what else do you see in your future? A family, maybe?"

"You're not just going to let me get away with saying I don't know, are you?" Expelling a breath, Neil reached out to finger a stand of ginger-colored hair waving past Jo's shoulder. "Why should I think about the future? My future has always been set in stone. Politics? Yes. Family? I suppose. A well-educated, discreet wife with political connections, and two point two kids to ride in parades."

"Is that really what you want?"

He shrugged. "What I want has never been an issue. What's expected of me, now *that* I know."

"And the Nancy Reagan wife and kids is what's expected of you?"

He nodded.

"Anything else?"

"Let's see..." As his hand dropped from her hair, he ticked items off on his fingers. "Don't rock the Hawthorne boat; keep up appearances at all costs; take the lieutenant governor appointment when it's offered even if you don't want it. I'd say that about covers it."

"What?" Jo sat up straighter and pulled him around so that he'd have to look at her. "You let that slide into the conversation like it's nothing, no biggie. Lieutenant governor? Are you kidding? When is this happening? How? Aren't you excited or scared or anything?"

"I don't kn—"

She cut him off with a finger to his lips. "If you say you don't know, I swear I'll smack you. You must know when and how. Is it for sure?"

"When—soon, a couple of months, I think. How—my uncle is ill and he's going to resign. Helen Lindquist will move up to the governor spot, creating a vacancy at lieutenant governor. My father and some of the other party bigwigs are pushing me into the appointment."

"You say this all so matter-of-factly, like you don't even care."

Jo was prepared to display a frenzy of enthusiasm. Heavens! Neil was bucking for the state's second-highest office! But how could she get excited if he was so apathetic?

Glancing down, Neil grappled with the question of why he couldn't seem to put a cork in it. Information was flowing out like he'd been given truth serum.

As casually as if his innermost thoughts were common knowledge, he heard himself say, "I'd be happier about it if it were anything but a standard political shuffle. They want me because the Hawthorne name guarantees electability later on. I'm a known quantity and a team player, and the chances are slim that I'll blow up in their faces down the line. Those are the important things."

"I don't believe you."

"It's true." He smiled bitterly. "They wouldn't care if I had an IQ of four and couldn't tie my own shoes."

"Nonsense." Working up a full head of steam, Jo slipped into her most persuasive mode, the one she only used when she truly believed something with every fiber of her being. "They want you because you're smart and savvy and because you care so much about people and issues. You're honest and gentle and a wonderful person. Of course they want you!"

His answering smile was wan. Honest? Gentle? Who was she kidding? "You ought to be the politician, Jo. You've even got me believing you, when I *know* you're crazy."

"No," she said firmly, clasping his hands in hers, "I'm not crazy. You'd do a great job as lieutenant governor."

"Actually, I probably would. But that isn't the issue. No matter what kind of job I'd do, the appointment would be offered for all the wrong reasons."

He pulled his hands away, and slid them into his pants pockets as he rose from the bench. Wheeling abruptly to face the lake, he was framed against a backdrop of dark, tall trees and deep, unfathomable water. Behind him, a sliver of moon glowed soft white.

"But don't worry," he said grimly. "I've been trained well enough not to walk away from an opportunity like this. When they offer the position, I know better than to refuse."

Jo scrambled to her feet to join him. "Don't you see that it doesn't matter why they offer it? Even if it's only because of your name, which I don't believe for a minute, you'll still be able to do a lot of good once you're the lieutenant governor. The very thing that makes you uneasy about taking it is what will make you so great at the job." Her hand slipped up to cradle his jaw. "You have a conscience, Neil, and that's wonderful."

He closed his eyes, savoring the feeling of her small hand against his jaw. "A conscience?" he muttered, and shifted away from her touch.

If only she knew what she was suggesting. If he had a conscience, he never would've considered infiltrating her group, or lying to her every day that he didn't tell her his true motives. His lips twisted into a mocking line.

Right now, Jo didn't have a clue as to what he was really like.

He turned away completely, gazing out at the still water, but seeing only a reflection of himself. Jo's faith in him, and the rose-colored opinion she seemed to have formed, touched him deeply. He found himself wanting to try his damnedest to live up to her vision of him, to shed his skin and become the Neil Hawthorne she saw when she looked at him.

But he couldn't. He was only a very imperfect man, and he couldn't unburden his soul or throw in the towel at Water Works, or tell his father to take the lieutenant governor appointment and shove it. He was the man his father had brought him up to be. And that package did not include a conscience.

"It's late," he said finally. "We'd better get some sleep. We've got a long drive ahead of us tomorrow."

"Too hot to sleep."

"There's a breeze off the lake now. It won't be so bad with the flaps open."

Jo grimaced as an unpleasant trickle of perspiration slid down her neck. "Let's take a swim first."

"A swim? In a lake that may be toxic? Have you forgotten why we're here?"

"Pooh. There's nothing wrong with this lake." Jo's brows came together darkly. "The birds and the fish are all fine, aren't they?"

He threw her an exasperated look. "I don't know anything about how toxic waste affects birds and fish, and neither do you. You're not going swimming in a lake that may kill you."

"Neil, Neil, Neil...what am I going to do with you?" Jo shook her head. "Sometimes you have to trust your instincts; you have to have a little faith. My mind may admit that there's a slim possibility of pollution, but my heart tells me there's nothing wrong with that water." She lowered her voice to a hushed whisper. "I know that the water will be cool and wet and clean...and it couldn't possibly hurt me. I know it the same way I know you could never hurt me. It's trust and faith, Neil—can you feel it?"

"No," he said flatly. He clenched his jaw, willing his body to pay no attention to Jo's words. "I'm not going swimming."

"But—"

"No," he interrupted, holding up a hand to forestall further argument. "Even if I wanted to I didn't bring a suit."

The startlingly clear image that comment created in Jo's mind was one she couldn't have shared with her best friend. Lean, gorgeous Neil, dripping as he rose naked from the lake.

"A suit?" she said softly, as if it only now occurred to her. She felt the warmth in her face flush even hotter. "Neither did I."

Neil's groan was audible. "Why are you doing this to me?"

Jo surmised that his thoughts were leaping and gawking along the same bare lines as hers. The idea that he might be as stirred as she was made her pulse jump and her breath unsteady. She leaned up to frame his face with her hands, feeling his jaw clench under her fingers. "I'm not trying to do anything to you," she whispered. "I just want you to trust your instincts. I want you to trust *me*."

He removed her hands from his face. If he trusted his instincts right now, the water would boil around their naked bodies. Instead, he mumbled, "I trust you. But I'm not going skinny-dipping with you."

The tension between them was unbearable, and she knew she had to break it. She had to end the pained expression on his face and stop the awful ache inside her. A joke was her only hope. "So wear your clothes, nerd." With forced laughter trailing behind her, Jo raced to the tent and poked around inside. She came back a few moments later, carrying two towels. With a friendly grin, she tossed one at Neil and then ducked down the path to the water.

"She's absolutely off her rocker," she heard Neil say to no one in particular. But tiny pebbles came tumbling down the path, and she knew he was following her.

"Oooh," she moaned, and sank like a rock. It was wonderful. Indeed, the water was cool, and briskly exhilarating. Jo felt like a new woman, even saddled with a T-shirt and shorts while she sliced in and out of the water. Neil had removed his shirt, but he was swimming in his trendy khaki pants with the little gathers at the waist, and the very idea made Jo smile.

She reached out and splashed him, and then dived back in before he could return the favor, so he came after her instead, grabbing for her ankle as she slipped past. The fleeting touch of his hand on her cool, wet foot was tantalizing. If she'd thought cold water would douse her desire, she was very wrong.

Inside the dark lake, Jo tingled and trembled, feeling him flash past her here, dip just out of her reach there. As they flipped and circled, her fingers trailed down his smooth chest, but then he was gone. His hand slid up her leg, but she kicked smoothly away, gasping for breath. She was trying her best to elude him as part of their splash-and-run game. Yet she wanted desperately to catch him as part of a different game entirely.

Finally, she stood up and shook her dripping head from side to side, raining water droplets out in every direction. "Time out," she said breathlessly.

"You know, I think you're the strangest woman I ever met." There was something close to awe in his voice.

"You must know some pretty dull people."

He gave her a crooked smile. "I wonder what you would've done if I'd just stripped off and dived in when you suggested swimming."

She couldn't breathe. "Dived in after."

He reached out for her hand, drawing her up against him. "No, you wouldn't have."

"Oh, yeah?"

They were hip-deep in lake water, and the only light came from a narrow crescent moon and the tiny dots of a hundred stars. It was dark, too dark to read the expression in his eyes, but his body was sleek and warm next to hers, and Jo knew what she wanted.

With her pulse pounding and her lips parted to allow her to draw an unsteady breath, she thrust her hands into the short, soft hair at the back of his neck and pressed herself up more closely, molding herself to the contours of his wet, wonderful body.

He asked me before if he could kiss me, she thought. *But I'm not that polite.*

And so she tilted up and pulled him down and kissed him with a hungry impatience she hadn't know she was capable of feeling. But she wanted him, all of him, now. Their lips met, warm and soft and sweet, and when his tongue tipped hers, she sighed with the perfection of it all.

Desire curled inside her with aching insistence as she tightened her arms around his neck, rubbing her small breasts against him, whispering his name. His bare torso inflamed her and soothed her at the same time, and she slid her fingers down his chest, committing the slick feel of his skin to her memory.

"Oh, Jo," he murmured. He bent his lips to the slope of her neck, and he heard her shiver underneath him. Her slippery little body did all kinds of wicked, intoxicating things to his mind and his body. Did she have any idea what she was starting?

This wasn't supposed to happen, he thought, groaning as he brushed his lips from the soft line of her jaw to the pink tip of her ear. He was throbbing, he was ready, and it wasn't supposed to happen. They were too different, weren't they?

There were too many obstacles standing between them. But it *was* happening.

Before he could convince himself not to, he swept her up in his arms and stalked up the path to their tent.

Just outside the tent, he set her carefully on the ground, but she immediately moved to bridge the small gap. She looped her arms around his waist, trying to pull him backward into the tent and the sleeping bags.

"No."

The single syllable was muffled and indistinct, but she heard it. She relaxed against him, no longer trying to tug him inside, as he held her gently in the circle of his arms, and his jaw brushed the top of her head, back and forth, ruffling her hair.

He wondered how in the hell he was going to extricate himself from this one. He'd almost lost it altogether, but the wrongness of his actions had hit him in the face when she tried to pull him inside the tent.

"Jo?" he ventured. "I think this is probably not a good idea."

She looked at him with wide, soft eyes. "Why?"

"It just isn't."

She swallowed. "Okay."

Not knowing what else to say, Neil suggested, "Let's get into dry clothes. I'll hang up the wet ones."

Silently, they slipped inside the tent, careful not to touch each other. Neil grabbed some things and bolted from the tent, and Jo wrestled out of her wet clothes and into dry ones as soon as he was gone. She had long since finished when he came back in a different pair of khaki pants and a pale yellow polo shirt. She tossed him her wet things and then waited again for him to return.

"Neil," she said patiently, even though she could tell he was avoiding looking at her. "Do you want to talk about this?"

"Not particularly."

She persevered. "If what you're trying to say is that you're not attracted to me, I can handle it." Her stomach tightened into a knot. "Just tell me, okay?"

"Good Lord." Leaning back on his sleeping bag, he covered his eyes with both hands. "How could you possibly believe me if I *did* say that?"

She took that as a reference to certain physical evidence that she had, as a matter of fact, noticed, and she felt herself blush under her freckles. Hiding behind a brave front, she asked, "So what's the problem?"

He met her gaze with an annoyed green stare, but he didn't answer.

"You know," she said cautiously, "there's a big range in between, well, everything, and nothing. I'd like to think that we would've found the right place in that range, even if it wasn't, well, everything."

"Nothing, everything," he muttered to himself, wondering where in the hell she came up with these bizarre ways of framing delicate issues. "Anything between nothing and everything is too much for us, Jo."

There was nothing in the tent to throw at him, but she certainly felt like it: Jo Wentworth, reduced to using petty violence when discussion proved fruitless. Sad days indeed.

"I don't understand this," she said rather loudly, trying not to shout. "I want you to tell me why there can't be anything between us. I like you, and I think you like me. No, I *know* you like me. You even let down your guard and talked to me tonight so you must like me. And if we like each other and we're obviously attracted to each other, what's wrong with getting to know each other better?"

"Oh, no," he returned. "Not me."

For one thing, he had entered her life because of a lie. He was certainly not going to get involved with her, knowing that, and knowing if she ever found out, she'd scream murder that he was a rat fink and a heel. He didn't plan to let himself in for that kind of merry-go-round. Besides, he had enough headaches as it was. Fooling around with Pollyanna was really asking for trouble.

"But why?"

He said, "Because you're too nice, okay? And I'm not particularly nice. I don't think it's a good match."

"Ha!" Now Jo was really rolling. All of her theories about Neil's childhood and its damaging effect on his psyche came racing to the front of her mind. "You're just scared to death of someone getting close to you because you haven't had enough love and affection in your life."

"First it was an Oedipus complex and now it's fear of intimacy." Neil shook his head wearily. "What will you throw at me when you run out of talk-show topics?"

"That's a cop-out."

"Jo," he said carefully, trying not to get angry, "you tend to idealize things. I think I can be included in the list of things you've sugarcoated. All that stuff you said about me being honest and gentle and whatever else . . . It's wrong, okay? I'm not the Easter Bunny."

"The Easter Bunny?"

"Okay, try this on for size. You are an idealist. I am a realist. Someday, somewhere, someone is going to shatter your pretty little illusions." He smiled, so cynically she winced. "But it isn't going to be me."

"You," she said under her breath, "are a jerk."

She threw herself into her sleeping bag with a good display of rage, but even while she was doing it, she knew she wasn't really mad at him. How could she be angry with a man who thought he was saving her from himself? The nobility of the gesture really appealed to her. In fact, it dovetailed perfectly with the image she already had of him as a sweet, caring man. Even if he did think he wasn't a very nice person.

Now if only he weren't so stubborn. Or if only she hadn't gotten so overwrought tonight, before she had time to convince him she didn't need to be saved from him and his dreaded realism. Unfortunately, her mind and her body both knew he was only a few feet away, and both kept reminding her of what his bare chest felt like when it was wet and slick against her, of what the short, soft hair at the nape of his neck felt like between her fingers, of how his arms felt around her, of what it sounded like next to his heart.

She sighed and unzipped her sleeping bag, throwing back the top half. The night air was getting cooler, but it was much too warm to be inside the bag.

As if in response to the sigh, Neil leaned across the gap between their sleeping bags and took her hand in his, squeezing gently.

He whispered, "I'm sorry, Jo. But this is the right thing to do."

Jo smiled into the darkness. The man was a sweetheart, no matter what he thought. Yep. She had his number, all right.

Chapter Ten

Within twenty four hours of returning from Creosote, Neil found himself an object of scorn and derision at the Water Works office. Immediately, the other members of the staff figured out that the trip to the north woods had caused a rift between Neil and Jo, at least as far as Neil was concerned, and they began to whisper and sneer in his direction.

"Jo keeps trying to be friendly, poor dear," he heard Fern sniff loudly behind him. "And high-and-mighty Mr. Hawthorne brushes her off like a fly. It isn't right, if you ask me."

"Jo deserves better," Chris grumbled. "Much better."

After which Fern contributed, "Someone ought to tell him never to blacken our door again," and Neil made a point of concentrating on the papers in front of him. But the two of them didn't give up; they crossed their arms over their chests and stood there glaring at him. As volunteers arrived for work, the story spread, and the group glaring at him began to grow.

Neil felt his long-dormant temper stirring into life. Where in the hell was Jo? She'd left on an errand hours ago, and he was unaccountably peeved with her for not being around to defuse the wrath of her supporters.

"Okay, okay," he said finally, standing up and meeting the angry stares. It was obvious that he wasn't going to be able to conduct his covert investigation under these conditions. "I give up. I'm leaving."

Scattered cheers sounded behind him as he slammed out of the office. He wondered what Jo would think when she got back, if she would rail at her co-workers for being mean to him and insist that he come back to Water Works.

As the hours passed after his abrupt departure, he realized he wasn't going to be begged back. He sat in his rapidly darkening apartment with his hand on the phone as time slipped by and she didn't call.

Just as well, he decided, knocking the phone off the hook. It had been a mistake to go inside Water Works in the first place; what he needed was some distance.

"I'm going to find out who's behind this," he growled into the empty apartment, "and be done with Jo Wentworth and her damn group once and for all."

He snatched the phone up off the floor and pounded in a number.

"City desk," he snarled. "I need a favor, Dick, and you owe me one. You tell me who wrote the stories on illegal dumping a few months ago, and I'll give you an exclusive on the next Hawthorne campaign."

It was an easy bargain. Neil spent the next several hours on the phone, scribbling notes on a legal pad as he talked to the reporters. If he succeeded in getting background on the dumping incidents, it was also likely he'd aroused the suspicions of the reporters he'd pumped for information. He only hoped he figured things out before they did.

His life became a blur of sleepless nights, hours spent scanning reels of microfilm at the newspaper library, and calling in favors to get surreptitious copies of police reports.

Soon he was sprawled on the living room floor of his apartment, with files and notes spread around him, drowning himself in coffee as he checked and rechecked every angle.

Even on paper, Jo was everywhere. Her name appeared again and again in the news stories and police reports. Forcing himself to be objective, he put her on top of the list of suspects, even knowing it was insanity.

But if he didn't want to suspect Jo, he would have to find someone else. Like Fern, for instance. So he shaved and dressed and took off for Westlake Heights, Minnesota, where Fern had come from. Maybe he'd find some answers there.

It was a two-horse town, with a post office and a public library conspicuous on Main Street. He chose the library. Luck was with him; it was manned by a gregarious woman who warmed to him immediately when he made up a story about researching the clean-water movement in Minnesota. He mentioned Fern, Stanley and Chris, all from Westlake Heights, to see what kind of reaction he'd get.

"Well, you know, I went to school with Fern and her sister Madge. Sweet girls, both of them. Of course neither one has the sense of a goose, but they're friendly all the same."

Soon he knew the name of Fern's pet poodle and who she went to the prom with in 1942. He tried to keep smiling as the high school yearbooks came out.

"Who else was it you asked about, dear?"

"Stanley Hoffmeyer and Chris Henry. Do you know them, too?"

"Oh, of course." The librarian beamed at him. "And such nice boys. Stanley used to live out on route eighty-one, until his parents died and he sold the place. An only child, you know, so he inherited the whole kit and caboodle. Quite a catch with all that money. Too bad he moved to the city after the bad-water scare." She shook her head sadly. "We lost a lot of folks then, what with all the uproar. Nobody died or anything, but a few people did get sick, and there was a big hoop-de-doo." She hastened to reassure him, "Of course, it all turned out all right, and our water's fine now."

"Glad to hear it." He smiled dryly as he jotted down "Stanley rich?" and "no casualties from water poisoning," still mining for anything surprising. "And what about Chris Henry?"

"Chris must have moved about then, too. Such a scandal, you know."

His ears pricked up. "Scandal?"

"Why, the boy's been married three times," she confided, leaning in close. "He had to move away because there was nobody left who'd have him."

And that titillating bit of info was the most suspicious thing he found. Fern hadn't the sense of a goose, Stanley had money, Chris had three wives, and, coming from Westlake Heights, they all had the same motive. The town and its librarian might have been entertaining, but they didn't pin the publicity scheme on anyone.

As he returned to the Cities, Neil weighed his options. Finally, the only thing that made sense was to go to the Water Awareness festival—a celebration marking the end of the Water Works' formal fundraising season—to watch and wait for one of his suspects to make a mistake.

But the minute he saw Jo, he knew why he'd really wanted to come to the festival.

She looked slightly wild and slightly crazy, her hair every which way as she checked people off on a clipboard. She was smiling, but her smile faltered when she saw Neil.

"I didn't expect to see you here," she said softly. "I thought you quit."

As always, the lie came easily to his lips. "I know this is your big event, and I thought you might need me."

"Really?" Her eyes lit up with pleasure, and she brushed his arm gently. "It's awfully nice to see you."

He cleared his throat and backed away, avoiding her eyes. She understood at once that nothing had changed, that Neil's mind was still made up, and she assigned him a few jobs quickly and turned away before she lost her patience and throttled him. Sometimes it wasn't easy being a person who didn't believe in violence.

As he did the tasks he'd been given, Neil followed Jo with his eyes. It wasn't even a conscious thing, but she always seemed to show up in the middle of his focus, no matter which way he turned.

He hardly noticed when Jo's sister Kit, magnificently angry in a knockout yellow dress, appeared from out of nowhere and shook her finger in his face. "You know, of course, you're a moron to pass up a woman like Jo."

"I—I—" he tried to say, but with a "hmph" and a sweep of pale hair over her shoulder, Kit disappeared into the festival crowd.

Peeved, he considered adding her to his list of suspects. Like the rest of that cockamamy family, she certainly had the temperament to do something outrageous if she thought her beloved sister would benefit.

Neil had scarcely recovered from Kit's verbal abuse when Chris growled at him as the two of them worked on the makeshift stage that would hold RoRo and the Boats when they did their benefit performance later. Then Fern pursed her lips and loudly proclaimed, "People who live in stone houses shouldn't throw glass," as if that was supposed to mean something.

He actually toyed with the idea of smacking the old lady. What had Jo told these people? Determined to find her, he trampled a volunteer or two in his haste to get to Jo.

But then he saw her and his determination evaporated. She was down by the river, crouching as she plastered an I Care About Clean Water raindrop-shaped sticker on a little girl's T-shirt. She smiled as she tweaked the child's pigtail.

She looked beautiful. Neil gritted his teeth and cursed them both.

As she stood up, she felt the pressure of Neil's eyes on her once again. Why did he keep staring at her? What did he want? She met his gaze, asking her questions silently, but he crossed his arms over his chest and turned away. "Coward," she muttered under her breath.

Behind him, Jo saw Alex and Stanley waltz arm-in-arm around the corner of the stage. As Alex caught sight of Neil, she stopped dead in her tracks and began to gesture vigorously, as if urging Stanley to go over and punch him, but Stan was shaking his head, refusing to get involved. With a venomous glare, Alex stalked up to Neil herself.

Knowing this meant trouble, Jo dropped a whole packet of raindrop-shaped stickers and ran up the incline to the performance area. She got there just as Alex raised an open hand and slapped Neil across the face.

With heightened color and flashing eyes, Alex thundered, "How dare you reject someone as sweet and caring as my sister?"

Jo interrupted with "Neil, are you all right?" and "Alex, how could you?" as Stanley put his arms around her enraged sister to keep her from striking any more blows.

Taking Jo's elbow, Neil said meaningfully, "I need to talk to you," and he pulled her around the corner and behind the stage platform. "Okay," he announced, glowering down at her. "I want to know what you've been telling these people."

"Nothing. Nothing at all."

He cast her a skeptical glance. "Then why have I been bawled out, grumbled at, insulted and now slapped? Do you have an explanation for that?"

Jo colored. "I'm really sorry about the slap. At least the red marks on your face are fading."

"Wonderful."

"And, as for the rest, I'm sorry about that, too, but it really isn't my fault." Jo stuffed her hands in the pockets of her embroidered overalls, wishing he wouldn't glare at her that way. She tried patiently to explain. "I didn't ask anyone at the office to take my side—I didn't even tell them I had a side to take. I swear. Not one other word. And as for my sisters, well, I had to say something, didn't I?"

"What did you say?"

She lifted her chin. "I said that I had expressed an interest in you but that you made it very clear you weren't interested in me."

"Oh, Jo..."

"Well, it was the truth, wasn't it?"

"No," he managed between clenched teeth. Not interested? He was dying for her. He had half a mind to cast away all of his good intentions and let the fire between them rage higher and hotter than ever. Maybe a blaze like that would scorch Jo and her innocence right out of his system.

Looking down at her stubborn mouth, he said with a sigh, "If you can, will you please put a stop to this and call off the dogs? I don't want to risk splashing a blow-up in my personal life across the front page, when that is exactly what I was trying to avoid in the first place by staying away from you."

"That's it?" Jo's eyes spit fire. "That's the reason you said no? Because of your stupid public image? Sounds to me like you might as well quit worrying, because your personal life is already a shambles, and any reporter worth a nickel could figure it out. What have you got to lose?"

Neil didn't answer. He shook his head, looked at the sky for a few seconds and then walked away.

"And quit staring at me!" Jo yelled after him. Her voice trailed off. "I don't know why I even bother with that man."

She picked her way back down the slope to the scattered pile of I Care About Clean Water stickers and groused as she collected them together. If she were fair, she wouldn't blame Neil for being angry, especially given the imprint of her sister's hand on his cheek. But to hell with fairness!

If he hadn't been so pigheaded, none of this would've happened. The two of them could've been enjoying the festival instead of getting into fights. Instead, everything was a mess, and it was his fault.

Spending the hours of the Water Awareness Festival looking over her shoulder was not her style, but Jo found herself doing it anyway, sending furtive glances whenever her path crossed Neil's, and getting a few in return. As the day dragged into evening, her plastic smile didn't fade, even if her stomach was churning and she kept dropping the stickers she was supposed to be giving out to good little boys and girls.

She did manage to gather her sisters together. "It has come to my attention," she said firmly, "that you are giving Neil a hard time. Cool your jets, will you?"

"But, Jo," Kit protested, "it's only because we love you."

That made her relent a little. She patted Kit's arm. "I know. And I appreciate the sentiment, really. But Neil didn't do anything wrong and I don't want you hassling him on my account and making things worse when there's really no reason, okay?"

"Didn't do anything wrong?" Alex demanded, widening her beautiful eyes with horror. "Giving a Wentworth sister the brush-off is nothing wrong?"

Maggie interceded in a warning tone. "If Jo tells us to butt out, I think we should butt out."

"Pooh!" Alex and Kit chorused, as Eliza ventured, "Does this mean Neil is fair game?"

Jo wanted to scream. Instead, she gave up her sisters as a lost cause, and kept smiling, kept pasting stickers on children, kept acting like a mature adult. Even when she saw Maggie approach Neil, Jo didn't interfere. But she couldn't help hovering in the general vicinity, dying to know what would be discussed.

"Oh, no, not another one." Neil's expression was grim as he backed away from Maggie.

"I'm not going to yell at you," Maggie assured him.

His eyes narrowed. "Then why are you here?"

"I thought I'd suggest something practical, as a solution to your dilemma."

"And what exactly is that?"

"I think you should quit fighting so hard." Maggie gave him an easy, reassuring smile. "Take Jo out to dinner or somewhere quiet, away from all these distractions. If people see that you two are friends again, they'll relax."

He exhaled a ragged breath, and then spoke rapidly, shaking his head. "I'm sorry, but I'm not getting myself into a situation I can't handle just to make Jo's friends feel better. Thanks for the suggestion—I appreciate your trying to help—but being alone with Jo isn't a good idea right now."

"If you think you can't be alone with Jo, then that's all the more reason you should be alone with Jo." Maggie sounded as if she found all this quite logical. "Obviously, avoiding her hasn't solved anything."

"That's true enough," he muttered.

Eavesdropping shamelessly, Jo had to strain to catch Neil's last words. *Damn Maggie for getting me in the middle of this.* What made her think Jo would go along if he wanted to be alone? She had *some* pride, didn't she? They must all think she was the biggest doormat in the world.

RoRo's manager had been signaling frantically for several minutes, and Jo could no longer ignore the fact that it was time to get the show on the road. Tearing herself away from Maggie and Neil, she raced behind the platform,

checked that everything was set for the Boats and then
dashed out on stage herself to make the introductions. It had
been quit a coup to get such a popular group for a charity
function, and Jo would've been pleased with herself if she'd
had time to think about it. As it was, she hadn't even had a
chance to decide what to say to introduce them, and here she
was, standing at the microphone.

But somehow she muddled through, holding up her hands
to get the crowd's attention, then smiling and thanking an
assortment of people who had made the festival a success.

"Last but not least," she said loudly, but she stopped
when her eyes caught and held Neil's rapt gaze. He was by
himself again, off to the side of the audience, and she
wanted to touch him with her fingers, not just her eyes. She
wanted to slap him. And then she wanted to ravish him, to
see if he and his body were worth all this emotional upheaval.

Caught in the path of his gaze, she faltered, blocking out
the reason she was up here on this stage in front of all these
people. She felt dizzy and hot and more aware than ever of
Neil and the uncontrollable emotions he stirred up. A public moment had turned quite private.

But the buzzing of the empty microphone, and the confused whispers in the crowd finally penetrated. Pulling her
eyes away from Neil with considerable effort, she focused on
a perfect stranger and announced, "Last but never least,
let's all say thank you to RoRo and the Boats!"

The band came running onstage, and the audience
whooped it up, cheering and screaming. With nerves raw
and exposed, Jo raced away from the performing area, as if
the devil were nipping at her heels. She was determined to
salvage this festival and enjoy the rest of the evening with
her family and friends.

Her sisters and some of the clean-water folks had staked
out a patch of grass from which to watch RoRo and the

fireworks, which would cap the end of the performance. Jo joined them, sitting Indian-style on the edge of the blanket and stealing a sip of Eliza's lemonade. She laughed and nodded at what she hoped were appropriate times, but her gaiety was hiding an incoming tide of hysteria. Maybe it was the crowd—a latent streak of claustrophobia—but she couldn't breathe.

Sneaking a quick glance, she saw that Neil had left the tree where she'd spotted him before. Where had he run off to? Not seeing him, yet feeling his presence so strongly, was nerve-racking. She trusted the instinct that told her he wasn't far away, as surely as she'd trusted her instinct that Loon Lake was clear and clean, as surely as she knew she wanted Neil even if she couldn't have him.

Jo reminded herself that she was staying cool, giving him space, but she was trembling with the need to track him down, shake him by his button-down collar, and demand to know what was going on inside that handsome, complicated, muddled head.

She flinched every time someone got up or sat down near her, sure it would be Neil and it would be all over, one way or the other. Only it wasn't Neil. She fanned herself rapidly with a clean-water flyer, trying to concentrate on the meaningless words of "Rock Out," the Boats' newest and loudest hit.

He was behind her. He knew she couldn't see him, and it was better that way. Damn. If only it were as easy as Jo's army of protectors thought, that the problems they faced would vanish if they just talked it over. He jammed his hands in his pockets and watched Jo laugh with her friends. She looked so right, with her hair a little bit crazy in the breeze, wearing a pink T-shirt under embroidered overalls with a bright blue happy-face raindrop stuck on the pocket. What she looked like or what conclusions other people might draw from the way she presented herself didn't matter to Jo in the least.

She was like an alien species to him, and it would never work.

So why did he find himself edging closer, hungry to be near her? Like a voyeur, he crept in a few more inches, never losing sight of Jo.

A hand descended on his shoulder, and Neil jumped.

"Stanley," he said, a shade too heartily as he brought himself back to reality. "You surprised me."

"I saw you watching her." Stanley stroked his beard and chewed his lip. "Why don't you just tell her how you feel?"

"I think you've misunderstood something," Neil said with a careful smile, taking a few steps away. "See you later, Stan."

"Believe me, I understand," Stanley volunteered, pulling him back by the shirt. "And I agree with Maggie that avoiding Jo isn't the solution."

Quietly, Neil said, "So Maggie shared her theory with you?"

"Well, not exactly. Maggie told Kit, and Kit told Eliza and Eliza told Alex. Then Alex told me."

"Right." His personal life was now undoubtedly gossip fodder for the entire Twin Cities metro area.

Young, tall, skinny Stan was beginning to come off like a father figure. He drew his brows together sternly and draped an arm around Neil, who didn't know whether to laugh or punch him.

"If it were me and Alex," Stanley said sagely, "I'd sweep her off her feet and out of town for the weekend. Whatever the problem, I know the two of us could figure it out, given the chance."

Neil didn't need a chance; he needed some peace. He needed to spend a weekend in a dark cave blindfolded, not a weekend in Jo's arms. He winced as the picture of what a weekend in Jo's arms could be like sprang fully formed into his mind, left over from any one of several sleepless nights. Those kinds of pictures he didn't need.

"Come on," Stan coaxed, punching him lightly on the shoulder. "Come up and watch the fireworks with the rest of us. You can stay on the opposite side if you don't want to be too close to Jo."

He knew it was a bad idea when he agreed to it, but he wanted to see her a little better, and she wouldn't even have to know he was there. There were fifteen or twenty people in between them, and he could stay in the shadows, on the fringe.

RoRo and the Boats finished up their song and scattered, but scores of matches and cigarette lighters flashed in the darkness, demanding an encore. Everyone was surprised when the Boats reappeared to do a surprisingly decent version of "Old Man River" in honor of the festival's theme.

As they coasted into the last verse, the fireworks began, and the eyes of the crowd turned skyward. The display started slowly, so that by the time the musicians were finished, the oohs and aahs were only beginning to build momentum.

Neil, too, concentrated on the bursts of color in the sky, tuning out the whispers and jostling that surrounded him on the ground, steeling himself not to look in Jo's direction, even though his body seemed to be tugging him that way of its own accord. The fireworks were a convenient excuse.

There were so many people standing that Jo's view was blocked and her claustrophobia worsened, so she got to her feet to be able to see and breathe. One of her sisters pulled her over to the side, hissing something about getting trampled, and Jo let herself be dragged, paying more attention to the spectacular burst of red that crackled and boomed and then showered the sky with sparks.

"Oooh," she murmured, shivering, feeling the explosion vibrate along the lines of tension in her body. She noticed for the first time an absence of sound around her.

Startled, she darted glances right and left. There was no one there; the entire crowd of family and friends had vanished.

Except for Neil.

She should've known. She should've experienced some warning signal, some heightened awareness of his presence. But the fireworks were so loud and her insides were already coiled so tightly, what alarms were left to ring?

With her hands twisted into fists, she switched her gaze back to the sky, trying to remember to breathe in and out regularly as she waited for him to figure out she was there.

She felt his eyes, and slowly, carefully holding together the tattered scraps of her self-control, she turned to meet him. "Well," she said softly, "what now?"

"Damn."

Her eyes were wide and luminous, hazel flecked with a pure gold the fireworks couldn't hope to match. He was sunk, and he knew it. Every good intention he had went out the window.

There was such weariness and despair in his expression that Jo's heart flip-flopped. Without thinking, she moved to him and put her arms around him. "Don't be sad," she whispered, closing her eyes and laying her head on his chest. "It will be all right."

"Sad?" He laughed out loud. "Sad?"

Something broke inside him, cracking apart the last vestige of his control. He felt like howling at the moon and he didn't care who saw him or where they reported it. He didn't give a damn about Water Works or illegal dumping anymore. This had to come first. He was rocking on the edge of something very important, a watershed in his life, and he didn't have the wits to deal with anything else.

He pressed his hands into her shoulders. "I'm not sad, you idiot. I'm delirious."

Something snapped inside her, cracking apart the last trace of her control. She had been so patient with him and he was calling her an idiot. She felt as if nothing she did reached him.

Blinded by white-hot anger, she stomped on his foot. "How dare you call me an idiot? You're nothing but a chicken and...and...a stooge," she declared, for lack of anything better. "You want to be with me as much as I want to be with you, and if you think I can't see it, you truly are crazy. You keep denying your feelings, and I'm sick of it. If you won't tell me what you want in your heart," she commanded, holding a fist to her own heart for emphasis, "you can take your public image and stuff it!"

He felt like a yoyo on a string, up one moment, down the next. First she was holding him, driving him out of his mind with soft sympathy. Now she was carping at him and beating up on him. He'd taken about enough of this today. Growling something incomprehensible, he grabbed her and hauled her against him, raking the metal buttons of her overalls up against the smooth fabric of his shirt.

And then he kissed her, with the fierce hunger of having spent two weeks with her image instead of sleep. If he had lost his mind, he might as well enjoy it.

His lips were hard on hers, but Jo equaled his intensity, needing to feel the harsh fury of the kiss to purge her frustration and anger. He made her feel so damned helpless, and so damned mad.

Almost against her will, the kiss deepened and sweetened. His lips, his tongue, his mouth were now soft and liquid moving against hers. She moaned into the kiss, wrapping herself in the luxury of feeling so close and so right. His fingers twisted through her hair, and she tipped her head back to meet his mouth more fully. She wound her arms around his neck and held on for dear life.

It had started as a battle, but mellowed into something far sweeter. She didn't want it to end, but she fought against that desire. Playing on the depth of her frustrated passion, he was getting away without answering her one more time.

"Wait," she said breathlessly, breaking away. She touched his cheek briefly, warming toward him once more, but she knew she had to be tough. "I was serious before, Neil. I have to be sure that you know what it is you want."

"No," he murmured, and pulled her back into his arms. "I need you."

"Oh . . ." The words were wonderful, and his mouth nibbling her earlobe was even more wonderful. "No, wait." She swallowed. "If this is a whim—if you'll hate yourself tomorrow for giving in—I don't want anything from you now."

He sighed, fingering a wayward lock of her red-gold hair. "I don't want to be crazy anymore, okay? I want some peace."

"From me?" she whispered.

"From myself." With one finger, he traced the embroidered edge of a rosebud on the bib of her overalls, gazing at the mixture of faded blue denim and pale pink thread. "All I've done since that damned camping trip is think about you. I can't get my mind on anything else. I want to talk to you and laugh with you and . . ." He stopped. They both knew what he was about to say. Looking deep into her eyes, he finished roughly, "And make love to you, with you."

She found her voice. "Me, too."

He inhaled sharply as he enfolded her in his arms, and he couldn't hold her close enough as he bent his head and kissed her again, tasting sweetness and passion inextricably mingled in her mouth. How was it possible to want someone so much?

He kissed her and she kissed him back until she was faint from lack of oxygen. She was thirsty for the taste of him, thirsty and needy, and the only thing that began to satisfy was the feel of her mouth and her arms entangled with his.

When she finally broke away for air, she wondered if she looked as shell-shocked as he did. She raised a finger to trace the line of his lower lip. He looked more desirable to her than ever, because she could see the depth of his desire for her.

"Take her home, mac," somebody yelled, and they realized simultaneously that the fireworks had ended and they were the only show left. Clumps of people were standing there, dangling blankets and lawn chairs, staring at the spectacle of two grown people so glazed over with passion they had blocked out the existence of the rest of the world. There were misty smiles and a few disgruntled frowns, and one woman had put her hands over her child's eyes.

Neil's lips curved into an irrepressible grin. "Uh, Jo, I think maybe we better get out of here."

Jo sent him a worried glance. "I hope there aren't any reporters here."

"I couldn't care less."

Arm in arm, they strolled away from the crowd as casually as they could manage, forcing back nervous laughs as they sped up over the last few yards.

"Jo," he said, unexpectedly serious as he looked down at her. "I'd like to take you away for the weekend. It was Stanley's idea, but it appeals to me all of a sudden. I want us to be alone, with no distractions, like it was at the lake. Can you do that?"

"I don't know." She hadn't thought ahead to the next thirty seconds, let alone the whole weekend. But he was looking at her so intensely, with such hope, she couldn't back away. "Yes," she breathed. "Yes, I'll come."

He grinned with triumph. "You won't regret it."

He was putting his key in his car door, when, abruptly, he spun around and took off, calling out something about needing to talk to her sisters.

"My sisters?"

She was mystified, but so jittery and hyped up she couldn't relax enough to legitimately ponder the question. Taking deep breaths, she waited in his car, telling herself it was nothing extraordinary to burst into flames or melt into puddles when a man so much as touched her. She knew, of course, that she was lying. This sort of thing never happened to her at all. Until now.

And the anticipation was killing her. Where were they going? What would they do? She felt like she was only inches away from unlocking his secrets and he was only inches away from finally letting her get close to him.

She remembered the touch of his hands, and she shivered. Getting close to Neil sounded like a fine proposition.

Chapter Eleven

When he returned, quite smug and mysterious, he whisked her off to downtown Minneapolis and tucked his BMW away in the underground parking lot of a skyscraper on a dark, quiet city street.

"My place," he said quietly. "Is that okay?"

"Oh, sure." She tried to sound like this was all a perfectly normal occurrence. "Perfect."

Jo's heart thudded as he took her hand and led her into the elevator. His eyes were intent on her, but she avoided him and watched the numbers on the digital elevator panel zipping past in a blur of lines and dots.

When the numbers rolled to thirty-five, the elevator made a high-pitched ding and then a dong and the doors slid open.

Jo murmured, "It's awfully high up here, isn't it?"

His gaze was kind, but there was a definite edge of amusement hiding in there, and Jo cringed. High up here... What an inane thing to say. Jo Wentworth could converse intelligently on hundreds of topics. And each and every one of them had chosen to abandon her at this moment.

He opened the door, and she went in first, determined to do a better job at being sophisticated and charming. She was alone with him, wasn't she? This was what she'd wanted, wasn't it?

"Interesting place," she managed.

It looked like a mini version of his parents' house, with the same low-key gray and white decorating scheme. The walls were eggshell white, splashed with black streaks at irregular intervals.

"Very different."

It was all open and rather plain, with low white leather couches that faced each other, and a chrome and glass cocktail table with a few tasteful magazines. She fingered the magazines as Neil pulled open the blinds.

Ah, now she understood the reason to have an apartment like this. Say what she would about the decor, the view was first-rate. The twinkling lights of the city lay before her, with dramatic gold bursts against the black of the night. The lights seemed to stretch forever, rolling away from her.

"What a view."

From behind, Neil wrapped his arms around her and drew her back against him. "That's the first time you've managed to put more than two words together since we got here. You don't like it, do you?"

She shifted in his embrace, and tilted up to graze her lips against his cheek. "I'm here with you. How could I not like it?"

He smiled, and it was a shy, heartbreakingly sweet smile she didn't remember ever seeing on him. It penetrated like an arrow to her heart as she thought she might finally be seeing Neil bereft of defenses.

She didn't have long to enjoy that glimpse of vulnerability. His telephone rang, and he left her at the window while he answered it.

"Send her right up," he said crisply into the phone.

"Who are you sending up?"

He touched a finger to her lips, and bent to follow his finger with his lips. Sharing the warmth of the kiss, Jo felt her body yield and yet grow tense with desire immediately.

It was as if the fires from the festival still burned, and only had to be stoked a little to blaze back in full force.

The doorbell rang.

Neil cursed himself for starting things at bad times, and he broke away to answer the door. A stack of white boxes and an old-fashioned wicker picnic basket were handed through the door, and Jo rushed to help Neil juggle all of it. The delivery person melted away before she saw who or what it was.

"What's this?"

He grinned. "A midnight picnic."

Poking through the food, Jo discovered it was to be a Chinese picnic, with delicious-smelling dishes in boxes bearing the distinctive markings of a favorite Twin Cities restaurant.

"How did you get all this stuff?"

"It pays to have friends in the catering business," he allowed slyly. "Your sisters got it."

"Didn't I tell you they were worth having around?" She sighed with happiness as she bit into a wonderfully rich wedge of shrimp toast. "And I can guess which one arranged this. Maggie, that little devil. She knows I can't resist Chinese food."

"Good. I don't want you resisting." He winked at her, sending tiny tremors to the pit of her stomach, which had nothing to do with food.

And then he took a red and white tablecloth out of the basket and swung it out under the window with the spectacular view. As he continued to unpack the wicker hamper, Jo saw little red plates and plastic silverware, a small silver ice bucket complete with ice and a cold bottle of Mumm's Cordon Rouge.

"Champagne?" he murmured, holding up the bottle. "Your sister has a romantic streak."

Jo shook her head as she filched baby corn cobs out of one of the cartons. "Not Maggie. She picked it for the red label. It fits the color sheme she's got going."

"You believe what you want to believe," he said, popping open the bottle with a whoosh and a ricocheting cork. "But I still say your sister has a romantic streak."

Jo discarded her shoes and padded across the carpet to the picnic spot. "I don't care if she does or doesn't. I'm just going to enjoy the feast. Funny, I'm feeling awfully hungry all of a sudden."

He filled a glass with wine and held it out to her. When she leaned forward to take it, the glass felt cold and smooth under her fingers, but he didn't take his hand away. His fingers were warm and pulsing, tip to tip with hers.

Jo caught her breath, jolted by the unexpected sensation of hot and cold, and she trembled, drizzling champagne over her fingers.

Quietly, Neil stripped the glass out of her hand and set it on the windowsill. And then he lifted her fingers to her lips, and licked the sticky champagne away. His tongue was soft and slightly uneven as he delicately brushed at the spilled wine.

Jo's knees wobbled. Each flick of his tongue on her hand sent sensation shimmering through her veins, dazzling her until she couldn't breathe. Her mouth dropped open, her nostrils flared, but still she got no air. "Oh, Neil. What are you doing to me?"

He pulled her hand around behind him and lowered his lips to the nape of her neck, sliding aside the radiant copper waves of her hair, holding her fast against him.

"Funny," he said roughly, echoing her words of only a few moments ago, "I'm feeling awfully hungry all of a sudden."

"Food?" she whispered.

"Good God, no."

Leaving the white boxes of food and red plates and forks scattered behind them, he knelt on the floor and drew her down to him.

She braced her hands on his shoulders, gazing down into his eyes, trying vainly to steady her erratic heartbeat and to regain a sense of control.

But there was no time for that. When her hand traced the line of his jaw, he pulled her down to his level and kissed her fiercely, urgently. Sliding to the floor, she took him with her, and he covered her face and neck with a deluge of small nips and kisses.

Jo was aroused and flushed, restless and eager. She felt her nipples grow taut inside the protective covering of her clothes, and she wanted more. Rolling, she slid on top of him.

His hand climbed to one of the top snaps of her overalls, and she helped him, slipping open the metal fasteners and letting the whole bib fall down in disarray.

It was much softer now between them, with the cotton of her T-shirt next to his oxford cloth. She rubbed against him, feeling the temporary relief of heightened sensation against the peaks of her breasts. She was tightening at the core of her body, even as she melted and flowed around him. But her overalls were hampering her movements and she peeled them off and kicked them away. Yes, much better to have free legs to entwine with his, much better to feel that much closer, that much bolder.

He moved away slightly, catching at her hand. "The bedroom," he muttered. "It will be more comfortable."

"No, stay." Her voice came out rusty and rough. "Please."

He shrugged. "If you want..." His eyes fickered over the length of her, small perfect Jo, wearing a T-shirt and bikini underwear better than most women wore silk lingerie. Kneeling, he ran a hand up her leg, testing the smooth, soft skin with his palm. She felt real. She felt sensational. Every bit of her was golden and dusted with tiny freckles. He had the crazy impulse to connect the dots and see where they led him.

She grew impatient and yanked him back next to her on the floor, laughing as she did so. But he saw that her fingers trembled and hesitated on the buttons of his shirt.

"Yes," he whispered, and together they managed to slip the damn things through their holes, although it seemed to take forever.

Finally, Jo thought, now she could fill her hands with the feel of him. Nudging his shirt off at the shoulders, she slid flat palms over his chest. She had never been so reckless with a man. She had never felt this all-consuming passion to acquaint herself with the hard angle of a man's shoulder or the inward curve of a man's rib. But these were part of Neil, and it seemed necessary and right to touch them, to want them, to know them, as much as she wanted him.

Clothes tumbled around them, summarily pushed out of the way as they reached for each other. Skin to skin, there could be no secrets and no regrets, and only one culmination.

When Jo felt the impact of Neil's warm skin next to her and around her, strong, demanding, and yet reassuring from head to toe, she tightened her own embrace. Still, it wasn't nearly enough.

Moaning, she hitched herself up to find his mouth, surging into his tongue as he rubbed her small nipple between his fingers, driving her wild. Frantic, she ran her hands up and down his back, feeling his tension under her fingers, urging him closer, trying desperately to satisfy the hunger that began so deep within. She was crazy with passion, out of control, and she knew it.

"Neil, please," she murmured, insinuating herself against his hardness. The connection between their bodies was tantalizingly incomplete as Neil stroked against her deliciously, touching the tip of himself to the center of her discontent. But the impact was profound and fast. Tremors toppled through her body, one after the other, until she was gasping from the effort of keeping up with these hard, rocking feelings.

As the sensation subsided, sating one need, the hunger to be closer intensified. She needed to feel him with her, inside her. But when she lifted herself to him, he shook his head and braced himself up on his arms, slightly away.

"No." He entwined one finger in a rather damp curl that had drifted across her neck. "Not on the floor."

And then he stood up, apparently unaware that she was staring. He pulled her to her feet, swung her into his arms, and carried her to the bedroom.

He tossed her on the bed and she bounced, and then he jumped in after her.

"Now," he growled, "where were we?"

"Play it by ear." She pulled his head down to hers and wound her legs around him.

It was a definite hint.

Neil had tried to turn off his emotions, to ignite on the living room floor into an erotic explosion that would put an end once and for all to his debilitating need for Jo. But as their bodies melted together, male to female, he simply couldn't hold himself back. Every part of his conscious being was concentrated on Jo. He wanted not just to feel her around him, but to feel her as a part of him. He wanted her to know him, down to the core, and to like what she knew. Moving faster, out of control, he couldn't stop himself; he held her and loved her and lost himself inside her.

Tangled into his bedclothes, content and exhausted, Jo found enough energy to search his eyes for clues. Was it for her alone that making love had become a mystical experience? The inevitability of it overwhelmed her. She had never felt so wise, so desirable, so thoroughly loved in her entire life. It wasn't supposed to happen this way.

She reached up and skated unsteady fingertips over his lips. "I don't know what to think," she whispered. "I've never felt like this before." She hesitated. "It's like now you're a part of me, and no matter what happens, I'll always have that part."

Had she read his mind? Those were exactly the feelings he was struggling with. With her hair a crazy jumble of reds and golds, and her small, lithe body dusted with gold, she looked like a wild fairy child in bed next to him, someone who would disappear in daylight. Perhaps mind reading was part of her repertoire. He traced the curve of her ear with the edge of his thumb, and his voice became low and indistinct. "How can you know what I feel before I know myself?" he mused to himself.

She yawned delicately, sliding her head to rest over his heart. "I am completely exhausted, do you realize that? I guess it's because I haven't been sleeping well lately."

Easing her head up to nestle under his chin, Neil smiled. "I haven't slept at all lately."

"You, too, huh?"

"We're nuts, Jo. Nuts."

"We can talk about it in the morning." She yawned again and snuggled in, curving around him.

"The morning," he murmured.

His body was satiated, drained and he was so damned tired. Holding her, he closed his eyes, if only for a minute...

"Aw, hell." He sat up and scrambled for a clock on his bedside table. "Only for a minute" had become three hours.

"What is it?"

"The limo. Damn it, I didn't plan...well, this." He sank back into the bed. "I underestimated things a bit. I thought we'd have our picnic and then I'd sweep you out of town in a limo.''

''Trying to impress me, hmm?''

''I guess I got sidetracked.''

Jo propped herself up on an elbow and grinned. ''Is that what you call it?''

''I don't suppose,'' he began, punctuating his words with little nibbles on her earlobe, ''you'd be interested in getting dressed and leaving in the limo that's been cooling its whitewalls out at the curb since midnight?''

She ran a proprietary hand down his flank, casting him a look brimming over with possibilities. She whispered, ''I don't think I'm ready to leave yet.'' Sliding her hand to the center of his body, she felt him rise and harden under her fingers. A wicked smile curved her lips. ''And I don't think you're in any position to leave yet, either.''

It was Neil's turn to smile as he pressed her down into his bed.

DAWN WAS STREAKING the streets of Minneapolis when they finally roused themselves enough to fall into the hired limo waiting patiently outside Neil's building.

After a quick—and very quiet—stop at the Wentworth house, they were on their way to the Hawthorne's lakeside retreat. If Jo had expected a rustic fishing cabin with outdoor plumbing, she quickly disposed of that idea. Her mouth dropped open when Neil helped her out of the limousine and she got a good look at the place. It was cedar and glass, modern and striking, set against a backdrop of woods on one side and shining water on the other.

Posh was the word.

Neil pulled an old Volvo station wagon out of the garage and took off to get groceries while Jo explored the Hawthorne's lake cabin. From the spacious living room with its beamed, vaulted ceiling to the balconied bedrooms, the place was huge. Lavishly done up in a sort of pseudo-hip American Indian decor, it had the facilities to comfortably entertain heads of state if they should pop in. There were thick Indian rugs, big clay pots sporting dried grasses and wall hangings that stretched from ceiling to floor.

She was in awe, and more than a little uncomfortable. She slipped outside quietly, preferring to sit on regular old grass and look for four-leaf clovers until Neil got back.

But she had to laugh when she saw the results of his shopping trip. There were three different kinds of chocolate ice cream, a gigantic box of Cap'n Crunch and enough meat to feed an army.

"Just how long do you expect to be here?" she asked, brandishing a package of six T-bone steaks under his nose.

He grinned, loosening up perceptibly now that they were away from the real world. "Long enough," he teased. With the T-bones caught between them, he tugged her closer and bent her over his arm. Then he attached his lips to hers, nuzzling sloppily.

"The ice cream's melting," she protested, trying to right herself.

He dropped her immediately, surprising her more than the original attack had. As he cheerfully stowed away the groceries in the big brick kitchen, Jo smiled. Somewhere between the T-bones and the wet kiss, she had stopped resenting the overdone house. After all, there were boats and trees and flowers here, and she could force Neil to rough it at least a little.

First, she talked him into a trip to the small island in the middle of the lake. It was, she told him, prime turf for the elusive pink lady's slipper.

"I don't believe this pink lady thing exists," he muttered after they'd tramped over every squishy, swampy inch of the little island.

"Why, Neil Hawthorne, I'm ashamed of you. This 'pink lady thing' is your state flower." She planted her hands on her hips and tried to look severe. "What would the voters think if they heard you?"

"They'd thing I was smart enough to find a better way to spend my time than looking for imaginary wildflowers."

"It isn't imaginary."

With that, Jo marched down another trail. Neil was left to shake his head, contemplating what the hell he was doing following her.

By nightfall, there was still no pink lady's slipper, and even Jo had agreed to stop looking temporarily. Clean and fed and warming up in front of a fire, Neil tried to convince her to partake of some of the sybaritic pleasures the place had to offer, like the hot tub.

"No," Jo said adamantly. "I refuse to do anything decadent."

"So what do you want to do? Toast marshmallows, I suppose."

"You don't need to be snide," she returned primly. "We could play charades or cards or tell ghost stories. Haven't you ever tried to be creative?"

"I wouldn't mind being creative." His smile was sly as he edged over toward her and whispered a lascivious suggestion in her ear.

"We'd catch cold! Besides, I think we should do something completely nonsexual for at least five minutes."

"Why?"

She narrowed her eyes. "Ghost stories."

"I hate ghost stories."

"Cards, then."

"Gin rummy." With an expert flourish and a rather smug grin, he fanned the cards out on the floor.

She was soon very sorry she'd brought up the subject of cards. Every other word coming out of his mouth was "gin."

"Are you cheating?" she asked testily.

Blinking, he glanced up at her in surprise. "Of course not."

"Well, I don't think it's nice to beat a person to a pulp, do you?" She threw her cards down in a huff. "I don't mind losing, but this is ridiculous."

"How about a different game?"

"Not on your life. I'm going to beat you at this one if it takes all night."

At that point, Neil's fortune took a mysterious turn for the worse. The game dragged on forever, until finally Jo discarded a card face down and crowed, "Gin!"

"It's about time," he mumbled.

"Wait just a minute here. You let me win, didn't you?" Standing, she kicked at the cards.

"Jo, stop that. I didn't count your points yet."

"You think I'm so pathetic and feeble you have to throw a game just so I can win one. Cheater!"

He tried to reason with her, but she refused to speak to him for a good ten minutes, until she turned back with fire in her eyes and her arms crossed over her chest.

"Poker," she said curtly.

"There are no chips in the house. Do you want to play for cash?"

"What about strip poker?"

He raised an eyebrow. "Fine with me."

They got down to business. She dealt first and drew three fours. The best Neil could do was two queens.

Her eyes danced as he removed his watch.

They played on. Her smile was menacing when he unbuckled his belt; she was still back at the barrette stage. Her pulse quickened when he peeled off his shirt. The sight of bare skin added a new dimension to the game.

"Pants next?" she asked coyly.

"Women have more clothes," he grumbled. "Strip poker isn't fair."

"Sore loser."

"Bare loser."

When she laid down a straight, all he had was a pair of nines, and they both knew his pants would have to go. Slowly, purposely making her squirm, he slid them down his long legs, revealing a pair of navy bikini underwear. Jo laughed nervously. Was this what she wanted?

Down to that one small article of clothing, he battled back like a champion. Every hand, the tension leaped higher, Jo's heart beat faster, and she didn't know which she feared most—Neil winning, or losing that damned pair of blue pants. But he didn't lose. And she kept removing things, one by one, until all she had left was a T-shirt, which she'd stretched down to mid-thigh for protection.

They were down to the last hand either way, and one of them was going to be very bare very soon.

He dealt. After drawing, she came away with nothing, king high. It wasn't much.

Her hands were shaking when she tried to set down her cards, waiting for the exact moment he did. Her eyes flashed over to his hand and then up to his face.

"You lose!" she screamed. "Nothing—queen high. And I had a king! You lose!"

He remained motionless.

"Are you going to take them off?" she asked huskily. "Or do I have to do it for you?"

Suddenly, without warning, he reached over and grabbed a handful of her T-shirt, pulling her up against his hard, aroused body.

"I win," she whispered.

"So do I."

Tossing the remnants of their clothing aside, they wrapped themselves around each other in the glow of the dying fire.

WHAT NEIL HAD ENVISIONED as a weekend away was swiftly turning into a week. They were sprawled under a tree, his head in her lap, while she fed him cold pasta salad with a plastic fork. Out of the blue, she dropped a bomb.

"By the way, did you ever sleep with my sister?"

He jolted upright, almost choking on a noodle. "Alex?" he managed weakly.

There was a pause. "I certainly hope it wasn't any of the others."

"Of course not. I mean, not Alex either. None of them," he added hastily. "I've always been very careful about my personal life."

"Careful doesn't necessarily mean celibate," she pointed out.

He considered that for a moment, casting her a pensive glance. Gently removing the fork and the pasta bowl, he took both her hands in his. "Jo," he began delicately, "is this your way of asking if I've played around?"

"Well, maybe." She evaded his gaze. "I mean, everyone knows what politicians are like, hopping from bed to bed on the campaign trail. And you're awfully good at…it. I mean, it smacks of practice." She amended that. "Lots of practice."

"You're hilarious."

"You're avoiding the issue."

He smiled, genuinely tickled by what he had to conclude was jealousy. And he didn't mind the compliment that he was some kind of expert, either. "Any relationships I've had were boring and serious. Not bed hopping. And not with Alex."

"Thank goodness," she said fervently. "All right then."
She gave him an encouraging smile. "Now you can tell me
about the others."

"Others?"

"The serious, boring ones."

"Oh, no," he groaned, putting his head back in her lap.
"I can't."

"You have to. Spill it."

And to his amazement, he ended up telling her, at least an
abbreviated version. "And that's it—that's all I'm saying."

"What did you like about them?"

"You don't give up, do you?"

She grinned, retrieving the pasta salad, and popped a
black olive into his mouth. "No."

"What if I asked about your love life? Let's see how you
like it."

"Talk about boring."

"That's no answer."

Sitting up, Jo shooed him out of her lap. "This total
honesty stuff isn't as great as I thought it would be."

"Now who's avoiding the issue?"

"Okay, okay," she said indignantly. "I'm just embarrassed, that's all."

"Tell me."

She colored slightly. "I've never told anyone, not even my
sisters."

"Tell me."

After a pause, she mumbled, "Well, there was a college
professor whose mind intrigued me. But it was no big deal."

"Did he at least give you an A?"

She stiffened. "Are you making fun of me?"

"Naah," he said softly. He hitched her over into his lap
and tightened his arms around her. "I'm the only one
you've ever told?"

She nodded.

"Thank you. I consider that a compliment." His face grew stern. "Now tell me about the rest of the guys in your sordid past."

"Baring of souls is tricky work, isn't it?" she mused aloud. "All right—let's start with Bucky Applegren in second grade..."

BY THE TIME Thursday dawned with gray skies and drizzle, Jo felt as if she had known him forever. She certainly felt like she had been waking up with him forever. Usually he woke first, but today she had the chance to spy on him while he was still sleeping peacefully between the designer sheets in the master bedroom.

She leaned over and pressed her lips to the soft skin of his cheek, just under the thick sweep of his eyelashes.

His eyes flicked open, pale green and sleepy. "Time to get up?" he mumbled.

"Nope." She settled in behind him under the covers. "It's raining, and we get to sleep in."

He sighed happily and closed his eyes, and Jo felt her heart fill with tenderness. She had the bizarre desire to coo and purr over him, to cover him with kisses, to tell the world that he was hers, that she loved him more with every tick of the clock.

She sat up straight in the bed and swallowed. Sure his touch was addictive, his lovemaking fascinating. She knew that he respected her, that he listened to her, that he seemed to bring out the best in her. But when had she taken the plunge into love?

She had always imagined that the man she fell head over heels in love with would combine the best of Martin Luther King, John Lennon and Mahatma Gandhi, all in one simple, unprepossessing package. They'd live their lives in blue jeans, raise non-sex-stereotyped children and grow their own vegetables without chemicals.

What a dumb thing to imagine. Because instead of this mythical folk hero, her heart had somehow settled on Neil. He was a nice man with a cynical streak, and not a super-hero. Critically, she realized that he was very good-looking, perhaps too good-looking. It made her feel as though she might be giving up her principles in favor of going for a gorgeous exterior. And he was in dire need of rehabilitaton and reconstruction in several areas of his political thinking. Of course, she could work on that. She chewed her lip thoughtfully as she gazed down at him. Maybe she could get him to compromise on the CIA if she hedged a bit on the Sandinistas.

She shook her head. The point was not how many issues they agreed or disagreed on, or how much she enjoyed his company, or even how much she respected him as a person. The point was that she had fallen in love with him. Neil. The way he was. And she should've known a long time ago—when her heart and her body pushed her into his arms, when the love they made was so special. How could it be any other way?

"I love you," she whispered, trying out the feel of it on her lips now, while he was asleep. As the words drifted past him, she thought she saw him smile in his sleep.

Pent-up energy pushed her out of the bed, and she changed into a swimming suit, deciding on the spur of the moment to take a swim in the rain. She needed time to think before she told him. It had to be handled in just the right way.

She dipped into the cold water, smiling to herself, feeling the strength of her emotions coursing inside her. She was happy—no doubt about it—but she was also scared stiff.

Love to Jo meant much more than a few days of playing house at a private lake. It meant giving her entire heart without looking back. It meant trust and hope and commitment. The commitment didn't have to equate marriage proposals, no matter what her mother might deem appropriate. But when Jo gave her heart, she expected that inner commitment, that trust, to be there.

She rolled over and floated on her back, pensively letting the rain spill over her face in an uneven rhythm. She was wet and clear-headed, but nothing had changed. Her heart told her to share her news with Neil the minute he woke up, to hug him and kiss him until they were both exhausted and naked and happy as clams.

Her head told her to keep her mouth shut. Her head told her to find out first if this love would be returned. But how could Neil begin to return it?

He wanted a politician's wife and perfect kids to ride in parades. Not only would he not contemplate a relationship with a political undesirable, but he shouldn't even be fooling around with one on a temporary basis. All that hoo-ha about not wanting to risk blowups in his personal life, which might damage his public image, made his feelings about a liaison with her clear enough.

Jo sighed as she slipped out of the water. She didn't like having doubts, especially about Neil. But could he possibly feel the things she did? Her mind wandered as she walked across the wooden planks of the dock, and she let her gaze slide up the grassy slope to the house.

And there was Neil. He was wearing jeans, no shirt, no shoes, with his thumbs hooked in his pockets and rain dancing over his body.

"Hi," he said softly. "I missed you."

Her knees went weak. "I missed you, too."

"How was the water?"

"Fine."

"Wanted to be alone, hmm?"

"Everybody needs some time alone," she said with a small smile.

"Come to any conclusions?"

She hedged. "That we're going to have to get back to reality soon."

"Hey, come on." He kissed her temple and draped a wet arm around her shoulder. "I'm supposed to be the realist here. You're supposed to be all dreamy-eyed, and lost in the fantasy that this will never end."

"I guess I blew my reputation, huh?"

"Maybe we should never go back."

His voice had become gruff and uneven, and she looked up in surprise. What could he be thinking?

He tightened his hold around her, staring off over her head. He had never felt more at peace with himself than during this week with Jo. It was like a precious and unexpected gift to discover that he might really be the person she saw in him, that the world could really be beautiful, and fixable, if flawed. This time with Jo had restored something in him he wasn't sure he'd ever had—faith. In her and in himself and in their being together.

He was becoming more of an idealist than Jo. His lips curved wryly. What a turn of events.

Without a word, he bent down to pick the tiny bloom of a violet nestled in the tall grass, and handed it to her.

"You're always giving me flowers," she said softly.

He wondered when he had begun to love her. There was no one moment, but instead a gradual deepening of his feelings over time. He remembered the stirrings of affection at his parents' house, when she was ready to take on his father on his behalf, and the tenderness he felt when she stuck a clean-water sticker on a little girl with pigtails at the festival. He grinned as he recalled the full-blown surge of infatuation that had pushed him to let her win at gin rummy.

Whenever it had begun, the feisty wildflower was now firmly rooted in his heart.

"I love you, Jo."

Jo blinked, breathed in and then out. "I—I don't think I heard you."

"I said that I love you."

He skimmed the contour of her cheekbone with the miniature flower, and his gaze held hers steadily. Love and affection shone in his pale green eyes, and she wondered how she could have been enough of an idiot to doubt him.

"Jo," he said patiently, "this is supposed to be good news. Why do you look like you're in shock?"

She smiled brilliantly through the downpour. "Because I'm not Nancy Reagan and I *am* shocked. I mean, I knew how I felt, but you're so hard to read. My emotions sort of run out my fingertips, but you... well, I never know what you're feeling. And I wasn't sure you could. Love someone like me, I mean."

He said, "Nancy Reagan's too old for me." And Jo hugged him hard.

"I love you so much," she said, feeling totally inappropriate tears well up behind her eyes. "I love the way you sleep, and the way you smile and the way you look when your hair's a mess. But I *hate* the way you play gin rummy."

He shouted in mock outrage and caught her in his arms, lifting her above his head. "I can't believe you doubted me," he chastised. "Thinking I'd prefer Nancy Reagan. I'm wounded. Don't you know, Jo?" He tightened his hold around her. "Sometimes you have to trust what you believe in your heart. Sometimes you have to have a little faith in people."

"I do," she murmured.

And then she kissed him while the rain poured down around them.

Chapter Twelve

If only they could have stayed at the lake a little longer. But by Friday morning, both of them knew that their impromptu vacation had lasted too long already. There were places to go, people to see, responsibilities to be met. Chances were good that both Grand Affairs and Water Works would by now need Jo's attention, and Neil was scheduled to put in an appearance at a party his parents were giving that night. Reluctantly, they called their limo back from the Cities to pick them up.

As they pulled into the driveway at her mother's house, Neil paused and then said, very casually, "I don't suppose you'd consider going with me to this party tonight."

She was extremely pleased he wanted her there. "Of course I'll go. Is this party important?"

"Could be." His voice was deceptively light. "I was thinking of telling my father that I would definitely take the lieutenant governor appointment." *And add that I can't investigate Water Works, even if there is a bad apple.* At this point he had a serious conflict of interest, and he didn't care, anyway. He felt sure he could be a viable candidate without tearing up Jo or her organization. If his father still wanted to clear his pals at ChemCo and Red Metal, he could find himself another stooge.

Lifting her chin, Jo announced, "You are going to be the best lieutenant governor this state ever had, and I would be proud to accompany you to your parents' party."

"Thank you, Jo. This means a lot to me." He reached over and squeezed her hand. "But there is one drawback. It's black tie. Can you find something to wear on such short notice?"

"Of course!" Her tone came out a lot more confident than she felt. But Alex had tons of things, didn't she? Somewhere in that vast wardrobe, there must be something that would fit Jo. She hoped.

She breezed in the door, paying no attention to her mother's sniff of disapproval and subsequent offer to clue Jo in on how to con a man into proposing.

"I'm fine, Mother," Jo said, patting Lilah's cheek fondly. "I had a lovely time and I'm not planning on conning Neil into anything, okay? Let's just let things take a natural progression."

"Hmph," Lilah trumpeted. "I daresay you imagine this will all conclude splendidly, without my interference. But, good gracious, Josephine, I can't help but be distressed that you've chosen to throw yourself at this man, no matter how eligible he may be."

"Don't get excited, Mother darling," Jo said soothingly. She scanned the living room. "Have you seen Alex lately? I need to borrow something really special to wear tonight."

Lilah's exotic green eyes lit up. "Oooh, how truly marvelous. A formal occasion, is it? And where is he taking you, dear?"

"To meet his parents."

It wasn't exactly true, and Jo experienced a twinge of guilt, but nothing too terrible. She knew the connotations of meeting Neil's parents would thrill her mother and quash her objections for the time being. She hid behind that thought.

Racing up the stairs, she found the house deserted. Alex no longer lived at home, so there were no convenient closets to rifle. Eliza tended to go for little-girl cute, and Jo was definitely leaning toward sophistication for her look tonight. She knew Maggie had a dress in the basic black mode somewhere, but Maggie was six inches too tall. Kit was also way too tall, and besides, her wardrobe was worse than Jo's. So what was Jo going to wear?

She was tripping back down the stairs, having decided to give Alex a ring and throw herself at her sister's mercy, when Alex herself burst in the front door, obviously in a tizzy about something.

"Oh, Jo, thank heavens you're home!" She fled into the living room and draped herself gracefully over the Queen Anne wing chair. "You're needed desperately, Jo, simply desperately."

Jo hovered in the door cautiously. "I'm glad to see you, too. I need to borrow a dress."

"A dress?" Alex demanded, as if she were scandalized. "There are more important matters to deal with, my dear sister, than dresses!"

When clothing had become immaterial to Alex, the world had turned upside down. "What are you so upset about?"

"There's been an incident." Dramatic vibration in Alex's voice underlined the last word.

"What kind of incident?"

"I don't really know, but Stanley is simply in a panic. He told me to find you at any cost and, thank goodness, I did. He gave me a note for you, as if I were some sort of courier service. The nerve."

"Okay, okay." Stanley was never in a panic. He was the most laid-back person she knew. So what was all of this about?

The note spelled it out. "Dumping," he had scrawled. "Tyler Markham Industries looks like the culprit." And there were hasty directions to a small lake on the western edge of the suburbs.

Dread and worry combined in her heart. "Have Stanley and the others already gone?" she asked quickly.

Alex nodded. "He took off like you wouldn't believe." Her emerald-green eyes shone with admiration. She sighed. "I love it when he's decisive."

Meanwhile, Jo was already halfway to the door, muttering to herself about what she should take with her. She reversed direction and grabbed the keys to the van off a hook in the hallway. "Alex," she called as she backed out the front door, "can you dig up a dress for me? Formal, but not too fussy, and remember, I haven't got any cleavage. Oh, and shoes, too, okay? To go with whatever dress you pick out. If Neil gets here before I do, tell him I'll be back as soon as I can. I promise."

With Stanley's note clutched firmly in her hand, Jo was off in the Grand Affairs van, rerunning the contents of the note in her mind. Good old Stan. His directions were a cinch. In no time at all, she was making the last turn, wondering what kind of scene would greet her.

She climbed out of the van and stopped dead in her tracks. There must be some mistake. This wasn't just terrible; it was a disaster. She had never seen anything like it. The water shone bright red from what must be chemical pollution, and there was the smell and feel of death in the air. As she stumbled down to the lake, not much bigger than a pond, Jo felt sick to her stomach. A few of the Water Workers were there. She saw tears running down Chris's face as he knelt next to a limp bird. She saw her own sister Eliza, covered with mud and slime, as she tried vainly to save a few fish from the hole of poisoned water. Two ducks floated head-down in red waves near the edge of the lake; dead fish lay everywhere.

She didn't know what to do. It didn't appear there was anything anyone could do. Stanley rushed past her with a camera, and she caught his arm.

"Stan," she said in a choked voice. "I'm here. My God, what happened?"

His mouth twisted grimly. "It was Tyler Markham Industries. We found drums with their logo on them overturned on the shore. We don't know exactly what they dumped yet, but we'll get those creeps. They won't do this again."

She licked her lips and cleared her throat. She couldn't keep her eyes away from the contaminated water. "Who found it? How?"

"I did." Stanley's face was bleak. "Alex and I were going to go sailing farther west. When we drove past here, I thought I saw red water through the trees. I came down and looked and I…" He faltered and ran a shaky hand through his dark hair. "I couldn't believe it. I still can't believe it. I took Alex home and came right back. But it was already too late for the wildlife. That lake is so toxic I'm surprised we're not all keeling over from the fumes."

"How could anyone do this?" she whispered.

"Lowlifes," he said fiercely. "You know what we ought to do? We ought to refill one of their damned drums with this poison and shove it down Tyler Markham's throat."

"Yeah!" someone else shouted, and around her, Jo heard others take up the call. Helpless horror was hardening into fury. This was something they could do. This would make a statement.

Suddenly, there was a blaze of activity. Two of the men grabbed a drum and they all helped fill it with polluted red water and dead fish and then dragged it up onto the flatbed of Chris's pickup. There was no thinking involved, no conscious plan. They just wanted to do something. So they tore off for Markham's headquarters, in a caravan seething with rage and recklessness. Individually, they were nice, caring people, none of whom supported violence. But they had been pushed too far.

Before they knew it, they were there, crashing through the door with their barrel and spilling its digusting contents on the pretty beige carpet of Markham Industries' lobby. The receptionist screamed, and the sound reverberated in Jo's mind where she stood near the back of the group. Dimly, she noted the presence of reporters and lights and TV cameras, recording everything. How odd that they had known to be there.

Stanley was at the front, shouting at the TV cameras, urging Jo to come up, too, and tell the world what Tyler Markham's company had done. But then the police came, and all of the volunteers were quietly taken into custody. Stanley shouted, "You haven't heard the last of this!" And the others cheered and chanted. Jo felt like a zombie, trailing along on the fringe of this determined crowd.

She was sorry, really she was, that they had trespassed and scared the poor receptionist half to death, and she said as much to the reporter who stuck a microphone in her face on the way to the paddy wagon. But she spared no remorse for Markham Industries and its ruined carpet when she remembered the horrible scene at the small lake. Someone had to pay.

It wasn't long before she was situated in an uncomfortable plastic chair in the waiting room of the police station, trying to be a good role model of civil disobedience. They were all looking to her to be strong and defiant, and she did her best as one after another of the volunteers was released into the custody of a friend or relative.

And then Neil arrived for her. He was wearing a tux.

"Thank goodness you're here," she said, rushing into his arms. "You're the only lawyer I could think of. This has been a nightmare. Can you bail me out? What's going to happen next?''

"Nothing," he returned tersely. "Tyler Markham's not pressing charges." He steered her toward the front door.

"Wait a minute. I'm not sure that's a good idea. What if we want the public forum of a trial?"

"We can discuss this later. Right now, we're getting out of here." He held open the door. "Now."

She lagged behind him on the police station steps. "What is it, Neil? You act like you're angry with me."

"I said we can discuss this later."

Her mouth dropped open. "You *are* angry with me. But you didn't see that place—how awful it was—the dead birds..." Her voice broke. "We had no choice."

"Fine," he snapped, as a television crew turned on them from the sidewalk. Neil shielded her from the cameras as he maneuvered her to his car. "Not only are we going to be late to the party, but we're going to be on the news again." He yanked the passenger door open. "Undoubtedly my father will hit the roof."

"I don't care what your father does." She didn't get in, but instead slammed the door shut with a satisfying bang. "I did what I thought—what I *knew*—was right. If your father doesn't approve, you can tell him I said to take a hike."

With a ferocious glare, Neil reopened the door extremely quietly. "Get in. I'm not going to fight with you, Jo. I just want to get to the damn party as quickly as possible, okay? I want my parents to meet you and I want us to have a nice time, and I want to forget today's fiasco, okay?"

She got in demurely. "By all means—let's go. I can't wait. It promises to be *such* a great time."

MAGGIE KNEELED on the floor with pins in her mouth, patiently marking the hem on a full-skirted metallic-gold party dress that belonged to Alex. Jo had to hold up the strapless top with her hands until they figured out a way to keep it there temporarily. Meanwhile, Alex was painting makeup on Jo's face, humming to herself as she brushed things on from a sort of artist's palette with cosmetics instead of paint. Kit was cursing a blue streak as she ripped out half of Jo's hair with a curling iron, and Eliza zoomed in and out with potential accessories.

Jo felt utterly ridiculous.

She had tried on at least ten splashy dresses, and this was the only one that came close to fitting. Once they decided on it, there were two choices: hem it fast, or find four-inch heels. Given the fact that Jo hated shoes of any kind and never wore heels over half an inch, they ended up doing a quickie hem as fast as the united Wentworth sisters action committee could get it accomplished, which was pretty darn quick.

With the dress's semipadded bodice literally taped together, Jo was uncomfortable, but ready. She didn't know why she was even going to the stupid party. She should've told Neil to forget the whole thing. But he had said this was important to him, and how could she let him down? Instead, she allowed herself to be treated like a human Barbie doll, and she was going to go with him to the stupid party if it killed her.

Which it just might.

Alex proclaimed, "Ta-da," and thrust Jo in front of a full-length mirror. A phony, icky person she didn't know looked back at her.

"The dress is perfect with your hair," Alex insisted. "It brings out the gold streaks. You look stupendous, darling."

"I don't think I've ever seen you with makeup." Eliza put her hands on Jo's temples and forced her head to the side.

"She's a dead ringer for Mia Farrow, don't you think so, guys?"

Jo sputtered, "Mia Farrow! I don't look a thing like Mia Farrow," while the others ignored her, fastened big gold earrings and a clunky bracelet on her, and pushed her out the door.

It was time to face the music. That meant Neil, who was downstairs sipping tea and sharing polite chitchat with her mother.

"You look beautiful," he said gravely, and Jo glared at him.

"I hate it."

Things went downhill from there. At the party, Neil quickly steered her over to where his mother and sister were standing.

"You remember my mother, don't you, darling?" He gave Jo an insincere smile. "And this is my sister, Diana."

The Hawthorne women were carefully coiffed and beautifully dressed. Jo was suddenly painfully aware that her dress was held together with adhesive tape. Two pairs of gray-green eyes, very much like Neil's, examined her as they murmured something like, "Charmed, I'm sure."

Casting about for something to say, Jo babbled, "So nice to see you again, Mrs. Hawthorne, and to meet you, Diana. I've heard so much about you."

They all exchanged polite nods as Neil said, "I'll leave you to get acquainted while I find Dad. Behave yourself, will you?" He kissed Jo on the cheek and then disappeared into the party.

"Was that comment about behaving directed at me or you, do you think?" Jo inquired.

Barbara Hawthorne said distantly, "I wouldn't know," and her daughter Diana offered in an equally languid tone, "Who can ever guess what Neil means?"

"Not me." Jo stared down at the floor and wondered what in heaven's name she was going to talk to these women about. "So," she said brightly, "what do you think about clean water?"

Barbara and Diana Hawthorne regarded her as if she'd grown horns and started to glow green.

At that moment, Neil was down the hall in his father's private study, being offered the inevitable cigar.

"Look," he began, "I may as well tell you right now that I know I was on the news again. Channel Four spotted us coming down the police station steps, and there was nothing I could do."

His father raised a hand. "It hardly matters at this point."

"What do you mean?"

"Your penchant for noisy publicity no longer matters, since the party has decided to go with Clay Swanson for lieutenant governor." The ex-senator's voice was cold. "You've had your fun at Water Works. And I hope you realize that it has cost you the appointment."

"I see." He couldn't blame his father. It wasn't the old man's fault if Neil had made a few too many public mistakes lately. "The timing is awkward, however." His lips narrowed in a cynical smile. "I was going to tell you I was prepared to go all out for the appointment. I had decided I would make a rather good lieutenant governor, regardless of the situation at Water Works."

The elder Hawthorne shook his gray mane contemptuously. "You have sorely disappointed me, Neil. This clean-water business should have been disposed of easily, yet you've dragged your feet since the beginning. And for what? To protect the misdeeds of a scruffy bunch of flower children who aren't worth ten cents all put together. I begin to wonder who exactly you're protecting. Is your little girlfriend the one with the bent for staged publicity?"

"Jo has nothing to do with this, and you can go to hell."
Neil's voice was low, but it sliced through the stuffy, cigar-filled air like steel.

"How dare you—" his father began, but Neil cut him off.

"I am sick to death of being your whipping boy. Did it
ever occur to you that I might do a better job of running my
life and my political career if you'd get off my back?"

The ex-senator held himself very still. "It was never my
intention to make you a whipping boy. I only wanted what
was best for you."

"What you wanted was to turn me into someone exactly
like you. We both know that—we've just never admitted it.
But we are different people, Dad." Neil stood and slid his
hands into the pockets of his elegant black tuxedo pants. He
said quietly, "I'm taking a stand. No more prepared
speeches, no more dodging controversial issues and no more
carefully preserved public image. I am what I am, and the
voters can take me that way or not at all."

Settling into the back of his leather chair, Byron Hawthorne regarded his son sadly. "I'm afraid that with that
attitude it will be not at all."

Neil shrugged. "Fine. I think I can find some way to occupy my time." A crooked smile lifted one corner of his
mouth. "Maybe I'll shock the law firm by actually doing
some work for a change."

"If you need my help—"

"I don't think so."

His father fingered the brass corner of his leather-topped
desk. "And what about Water Works?"

Neil's eyebrows rose in surprise. "What about them?"

"Are you going to let them keep playing their dirty
tricks?"

"After today and the Markham Industries fiasco, it won't
be long before they're discovered without me."

"Son," his father said gravely, "your name is now inextricably linked with theirs, by virtue of your recent appearances on the evening news. You can be as independent of me as you like, and I will respect that decision, but it won't stop your career from going up in flames. Your only chance is to blow the whistle before some reporter stumbles over the story and plays up your involvement for all the drama they can ring out of it."

"If I keep going, it won't be to save my own skin—or yours." Neil gazed steadily down at his father. "But you may have a point. If I can nab this person—and I'm getting closer—I can keep the lid on. The last thing I want is to see Jo hurt by the whole place blowing up in her face. She trusts the people she works with. They are her friends. If she has to find out in the papers or on TV that one of them is betraying her, it will devastate her."

"And you'd like to be there to soften the blow," Byron Hawthorne remarked carefully. "I begin to see this picture more clearly."

"Do you?"

"You think you're in love with the girl."

Neil smiled. "I am in love with her."

The ex-senator blinked and clasped his hands on the desk in front of him. "You have to do what you have to do," he said softly. "But you'd better make it fast. Your dirty trickster is getting more reckless, if today's escapades are any indication."

He glanced up, and Neil could have sworn he saw acceptance in his father's eyes. It was as if Byron Hawthorne had finally realized that he had a son, not a chess piece, to deal with. The ex-senator continued, in the same conciliatory tone, "Tyler Markham's outside at the party, and he's hopping mad about what happened today. He told me you talked him into dropping the charges, that you said you'd handle it. But if he has his way, the police will be crawling all over this before you have time to fix it up pretty for your gir—for Ms. Wentworth.''

Neil nodded curtly. ''I was waiting for the bad apple to make a mistake, you know. I hope that framing Markham will prove to have been that mistake.''

His father turned away. ''I hope so, too.'' There was a pause. He sounded old when he said, ''I apologize if it appeared I was trying to make you over in my image. I remember so long ago, thinking the same thing of my own father. I would never want to do that to you.''

Neil gazed down at his feet. ''Apology accepted.''

''Oh, and Neil . . . good luck. With the girl, I mean.''

''Thanks, Dad.''

A hint of a smile played around Neil's mouth as he let himself out of his father's study and returned to the party to find Jo.

She was easy to spot. She was the one in the shiny gold dress, going one on one with Tyler Markham. Neil's smile faded and he closed his eyes, cursing fate. He didn't need this right now.

''I told you, little lady,'' Markham shouted, pointing a fat finger at Jo, ''those drums were reported stolen weeks ago. You can go look up the police report if you don't believe me. You and that group of yours—that hotbed of liars and fanatics—stole my drums just to frame me. And it ain't gonna wash.''

''Oh, yeah?'' Jo trembled from indignation. ''We don't do things that way at Water Works. You're just covering up now because the whole world saw the baby ducks and fish you and your rotten company murdered with your poisonous chemicals. How can you sleep at night?''

''I've heard just about enough of your lies,'' Markham threatened, advancing on Jo. His normally florid complexion had darkened to a shade nearer purple.

"Hold on just a second, Tyler," Neil said calmly, stepping in between them. "The lady is misinformed, but she doesn't mean any harm. Why don't you cool off and go get a drink? I'm sure we can talk about this later. Don't you worry, Tyler; we'll clear up this misunderstanding."

Neil cuffed Markham heartily on the shoulder, while his mother took the red-faced man's other arm.

"Tyler, dear," she interjected smoothly, "I don't believe you've seen my collection of Ojibway artifacts. They're fascinating, really."

Markham grumbled a bit, but allowed himself to be led away by the elegant Mrs. Hawthorne.

"Misunderstanding?" Jo hissed. "He killed baby ducks, Neil!"

A strained smile covered Neil's face as he dragged her toward the door. He muttered, "Come on Jo. Give it a rest, will you?"

"No!"

Even in her anger, she noticed that everyone was staring at them, and she lowered her voice. "I'm sorry I made a scene. But he said we were fanatics and liars! How could I listen to that?"

"Okay, so he's not subtle. But try to look at it from his viewpoint. The man's company has been accused of some serious violations today. He's upset."

"Upset? *He's* upset? Who cares?"

"I care," he muttered, and steered her out into the hall.

"Don't tell me." She felt the tape start to slip inside her dress but she ignored it, holding her bodice up with as much dignity as she could muster. "Tyler Markham is no doubt a big contributor to the Hawthorne campaign coffers, so you have to defend him. Is that it?"

"That doesn't deserve an answer." He took her hand and pulled her down the hall and out the front door. "I'm taking you home," he said grimly.

She sulked on her side of the car, her arms crossed over her chest. "It really hurts that you would put a pompous jerk like Tyler Markham ahead of me and ahead of what's right. Your priorities are the pits."

"Markham may be a jerk, but he's honest. I've known him since I was a kid."

"Ha!"

He began to get very irritated. "And maybe I know a few things you don't."

"What is that supposed to mean? That you know Tyler Markham is a swell guy, and so you believe every pearl that drops from his swinish mouth?"

He hit his fist on the steering wheel and stared out into the darkness beyond his windshield. "What if he's right, Jo? What if his company was framed? Have you considered that?"

"No," she said coolly. "And I'm not going to, either. Who would do something that awful just to make Markham Industries look bad? Who would stand to gain? It just doesn't make sense."

He paused, but he couldn't hold it back. "Water Works would gain."

There was silence in the car. Finally, in a voice throbbing with suppressed emotion, Jo managed to say, "I can't believe you would even suggest that. That's the rottenest thing anyone has ever said to me."

"Oh, Jo..." Neil's lips pressed together in a thin line. There was no turning back now. "But it's true."

"It is *not* true! It can't be true! Don't you think I would know if my own people were doing something that low? Besides, they wouldn't. It's the absolute antithesis of everything we stand for."

Neil said nothing. He'd known all along she'd never believe this.

"Why, Neil?" she demanded. "For what earthly reason would anyone at Water Works steal Markham's toxic waste and dump it?"

"Publicity."

The word echoed around her. "Publicity?" she whispered. "You've been asking questions about our publicity for weeks. What is going on?"

The tires squealed as he took a corner too fast. "I've suspected for some time that things were being staged to get Water Works' name in the papers. The thing at the capitol and then the connection between Ed Bergstrom and Fern, the money in the bathroom, the anonymous tips that sent you guys running after ChemCo and Red Metal and now Markham Industries—it's all too pat, Jo. No group is that lucky."

"No," she said, shaking her head. "You're crazy. None of my people would do things like that."

Neil's voice was flat and toneless as he went on. "I talked to Tyler Markham before I came to get you at the police station. When I convinced him to drop the charges, he told me those waste drums were stolen from his St. Paul plant. He dug up the exact date they were reported missing. It was the weekend of July nineteenth. Does that ring a bell?"

"I—I don't think so. Should it?"

"That's the weekend we were at Loon Lake. Somebody sent us out of town on a wild-goose chase so they could get to Markham's drums without fear of us stumbling over them like we did at the racetrack."

"This is ludicrous." Putting a hand to her forehead, Jo laughed weakly. "It's preposterous. And who is supposedly masterminding this? Fern, right, because that creep is her brother-in-law? Or maybe Chris, because his social skills aren't the best? Or how about my sister Kit? After all, she's into publicity! The fact that she is also three months pregnant shouldn't put a crimp in your theory."

"Kit's out," Neil said wearily. "She wasn't at the race-track."

"Oh, fine. Well, Fern and Chris were. *I* was. Maybe *I* paid Ed Berstrom to throw slime at me. Am I public enemy number one?"

"Of course not."

"Who then?" Her voice shook with anger. "Who are you accusing, Neil?"

There was a long pause. Neil looked out the window. "I don't know," he said finally. "I still don't know."

"You don't know anything," Jo returned passionately. "You make all these wild accusations and you don't know anything."

"I keep waiting for the person doing this to make a mistake. I keep thinking that there will be a slip-up, and I'll finally know the truth." He ran a hand through his thick blond hair, grimacing with frustration. "Any small mistake could do it. If someone could just identify the voice that left one of the anonymous messages, like today's. Or if somebody really did take Fern to get her brother-in-law out of the drunk tank."

"What are you talking about? What do Fern and the drunk tank have to do with anything?"

He shrugged. "I know it's not much, but it would establish a connection to Ed Bergstrom for someone other than Fern. Unless Fern is lying about the whole thing just to shift suspicion."

Jo said indignantly, "Fern isn't lying. I remember that day perfectly well, and I'm not surprised she doesn't. She was practically hysterical. *I* asked someone to drive her."

"You what?" Neil shot up in his seat. "Then you know who it was?"

"Of course." Jo glanced over at him in surprise. "Not that it means anything, of course, because you've obviously got all your facts screwed up. Take today—there was no anonymous message about the Markham dumping today. One of the Water Workers saw the red water from the highway and went in to investigate.''

This was it. A mistake on a grand scale. Excitement lit Neil's eyes as he calmly, quietly pulled the car onto the shoulder and switched off the ignition. All he could hear was the beating of his own heart and the chirping of a few crickets as he turned to Jo. "Was it the same person? Did the same person who drove Fern that day discover the Markham dumping?''

''Well, yes, but so what?''

''Don't you see? The dirty trickster blew it. Whoever it was got tired of the anonymity of the phone calls and went for the glory today. Our friend pretended to stumble over the pollution he—or she—had created, just to be a hero. Tell me who it was, Jo. Tell me.''

Flustered, Jo mumbled, ''Surely you can't suspect... I mean, well, it can't amount to anything.'' She flashed Neil a wide-eyed look and whispered, ''Neil, it can't be. You can't suspect Stanley.''

Chapter Thirteen

"Stanley," Neil echoed, "It fits. He had access to Ed because he drove Fern to the drunk tank. He's from Westlake Heights, just like Fern and Chris, so he's got a motive. He was at the racetrack the day of the pay-off, and he just 'happened' to stumble across the chemical spill today." He let his head fall back against the headrest. "It's got to be Stanley."

"No."

"Don't you see, Jo? Stanley was even the one who talked me into taking you out of town last weekend, after the fireworks. He was probably setting up another scam, and he wanted us out of the way. Or maybe he was afraid we were close to figuring him out, and he wanted us preoccupied with each other. It damn near worked, too."

"No!" she shouted, turning to him. "I refuse to believe it. And what about the trip to Loon Lake? You said that was a wild-goose chase to get us out of town while he stole Markham's drum. But Stanley had nothing to do with who went to Loon Lake. I decided myself and then Alex suggested I should invite you."

"And Alex no doubt got a lot of support on that score from Stanley, who just happens to be her boyfriend."

Jo's head was spinning. None of this made any sense. "What you're forgetting is that Stanley is a sweet, nice per-

son. He's as committed to fighting pollution as I am. He
could never in a million years dump that stuff, knowing it
would kill the wildlife and poison the water for who knows
how long.''

He slid his fingers over her arm. "I'm sorry, baby."

"I'm not your baby." She shook off his hand. "And you
have no proof. All of this is conjecture. Okay, so Stanley
had a motive, and the opportunity to hire Ed. That doesn't
mean he did anything. That doesn't mean anyone did anything."

"Jo—" he began, but she held up her hand to hold him
off.

"You have no proof, no hard facts. For all you know,
every incident we've discussed has been perfectly aboveboard. Now start this car and take me home. I don't want
to hear any more."

He tried to be patient and understanding. "Not talking
about it won't make it go away, Jo. Something's going to
have to be done about Stanley. We've got a choice. We can
handle it ourselves, and try to clear it up quietly, or we can
do nothing. If we ignore it, the press and the police will figure it out eventually. And then all hell will break loose."

"There's nothing for them to figure out," she insisted.
"Just a string of coincidences."

One of the things he loved about Jo was her stubborn
faith in people. He didn't expect her to abandon Stanley
without a fight. But it would make things a lot easier if she
would give in a little.

"I'll take you home," he said softly.

EVERY TIME she looked at Stanley, she wondered if Neil's
stories were true. It made her feel disloyal and suspicious
and she hated it. She kept coming back to the basic premise
that her world was worth nothing if she couldn't trust her
own feelings about people. She'd known Stanley for years,

and he simply wasn't capable of the things Neil thought. But she still felt dirty, because a small part of her wondered every time she looked at Stanley. Her solution was to cut down the number of times she had to look at him.

But avoiding Stanley was no solution when she still saw Neil. And he insisted on talking about Stanley.

"No, no and no!" she finally exploded, rocking the porch swing violently. "I do not want to talk about this."

He sighed heavily. "But you can't keep pretending it doesn't exist. We have to do something about Stanley before he strikes again."

"I understand that you honestly believe all this nonsense." She patted his knee magnanimously. "But that doesn't mean I have to share that belief, because it simply isn't true, honest or not."

Her logic escaped him. "What can I say to convince you?"

"Nothing." She asked sweetly, "Can't we talk about something else?"

"No," he said stubbornly. "You have to face facts. If you refuse to believe me, I'm not sure we should keep seeing each other."

Jumping up from the swing, Jo sent him a shocked stare. "Is that a threat, Neil? I have to believe what you believe or we're through?"

"No, of course not. I just meant—"

"I know what you meant." Her small frame stiffened with pride. "Nobody dictates to me. Nobody tells me what to believe."

"But this is different," he insisted. "This is burying your head in the sand."

"Did it ever occur to you that I might be sick to death of you harping at me about Stanley?" Trying to keep a lid on her composure, she took a deep breath and set her hand on the doorknob. "You know, maybe you're right. If you can forget your crazy accusations, or show me some proof, then maybe we can still pull this off. Otherwise, I don't think we should see each other anymore.''

He hadn't meant the threat seriously. He'd only wanted to shock her into listening to him. "Come on, Jo. Don't do this.''

She lifted her eyes to meet his. "It was your idea. Chew on that for a while, Mr. Know-it-all.''

And then she slammed into the house while he cursed behind her.

Mulling it over, reviewing the argument logically and dispassionately, Jo wasn't sure she'd done the right thing. But she was fed up with his pompous lectures and superior attitude. Nobody—not even Neil—pushed her into believing something her heart said was wrong. Until she got a handle on things, she decided to while away the hours lying in the backyard in a bikini, drinking in the late August sun and acting like an apathetic, freckled sloth. Her sisters agreed to intercept Neil's phone calls until he either apologized or furnished proof. So far, neither had happened.

There she was, switching from baking her front side to her back side, when she heard the phone ring through the screen door. Figuring it was Neil again with more lectures about Stanley, she ignored it.

Inside, Alex was applying the finishing touches of her fuchsia nail polish. The telephone rang again, and she swore at it, shouted, "Somebody answer the phone," and then ended up picking it up herself when it blared again.

"Jo?" someone asked anxiously.

"Heavens, no," Alex drawled, blowing on her nails. "This is Alexandra."

A haggard sigh puffed over the line. "It's Neil," he said grimly. "I suppose she won't talk to me."

"Bingo," Alex responded cheerfully.

"Alex, you've got to help me. How can I get through to her?"

"I haven't the slightest." In the background, the doorbell started to buzz, and Alex offered lazily, "I'd love to stay and chat, Neil dear, but Stanley's here to take me to the fair. Ciao, sweetness."

The phone cut off with a clunk in his ear. He was getting awfully tired of this. He had half a mind to call up the *Star and Tribune* right now and turn over the whole ugly story. But he knew he wouldn't. A part of him clung to the idea that Jo would believe him and the two of them would handle it together, if only he could force her to discuss it. He shook his head at the depth of his own foolishness.

So Stanley and Alex were on their way to the fair. Charming. The state fair, no doubt. Stanley would be with the woman he loved, eating Pronto Pups and deep-fried cheese curds, while Neil and Jo's feud raged on. Since it was Stanley's fault that this had happened in the first place, the situation really didn't seem quite equitable.

Neil threw the receiver back onto the hook with more force than was absolutely necessary. Damn Stanley, anyway, taking a day off from his nefarious activities to take Alex to the fair.

But wait a second. Neil rustled around in his desk drawer for a street map of the Twin Cities. Stanley and Alex were going to the state fair, and the fairgrounds were awfully close to Markham Industries' St. Paul plant. If Stanley were getting cocky, couldn't he be planning another toxic-waste heist under cover of an innocent trip to the state fair with his girlfriend?

Neil grabbed a jacket and was out the door in a flash. If he was right, Jo would have to listen. If he got lucky, she would see the truth right before her very eyes.

No one answered the Wentworths' front door, so he let himself in. That's what they got for leaving their door open.

Nonetheless, he proceeded carefully, trying not to make any noise as he poked around the rooms on the first floor, looking for Jo. He had just reached the swinging door into the kitchen when the telephone rang from the other side. He flattened himself against the door and froze where he was.

The phone rang again and again, until finally the screen door to the outside slammed and he heard someone jerk the phone off the wall.

He eased the kitchen door open an inch or two, just enough to see who had answered the phone. She seemed to be hesitating, holding the phone but not bringing it up to her ear. Eventually, she brought it closer, snapped, "Hello," and then shouted, "No, I don't want to buy any carpet," before smashing it back into place.

He opened the door and strolled into the kitchen. "Hi, Jo."

She spun around, choked and laid a hand over the bosom of her bikini, all in the same motion. "What are you doing in my house?"

"What are you doing dressed like that?"

She blushed. "None of your business."

He scowled. "Did anyone see you?"

"How should I know. Who cares?"

"*I* care."

Lifting her chin, she removed her hand from in front of her breasts and stood stiffly under his gaze. "And I'm certainly old enough to choose my own sunbathing attire."

"You're old enough all right," he murmured warmly, surveying the curves of her small breasts inside the abbreviated bikini, the golden glow of her sun-sprinkled body and the defiant spark in those innocent eyes. "The question is, old enough for *what* exactly?"

"Old enough to tell you to scram."

He advanced on her. "Come on, Jo. It isn't really fair to shut me out because I forced you to face a few unpleasant truths."

"Or a few unpleasant lies," she retorted, backing up into the kitchen cabinets.

"Give me a chance to prove it."

He was right on top of her. "Prove what?" she asked breathlessly, holding in her stomach so that it wouldn't graze his jacket where it fell open. It did, anyway. She closed her eyes.

"That I was right about Stanley."

Opening her eyes, she pushed ineffectually at his chest. "How are you going to do that?"

"I'm going to take you to the fair. I'm betting that Stanley is going to pull something there. Today."

"The fair?" she ventured, fingering his lapel. "I'd kind of like to go to the fair."

He smiled, set his hands on her shoulders, and drew her up against him. Her skin—and there was a lot of it handy— felt sizzling hot and slightly sticky under his fingers. She smelled of sun and grass and summertime. It had been several days since he'd touched her, weeks since they made love. It felt like years. Who cared about Stanley? Having her so close was intoxicating.

His fingers were cool against the flaming skin of her shoulders. His eyes were a curious smoky green, and his lips curved upward in an amused, mocking smile. She wanted to wipe that smile off his face. She wanted to kiss that smile off his face. It had been so long since he touched her. Who cared about Stanley? Having him so close was tantalizing.

"I've missed you," he murmured, tracing a line with his index finger from the curve of her shoulder up along the slope of her neck. Leaning in, he nibbled gently on her earlobe. "Go change your clothes," he whispered into her ear. "I can't take you to the fair half naked."

"You have a one-track mind."

"I wish I did." He stepped back and released her. "I can think of at least one thing I'd rather be doing than going to the fair at this moment, but I don't have a choice. If we don't go, you'll never believe me about Stanley."

She slipped past him and headed toward the stairs, and he followed her into the hallway. On the landing, with her hand on the newel post, she turned back. "I want you to know that the chances are very good I'll never believe you about Stanley, anyway, no matter what happens at the fair. He's my friend and I trust him."

Sighing, he loosened his tie as he studied the contrast of her small hand against the dark wood of the banister. He said quietly, "I know."

She just looked at him for a long moment, and then she ran upstairs to shower and change as quickly as she could.

When she came back down, she was more respectably covered in baggy shorts and a faded Hard Rock Café T-shirt. She tied on her tennies and silently led the way outside.

It was only when they entered the fairgrounds that Neil realized how impossible it was going to be to find Alex and Stanley in the crowd. There were people of all sizes and descriptions, carrying shopping bags of junk they'd collected at the various exhibits and toting garish stuffed toys won on the Midway. It was a blur of noise, smells and frantic motion, and it hadn't occurred to him that he'd have to spot his targets in the midst of all this.

"Where do you think Alex is most likely to be?"

Jo glanced up at him with undisguised annoyance. "This is all so incredibly silly."

"Humor me."

She rolled her eyes, but played along. "Well, she's not the state fair type, so it's hard to say. But she does have a thing about ice cream, so I guess we could try the dairy barn."

They wound their way through a thick clump of people blocking the entrance to the dairy barn and quickly scanned the various milk-oriented booths inside the cool, all-white building.

"Want anything to eat?" Jo asked brightly. "I'd love a milk shake."

He wondered whether it was really Alex or just Jo who had a thing about ice cream, but he stood in line and forked over for her milk shake, all the while searching the crowd for Stanley's tall, dark form or Alex's bright hair. "Well, well, what do you know?" he remarked, handing Jo her shake.

"You saw them?"

"Naah." He laughed and pointed at a strange glass booth that was revolving in one corner of the exhibit hall. "Isn't that Miss Fish Fest?"

Sure enough it was. The beauty queen was wearing a ski jacket and mittens, and she was sitting on a stool inside a refrigerated compartment. There was a sculptor opposite her in the booth, and he was carving Miss Fish Fest's likeness on a head-sized block of butter.

"Oooh, it's gross." Jo muscled her way to the front of the crowd watching this butter-sculpting exhibition. "They're making busts of the candidates for Queen of the Milky Way," she whispered, pointing to four or five completed butter heads revolving around Miss Fish Fest and the sculptor inside the refrigerated glass case.

Neil laughed out loud as he came up behind her. He hadn't been to the fair since he was a kid, and he'd forgotten all about the Queen of the Milky Way and the nonsense that went with it.

With an arm casually draped around Jo, he bent over to get a closer look at the unflattering likeness of Miss Fish Fest currently underway.

"Looks just like her," Jo said with a nasty twinkle in her eye, slurping through the straw of her milk shake.

Neil laughed again, catching the reflection of his own image next to Jo's in the glass of the booth. Then the glass shone with a flash of red hair from the crowd behind them. Whirling, he got a glimpse of Alex's flaming mane bobbing out the door of the dairy barn.

"Come on," he said, grabbing Jo's hand. "I saw them."

From there, they zoomed in and around various booths and people, barely keeping Alex and Stanley within eyesight until the lovebirds stopped at a Pronto Pup stand. Jo's stomach growled as she watched the other couple devour a couple of corn dogs.

"How about Pronto Pups for us, too?"

"Quit moaning and look the other way, or they'll see you."

"What if they do see me? She's my sister, for goodness sake. She's not going to die if she sees me."

Neil explained patiently, "But Stanley will know he's being watched and he won't do whatever it is he's going to do."

"You don't know that he's going to do anything," Jo reminded him. "I bet this turns out like the racetrack. He'll do something really suspicious like go into the bathroom, and you'll shout, 'Aha!' like going to the bathroom is a criminal offense."

"Keep your voice down and turn around, will you? They're looking this way."

A rather cranky man standing behind the counter of the souvenir booth where they were hiding interrupted, "Are you two gonna buy anything, or are you just gonna fight and take up my counter space all day?"

"Here," Neil said as he stuffed a bright red beanie, complete with propeller, over the top of Jo's thick, coppery waves, and thrust an inflatable airplane on a stick in her hand. He grabbed a hat for himself and picked up a pair of plastic sunglasses with little Minnesota shapes in the outside corners. "And two of these."

Jo started to giggle as she put on her sunglasses. "What is this stuff for?"

"Disguise," he returned soberly.

Jo's giggles turned into peals of laughter. "This is great. The heir apparent is wearing plastic Minnesota sunglasses and an 'I'd Rather Be Fishing' hat. Did you know you have a rainbow trout hanging over your ear? It goes great with the suit and tie. I wish I had a camera."

"Damn." He'd forgotten he was wearing work clothes. Peeling out of his jacket and shirt, and stuffing them into a souvenir shopping bag, he snatched up the nearest T-shirt and tossed more money at the stand's proprietor.

"Do you think it behooves a politician to strip in public?" Jo asked playfully.

"Cut the comedy. Alex and Stanley are moving toward the food pavilion."

"At least that way I can snag a brownie and a big bucket of French fries while we keep Alex and Stanley under surveillance."

"How can you keep eating that junk?"

Jo just shrugged and smiled and bit into a corn dog as they wandered after her sister. In spite of her mixed feelings about Stanley and Neil and the mess they were all in, she was having a great time today. She loved Neil's hat, especially the rainbow trout. And she loved being with him, even under these screwball conditions. She could almost pretend that they had gone to the fair like any normal couple, just to enjoy themselves.

They followed Alex and Stanley into an enclave of artsy-craftsy stands as Stan pointed Alex in the direction of a caricaturist's booth.

"Isn't that nice?" Jo remarked cheerily. "He wants a picture of her."

"What a guy," Neil added sarcastically.

Jo and Neil made themselves comfortable, pretending to examine the wares at the Daughters of Sweden souvenir shack while keeping an eye on the caricature booth where Alex was perched on a stool. The artist sat inside the booth and kept up a stream of chatter to entertain Alex for the thirty minutes his sign proclaimed it took to do the finished sketch.

"Will Alex really be able to sit still for thirty minutes?" Neil asked snidely.

"Thirty minutes? That's how long it takes?" Jo dropped a Swedish Christmas ornament and urgently pressed her hand on Neil's forearm. "If she's occupied for the next half hour, where will Stanley be?"

Even as she spoke, Stanley was edging away from Alex and the knot of people gathered to watch the artist at work. But Jo and Neil were hot on his trail.

"Hey, lady," a kid called after them, "you forgot your airplane on a stick."

"You keep it," Jo yelled back, barely holding on to her beanie as she and Neil dodged slow-moving traffic in pursuit of Stanley. Neil was pulling her along with one hand, while dragging his shopping bag with the other. Meanwhile, their quarry was disappearing around a fruit stand shaped like a giant strawberry, and they had to slam on the brakes a few booths away or risk discovery.

As soon as Stan was out of sight, they also raced behind the giant strawberry. But there was no sign of him.

Neil swore and kicked his shopping bag. "Where did he go?"

"Down there!" Jo shouted, gesturing wildly to the top of the chain-link fence that marked the edge of the fairgrounds. They watched helplessly as Stanley's dark head and lanky body vanished over the top and onto the other side.

"Well, I guess that's it." Jo took off her beanie and pushed her sunglasses up into her hair. "We can't follow him there."

"Why not?" Neil demanded. "If he can get over the fence, so can we. You first—I'll give you a boost."

"But there are spikes on that fence!"

Neil wasn't paying attention. After ditching his hat and funny sunglasses, he fished his jacket out of his shopping bag and tossed it up and over the top of the seven-foot fence. "Come on," he said impatiently, making a booster step for her with his hands.

There didn't seem to be a choice. Taking a deep breath, she hiked one foot up in his clasped hands and balanced herself against his shoulder. With him pushing and her leaping, she managed to get a foothold in the links near the top, and then she gingerly edged herself over the coat-padded spikes. In one enormous leap, she was over the top and flat on the hard ground on the other side.

"I hope I never have to do that again," she mumbled, brushing grass off the scrapes on her legs, as Neil came tumbling down beside her.

Feeling like half of a commando team, she ran along the fence behind Neil until they came to the place where they thought they'd seen Stanley. A ragged piece of chambray shirt fluttered in the breeze on the top of the fence.

"He tore his shirt coming over," Neil concluded. "This is the spot, all right."

There wasn't much to distinguish it from the rest of the area along the fence, expect that up over a slight rise, they could see the edge of one of the fair's many makeshift parking lots.

"The parking lot?" she suggested.

"Must be. Let's hope he has a long way to walk to his car, or we've lost him for sure."

The hill they climbed looked down on a sprawling field that had been converted to a parking lot for the duration of the fair. As they watched, Stanley jumped into a white step van and spun out of the lot.

"But Stanley drives a Toyota," Jo protested. "He's never had a truck like that."

"It appears there are a lot of things you don't know about Stanley."

Jo bit her lip and kept quiet. Up to this point, she hadn't really thought about the purpose of this mad dash after Stanley, or that her complicity in it would mean she had accepted her friend's guilt.

But that was exactly what it did mean. As hard as she tried to hold on to her belief in Stanley, she knew deep in her heart that innocent people didn't ditch their girlfriends at the fair and go leaping over fences into strange trucks.

"What next?" she asked softly.

"We wait. He's got to come back for Alex sooner or later. All we can do is hope he parks his truck back here when he does."

Jo dropped to the grassy knoll. "Where could he be going? He's only got a half hour to do it in."

Tugging her to her feet, Neil led the way down into the parking lot and into the open bed of a pick-up truck to wait for Stanley's return. "I'd guess he's going to Markham's St. Paul plant. It's off Energy Park Boulevard, not a mile from here, and that's too much of a coincidence for my taste."

Again, Jo preferred not to discuss it. She had already as good as admitted she believed Neil, but pure Wentworth stubbornness was keeping her from going over the line into overt acceptance.

She was leaning against Neil's shoulder with her leg in his lap, and he was examining the scratches she'd suffered on the trip over the fence, when Stanley's step van came barreling back into the lot.

Peeking over the side of their truck, Jo reported, "That's him. He's getting out now and going back up the hill."

"We're going to have to see what's in his truck, Jo. Can you handle it?"

She squared her shoulders. "I can handle it."

Using a penknife, Neil pried open the back doors of Stanley's van and then stepped back.

"Is it . . . ?" she asked anxiously.

He nodded.

Oh, dear. She was hoping against hope it would all be a big mistake, that Stanley's truck would be filled with "I love you, Alex" balloons or something of that ilk. But when Jo swung back the doors, she saw a load of neatly stacked Tyler Markham Industries drums, with the words Contains Hazardous Waste clearly stenciled on the sides.

"Oh, God." Jo backed up and sat down abruptly on the grass. "How could he? Poor Stanley."

Kneeling next to her, Neil set his arms around her lightly. "Poor Stanley? What about poor Jo, whose friend betrayed her?"

"No, you don't understand." She felt numb as she let her head fall onto Neil's shoulder. "Stanley needs help. He must be out of his mind. That's the only explanation."

"Okay, Jo, okay." He helped her to her feet carefully, sheltering her inside the cradle of his arm. "Let's go home. We have to figure out what we do next, now that you know."

"The first thing I have to do is tell Alex," Jo moaned. "But how? How can I tell her?"

"As gently as you can, I guess."

She shook her head. "I've never seen her like this. She keeps telling me how different Stanley is from the guys she usually dates, how he's so real and so sweet. He gave her an emerald bracelet a few weeks ago, and she's practically enshrined it. She adores him, Neil, and he must adore her, too, or he wouldn't be bankrupting himself to buy her presents."

"No, Jo." He shook his head sadly. "It's just one more thing he's apparently been hiding. Stanley is rich."

Her eyes were wide and full of pain, and Neil saw cracks begin to appear in the surface of Jo's abiding faith in people.

"How can I know him so well, and not know him at all?"

That was indeed the question.

Jo hadn't come up with any solutions by the time they got back to the Wentworth house. She was extremely relieved that Alex and Stanley weren't back yet, even though that gave her extra time to stew over her dilemma.

She stuck Neil in the chintz wing chair in the living room and paced back and forth in front of him.

And then Alex strolled in the front door.

Neil saw the panic leap onto Jo's face and he took her hand for moral support. At least Alex had entered alone and there was no Stanley to contend with. Neil would cheerfully have choked that jerk with his bare hands.

"Josephine Victoria," Alex sang out. "I have a bone to pick with you."

Jo was taken aback. This wasn't how the discussion was supposed to start. "What is it?"

Alex was wearing a funny smirk and carrying some sort of poster. Her eyes alight with curiosity, she shook a fuchsia-tipped finger at Jo. "I distinctly remember you telling me that Neil was going to be the next lieutenant governor. It isn't like you to make up fairy tales and foist them off as the truth, baby sister."

Jo's baffled eyes darted from Alex to Neil and then back to Alex. "It wasn't a fairy tale."

"Sure, sure, Josie, dear." With a dramatic flourish, Alex whipped her poster around to reveal the front. She read aloud, "'Lindquist and Swanson—United for a Better Tomorrow.' Funny, I don't see any Hawthorne in there. They were giving these posters away at the party's booth at the fair." With a satisfied smile, Alex sent Neil a long, appraising look. "Looks like somebody's pulled a fast one here."

"What's going on, Neil? I thought you told your father you wanted the appointment."

"I did." He inclined his head toward Alex. "Can we discuss this privately, Jo?"

"Oh, heavens," Alex drawled, withdrawing gracefully. "Far be it for me to hang about like an extra appendage. Tata, kids."

"What is it, Neil?" Jo drew him over to the Chesterfield sofa with her. "What happened? And why didn't you tell me?"

He offered glibly, "No biggie. I was dumped. They chose someone else, that's all."

"But why?"

"Does there have to be a reason?"

He was avoiding her eyes, and she knew that something was very wrong. "For your own father and uncle to shunt you aside in favor of someone else, you bet there has to be a reason."

Shrugging, he patted her hand. "You'd have to ask my father."

Jo's eyes filled with compassion, and she squeezed his hand in between hers. "You don't want to tell me the reason because *I'm* the reason. They didn't want you because I got you on the news and made you look bad, and because I'm a political undesirable. That's it, isn't it?"

"Of course not."

"You poor thing," she cried, warming to her topic. "You volunteered at Water Works out of the goodness of your heart, and then stumbled over this whole ugly scheme of Stanley's, and I didn't even believe you! Now your political career is ruined because you're tied to me and to Water Works. How can you ever forgive me?''

"It isn't you, Jo," he pleaded. "It's me. My father gave me a project and I failed, okay? It's only peripherally related to you."

"I don't understand. What project did your father give you that is peripherally related to me?"

It was all coming out in bits and pieces, and he didn't want to tell her. He didn't want her to know the final betrayal. But when she gazed up at him with those luminous, trusting eyes, he didn't have a choice. He couldn't let her blame herself when the problem was *his* deceit.

"I didn't volunteer out of the goodness of my heart, Jo. And I didn't stumble over the publicity scams any more than Stanley did." He swallowed, but he had to go on. "My father sits on the board of the Minnesota Corporate Charities Fund. You should recognize the name."

"They're one of our biggest contributors," she whispered. Where was this going? What could he tell her that could be worse that what she already knew?

"He also has friends at ChemCo and Red Metal Manufacturing. Both companies claimed their dumping accidents were set up, and my father sent me to Water Works to investigate."

"But why? Why should *you* investigate Water Works?"

He smiled. It was a hard, cynical smile that pierced her heart. "Publicity. What else? I needed to look like a hero to justify getting the lieutenant governor appointment. Uncovering dirty laundry at Water Works was just the ticket."

"Oh, my God." Jo rose from the sofa and stumbled away from him. Her throat felt like it was closing, and the portrait of Great-grandmother Fitzgerald on the living room wall was threatening to fall in on her. Could no one be trusted? "Publicity," she choked. "You're no better than

Stanley. You wanted to destroy me and kill Water Works just so you could look like a hero.''

He stood by the sofa with his hands in his pockets, but made no effort to defend himself.

''You knew that honesty and trust were the most important things in the world to me. Yet you've lied to me since the first day.'' Huge, accusing eyes focused on him. ''You lied to me and you used me. You betrayed me, Neil, in a way far worse than Stanley ever could have. Because I thought I loved you. I gave you my heart.'' She felt tears well up in her eyes, and she blinked, letting them fall freely. ''All you wanted was publicity.''

''Now, wait a minute.'' His own eyes shimmered with anger. ''I told you we shouldn't get involved. I tried to stay away. I told you that someday, someone would shatter your pretty little illusions.''

She raised her chin defiantly. ''And you said it wouldn't be you.''

''I didn't want it to be me.''

He cursed out loud in frustration. He'd known from the start that he had no business running after Jo. Destroying her trust in him was like destroying himself. And he hadn't missed her words. *I thought I loved you.* Not ''I love you'' or even ''I loved you'' in the past tense. He felt like hell. And he wanted out of this place.

''Ah, well,'' he said in a bitter tone, ''at least I know how to make a graceful exit.'' In the doorway, he paused for one more look at her. ''I should have known it would never work out between Pollyanna and the Big Bad Wolf.''

''You jerk,'' she shouted into empty air. ''Pollyanna and the Big Bad Wolf aren't even in the same story.''

Chapter Fourteen

"Are you out of your mind?" Alex shrieked. "Stanley? This has got to be some kind of sick joke."

Telling Alex about Stanley wasn't going well. Draping an arm around her sister, Jo tried to be gentle. "Alex, I'm so sorry. But I saw it with my own eyes—when he left you at the fair, Stanley was collecting toxic waste to dump and blame on Markham Industries."

"You saw this with your own eyes?"

Jo nodded.

"This is bizarre." For once, there was no artifice in Alex's voice. "Stanley?" she said again. "How can it be?"

"I don't know, Alex."

"The fink. Taking me to the fair as a cover." Leaping to her feet, Alex began to sound more like her usual self. "Why, I'll kill the creep with my bare hands."

"No, you won't," Jo murmured soothingly.

"He was using *me* as a dupe. The nerve!" Alex's eyes narrowed to glittering green slits. "But I know what to do. I'll go see him, looking knock-down, drag-out gorgeous. He'll drool, he'll beg, he'll plead and I will laugh in his disgusting rodent-like face!"

Blazing with righteous indignation, Alex swept from the room, only to return in record time. *"Voilà!"* she exclaimed, spinning around for inspection. "The woman scorned."

Basic black had never looked like this. Her dress was black silk, tight enough to make breathing difficult, with a slit well up the thigh. A snippy little hat with a veil made her hair seem as though it was on fire in contrast.

"You look like you're going to a funeral on *Dallas*," Jo said dryly.

Alex rubbed black-gloved hands together. "I'm going to hit him where it hurts."

"Good luck."

"Oh, you're coming with me. I need the moral support. Besides, you're the eyewitness who will shame him with the truth while I look on and laugh." She smiled gaily. "I've got it all planned."

"Oh, no—" Jo protested, but her sister was already dragging her out of the house and into the Grand Affairs van. "He may have already been arrested," she continued as they were driving.

"Don't be silly." Alex made a left and parked the van in the driveway of a well-kept Tudor home. "His car's here, and the front door's open."

After adjusting her hat in the rearview mirror and applying a fresh coat of blood-red lipstick, Alex slid demurely from the van and marched into Stanley's house.

"Stanley, you swine!" she shouted. "Show yourself and prepare to be unmasked as the viper you are!"

First rodent, then swine and now viper. Alex was covering the entire animal kingdom. Jo hid behind her sister meekly as Stanley shuffled into the room in a grubby T-shirt and shorts.

"What's going on?"

Alex sizzled him with a contemptuous stare. "I know what you did. You used my sister, you used Water Works and you used me. But Jo and Neil saw you steal the Markham drums while I was getting my caricature done. You are scum, Stanley Hoffmeyer!''

Stanley ignored her. ''Why, how tricky of you, Jo,'' he said calmly. Looking pleased with himself, he fingered his scruffy beard. ''But I accomplished what I set out to do. I'm not sorry.''

''You don't even deny it?'' Jo gasped.

His eyes flashed with annoyance. ''Of all people, you should understand. It was for a good cause. I did it for Water Works.''

For a good cause. Unbelieving, Jo heard the words she used so often.

''But you used me as a smoke screen!'' Alex interrupted. ''How dare you?''

''I did like you, Alex,'' he allowed. ''But this was business. You were for fun.''

''Fun?'' she choked. ''I'll kill him.'' With her teeth bared and her hands twisted into claws, Alex advanced on him while Jo tried to wrestle her back in the opposite direction.

''Come on, Alex, let's leave. He's not worth the trouble; he's obviously off his rocker.''

Stanley's face flushed with anger. ''Who cares what you think? I won, didn't I? I fooled you, all of you. I got more publicity for Water Works than you ever dreamed possible. I hired Ed and I engineered everything—ChemCo, Red Metal and Markham Industries. I even pushed you and your pretty boy Hawthorne together. You should thank me.''

Pushing her vengeful sister out the door, Jo turned. Her head was held high with dignity. ''We'll see who gets the last laugh when you're behind bars.''

Curses echoed behind them as they raced into the van. Jo was more than happy to see the last of Stanley.

''I can't believe it,'' she murmured. ''He was always so sincere, so committed.''

"I can't believe it," Alex gritted between clenched teeth. "He never even said he was sorry. Not one plea for mercy. The slime."

As Jo started the car, Alex ripped off her gloves and hat and threw them out the window. "Just goes to show you should never trust a man."

Jo wondered how long Alex would be singing that tune— until the next good-looking man crossed her path, no doubt.

ALEX PROVED to be relentless. Stanley's arrest and the subsequent news stories only added fuel to her man-hating fervor. Every time Jo turned around, Alex was spitting venom about what rotten beasts men were.

It got to the point where Jo couldn't stomach another word. "Alexandra Jane Wentworth, you stop that this instant!" she shouted, earning herself a series of shocked stares at the dinner table. "Think how many men you've mistreated in your time. You've two-timed them, dumped them right and left and made fun of their feelings. Maybe turnabout is fair play."

"What?" Alex jumped up and bumped the table enough to slosh the soup. "This from my own sister? My own flesh and blood?"

Already regretting her words, Jo started to say, "I didn't mean to—"

"Ha!" Still standing, Alex glared down her lovely nose. "I think the truth of my words is simply too painful for you to bear since my situation so closely parallels yours. Deception, betrayal, treachery—thy name is Neil as well as Stanley, *n'est-ce pas?*"

At that point, Jo set her napkin next to her plate and rose stiffly from the table. "Excuse me. I'm going to my room."

Eliza giggled, Alex sniffed loudly and their mother boomed, "Now, Josephine, this won't do."

Jo left anyway, with Maggie close behind.

"Jo," Maggie said evenly, "this isn't like you."

"What do you know about it?"

"I know my sister Jo does not pick fights at the dinner table, no matter how much Alex deserves it. And I know she gives people the benefit of the doubt."

"I suppose you're talking about Neil."

"Of course I'm talking about Neil." Maggie pulled Jo down next to her on the Chesterfield sofa. "Don't you think he deserves a chance to atone for his mistakes?"

"No."

Although her voice never rose above its usual calm level, Maggie's displeasure communicated itself eloquently. "You sound as unfair as Alex," she said grimly. "I'm surprised at you."

Jo was stung. "What do you expect? I'm not Mother Teresa! I may not write off the whole male population, but I'm still not going to forgive and forget that easily."

Maggie tried to interrupt, but Jo rode right over her. "He lied to me. I consider that the end of the matter."

"How can you say th—" Maggie started, but Jo stalked off.

She didn't like hiding out from her sisters, whatever the reason, but she couldn't handle another minute of Alex's venom or Maggie's gentle remonstrations. Jo was willing to hide out forever if that's how long it took to get some peace.

She was up in her room with the door shut, lying on her bed and listlessly reading *War and Peace*, when Maggie knocked and asked to come in.

"I don't want to hear another lecture on forgiveness," she said testily.

"I'm not going to give you one. But there's someone downstairs waiting to see you."

"Who?" Her heart beat faster with the hope that it would be Neil, even as she struggled with whether she should agree to see him.

"Not him. His father."

She dropped *War and Peace* and opened the door to Maggie. "His father? What does he want?"

"To talk to you, obviously." Affection and concern softened Maggie's features as she reached out and rearranged a wayward lock of her sister's hair. "Just talk to him, okay? He's on the porch."

Jo nodded. She had no idea what this was all about, and Neil's father wasn't exactly a favorite of hers to begin with, but she supposed she might as well get it over with.

The ex-senator was posed stiffly on the rather dilapidated front porch. He had one hand in his vest pocket like a portrait of Napoleon, but he stood awkwardly, and his face was overtly sympathetic.

"Miss Wentworth," he said politely.

"Please, call me Jo." She took a seat on the porch swing and motioned to a white wicker chair opposite her. "Would you like to sit down, Mr. Hawthorne?"

"Thank you."

All this careful courtesy was stultifying. Jo smiled faintly. "Is there something I can do for you, Mr. Hawthorne?"

He leaned forward in his wicker chair, settling his palms against the knees of his perfectly creased trousers. She knew now where Neil got his taste in clothes; it was the same sort of stuffy suit Neil would wear. But his distinguished gray hair ruffled in the late summer breeze, puncturing his perfection at least a little, and when he impatiently raked a hand through it, he looked even more human.

Jo's initial impression of him threatened to mellow. "Yes, Mr. Hawthorne?"

He cleared his throat and began gravely, "I have two missions here today, Miss—er, that is, Jo. I hope you'll hear me out on both."

"Certainly." She met his gaze steadily, clasping her hands primly in the lap of her calico skirt.

"First, I have a rather unpleasant duty to discharge." His gray eyes were apologetic as he went smoothly through what appeared to be a rehearsed speech. "As you may or may not be aware, my son pled your case quite eloquently before the board of the Minnesota Corporate Charities Fund. He assured us that your Water Works organization was once more a trustworthy concern. Unfortunately, our board members felt that the amount of publicity generated by Mr. Hoffmeyer's arrest left them only one choice."

She had anticipated this, but it was still a blow. Without MCCF's support, there could be no hope of a resurrection for Water Works. "And that choice is to pull out their financial support, is that correct?"

"I'm afraid so."

"I can't pretend this is a surprise," she said gently.

"I suppose not." He scooted his chair closer to the swing and patted ineffectually at her hand. "I'm really very sorry, Miss Wentworth. I feel partially responsible for the way this thing has developed, and the furor it's created in the press. You have my sincere regrets, my dear."

Glancing up in surprise, Jo saw a kindness she hadn't expected. She was touched. "It wasn't your fault," she said softly. "We all know now that Stanley is the one who deserves the blame. You did what you thought was right for your friends at ChemCo, Red Metal and Markham Industries, and I admire your loyalty to your friends."

He smiled. It looked like one of Neil's smiles, almost shy and reluctantly pleased. The memory of that smile sent a sharp pang through her heart.

"And I admire your loyalty to your friends, also."

"Thank you."

He rose from the chair to look out over the porch railing into the park across the street. From the Wentworth porch, strollers and bicyclists and a few squirrels were visible on the grass and among the trees. It was a soothing, peaceful image.

Without turning, Neil's father murmured, "I have another errand, too. Of a more personal nature."

Well, here it comes, she thought. *Now he's going to want to talk about Neil and me.*

Jo looked down at her hands, wondering if she would now be requested to leave Neil alone into eternity to forestall further damage to his image. And she had just been starting to like Byron Hawthorne.

"I'm afraid you've rather thrown my son for a loop, young lady." Mr. Hawthorne clicked his tongue. "I thought perhaps I might intercede on his behalf."

She was shocked. "Excuse me?"

When he shifted back to look at her, he wore a more forceful expression. "Neil has accused me of trying to run his life, and I'm trying very hard to keep my hands to myself. Unfortunately, I find it difficult to see the two of you making yourselves unhappy when all you need is a push in the right direction."

"You don't understand, Mr. Hawthorne," Jo offered cautiously. "Neil and I both know it wasn't meant to be."

"Nonsense." He bent closer to her face, fired up with some of the oratorical zeal of his speech-making days. "I happen to believe that you have a good head on your shoulders, and you're refusing to use it. You won't find a better man than my son. He's not perfect, of course," he admitted, and then he slammed his fist down on the arm of the swing, sending it rocking with Jo in it. "But damn close."

Jo laughed as she steadied the swing. "You don't have to sell me on Neil, sir. And I do appreciate your coming—"

"Giving me my walking papers, are you?"

"Thank you again," she said firmly. She tilted up to brush a circumspect kiss on his distinguished cheek, and then shook his hand before directing him down the steps to the sidewalk.

"Well?" Maggie demanded, coming out the front door. "Did he talk you into going to see Neil?"

"Of course not."

"Why not?"

"Because, contrary to what everyone seems to think," Jo said self-righteously, "I am not a doormat or some naive little shrinking violet who hasn't got the sense to see what's staring her in the face."

Perched on the porch railing, Maggie looked down her nose calmly. "And what is that supposed to mean?"

"It means that maybe I'm not as trusting or as forgiving as you think."

"Oh, pooh—you are, too." Maggie's clear green eyes brooked no objections. "I've lived with you for almost twenty-six years, Josephine. I know you backward and forward, and I know you never stay mad at anybody longer than twenty-four hours. I *know* that in your heart you've already forgiven Neil. What I can't figure out is why you won't admit it."

"I have not forgiven him!"

Maggie rolled her eyes in disgust. "Oh, you have, too. Tell the truth, Josie."

"Well, okay, maybe I have," she grumbled. "But that doesn't mean I want him back."

"Why in heaven's name not?"

Jo swallowed and lifted her chin. "I may be willing to overlook the fact that he came to Water Works under false pretenses, and even that he kept his stupid undercover mission a secret for so long. But I *cannot* forgive the way he just gave up and walked out of my life without so much as a whimper."

"Oh, Jo . . ."

"No, I mean it." On a roll now, she left the swing and stalked back and forth in front of Maggie. "Did he ask me to forgive him? Heavens, no! Did he say he was sorry? Not on your life! He threw out some malarkey about Pollyanna and the Big Bad Wolf and then—whoosh—vanished into thin air. Did he come here today to talk things over like a reasonable adult? No! He sends his *father*. Good grief."

"I can call him," Maggie volunteered. "I can tell him you're willing to bury the hatchet if he comes crawling on his knees."

Jo narrowed her eyes. "Don't you dare. This time, the move—if there is one—has got to come from him. By himself. All along I've been the one with the faith that we belonged together, no matter what. But if he cares so little about me that he could walk away without a backward glance, then I truly believe that he doesn't deserve me. I've lost my faith that we belong together." She spun on her heel and slammed back inside the house.

"I don't buy that baloney for a minute," Maggie muttered to no one in particular.

NEIL WAS IN A RAGE. It was a beautiful day at the lake house, and it only made his mood worse. Why couldn't the weather cooperate and be as awful as he felt?

It wasn't fair. None of it was fair. Not the weather, not Jo, not the way it had all turned out.

For a person who had known for a long time that life wasn't fair, he was having a hell of a time dealing with the injustice of losing Jo. He knew well enough the world was out of balance most of the time. But this was too far out of whack to tolerate.

Against his better judgment, Jo had made him believe that things like truth and love could really exist. Even without her, he couldn't seem to shake those beliefs. He wanted his old cynical, jaded self back. *That* Neil would've accepted losing Jo as one more nasty trick of fate. *This* Neil expected a mischievous sprite to pop up out of nowhere and throw fairy dust on the problem.

His brain kept reminding him that he had lied to her and she hated his guts and that was the end of it. But his heart kept looking for some way around the obvious.

He'd been doing this for days, kicking himself around in circles. But what could he have done differently? It had certainly seemed like the right thing to do when he'd gallantly walked out of her life for her own good.

But who was he kidding? Nobility had never been his style. Ugly, dirty reality—now that was more like it. The ugly reality staring him in the face was that he wanted Jo back, no matter what he had to do to get her. Forget honesty and trust and all that other stuff. He'd use any low-down trick he could think of to con her back into his life. But what trick? What scheme would get him so under her skin she'd have to give in?

He shoved his hands into the pockets of a pair of gym shorts he'd dug up somewhere, and gazed out at the placid late-summer surface of the lake. It lay there, cool and unmoved, mocking his mental gymnastics. It taunted him, telling him that sometimes the best solution was the one that required the least amount of effort.

It suddenly seemed very stupid to be hanging around at the lake, wallowing in self-inflicted misery, when he could at least try to persuade her to forgive him. He might be deficient in several areas, but his one-on-one persuasive techniques were top-notch. He was a politician, for goodness sake. If he couldn't talk one small, contrary woman into trusting him for a few minutes, he didn't deserve the name Hawthorne.

As soon as he changed his clothes, he was heading for St. Paul.

JO WAS DIGGING in her garden with a vengeance. No wild-flower was safe today, and the creeping charlie might as well surrender without a fight. She dug her little fork in, spearing the stalk of a lily by mistake.

"Too bad," she mumbled, tossing dirt and leaves over her shoulder.

"Watch out. You almost hit me."

She spun around in time to see Neil neatly sidestepping a ragged pile of weeds. Holding her breath, she stared at the sky for a minute or two, until her pulse came back down to normal, and the hot color on her face cooled. Savagely, she shoved her gardening fork into the ground.

It would have been nice to feel beautiful at this moment, to be drop-dead gorgeous and worked up into a fury all at the same time. But instead, she was less than stunning in grubby overalls and a T-shirt, with filthy hands, bare feet, uncontrollable hair and a pink face. The worst part was that she had to summon up the most meager feeling of annoyance with him. He looked great. He looked delicious. His pale yellow polo shirt made him look tanned and blond, and his legs were long and lean inside khaki pants. And she wanted to be mad at him about as much as she wanted to crawl to Minneapolis on her knees.

"You haven't said hello," he announced grimly.

When she found her voice, it came out husky and weird. "Uh—hello."

"Look," he said, slamming his hands into the pockets of his trendy khaki pants, "I came here to talk to you and I'm going to do it whether you like it or not."

She swallowed with difficulty, rose and brushed her hands off on her overalls.

"I love you, Jo."

His eyes were hot and full of pain. His voice was shaky. She saw his hands struggle against the fabric of his pockets.

"I love you," he whispered. "I'm so sorry for what happened. More than you know. You have every right to hate me, but I'm hoping you can get past that. I know you can forgive me if you try. Will you try, Jo?"

Her throat threatened to close. "Oh, Neil..." She didn't know what to say. Of course she could forgive him. What kind of monster did he think she was?

"No, don't say anything yet." He held up a hand to hold her back. "I had this all planned—I ran it through my head on the drive down from the lake—but I'm not getting it right at all."

She started to smile.

"Look, Jo," he said again. "I know that honesty is very important to you."

He edged closer, reaching out tentatively to barely graze one finger against her cheek. She closed her eyes, drinking in the small but amazingly powerful sensation, and she heard him inhale sharply above her.

"Honesty," he murmured, laying his whole hand against her cheek. "The honest truth is that we belong together. We may not be a perfect match—we may never be a perfect match—but there is something very strong binding us together. And it would be the worst lie of all to deny it."

She licked her lower lip. She nodded. "Maybe."

"Not just maybe, Jo. You have to say yes."

She moved away from his hand and looked down at the ground. She knew she was too stubborn for her own good, but she had to be sure their problems were resolved. "Yes to what exactly?"

"Yes that you love me. Yes that you'll marry me."

Her eyes widened. "Marry you? Where did that come from?"

It was his turn to look surprised. "But I love you. I've been thinking about buying my parents' lake place so you can have your house in the country. I want to have the kids and the cats and the wildflowers and all the rest of it. What do you think?"

"I don't know. A discreet affair, maybe." She backed away, more confused than ever. "I'm not the type to be a political wife—we both know that. I've practically ruined your career already and we were only dating. Think about the damage it would do if we got married."

"Who cares? I don't need a political wife. I may not even stay in politics." Framing her face with his hands, he forced her to look up at him. "Do you love me, Jo?"

Her voice dropped low. "Of course I do."

"And will you forgive me for lying to you about Water Works?"

"I forgave you a long time ago."

"Really?" he whispered, searching her eyes for confirmation.

She softened. "How could I not forgive you? I love you. It's almost like you were a different person then. But I know that the person you are now would never deceive me like that." She paused. "Would you?"

His face grew very serious. "No."

She believed him. But something held her back from throwing herself into his arms.

"What in the hell are we doing apart?" he asked impatiently.

Moistening her lips, she gazed straight into his eyes. She wanted so much to feel his arms around her. But it was vitally important that she be sure about one thing. "Do you truly believe," she asked intently, "with all your heart, that the two of us belong together?"

He replied without hesitating. "Absolutely."

"You know," she remarked in surprise, "me, too." She laughed and glanced up at him. "I guess sometimes you have to have a little faith in people." Her eyes danced with the mischief of a fairy child, and she slipped her hand inside his. "I love reclamation projects. I think we should get married."

Laughing a good, clean, ringing laugh, Neil swept her up into a hard embrace. "You won't regret this, Jo. We're going to have a lot of fun together." And he dropped a delicate kiss on the tip of her freckled nose.

"One thing, though," she warned, settling into the firm circle of his arms and paying no attention to the dirt she was smudging across his spotless yellow shirt. "My children are not growing up in a hothouse environment. You can be Joe Senator if you want, but my kids are not going to be polite little things who ride in parades."

"You bet." He kissed her again, on the mouth this time, and got out his handkerchief to swipe at a streak of dirt on her chin. "I want them to be more like you—feisty little wildflowers with roots that dig in deep."

"Dandelions," she returned happily. "Or maybe wild roses. That has a nicer ring to it."

"What are you guys doing down there?" someone shrieked from up by the house.

Disentangling slightly, they spun around to see who was shouting at them. From the third-floor sun porch on the back of the house, the three other Wentworth redheads were arrayed. Eliza waved gaily, shaking her pretty strawberry curls in the breeze.

"Having fun?" she squealed.

Next to her, Maggie put a hand over Eliza's mouth, and made as if to drag her inside, but Alex shook her fist and called, "Don't give in too easily, darling. Give him hell."

Then Kit came up behind the three of them, her long blond hair streaming around her as she beamed down into the backyard. "Pay no attention to her, Jo! I think you should grab him."

Maggie said loudly, "You guys! Leave them alone!" and the others surrounded her with various arguments and pithy comments, waving their arms and gesticulating madly as their voices trampled right over one another in the high-spirited struggle to be heard.

Both of Neil's eyebrows rose in disbelief as he cast a glance at Jo. "What is this?"

"If you're going to join the family," she offered innocently, "you might as well get used to it."

Epilogue

Jo heard the first chords of the "Wedding March" echo in the cavernous chapel from the hall, and she got a serious case of panic. From the circle of assorted wildflowers on her head to the tips of her white satin pumps, she was suddenly frozen. She dropped her bouquet.

"Calm down," Maggie said quietly, retrieving the bunch of flowers and sticking them back into Jo's stiff hands. "Everything's under control, Josie. Take deep breaths."

Eliza came swirling in the door to the bride's dressing room, looking smashing in dusty-mauve satin, lace-edged and off the shoulder, with big puffed sleeves and yards of skirt gathered at the high waist. Her bouquet and the flowers in her hair were sweetheart roses.

"There are a million people out there, Jo. I swear Mother invited every single person she ever met in her whole life, and you should see Neil's mother. Mrs. Hawthorne is wearing..." Eliza paused in her excited narrative to increase the drama. "Are you ready for this? A Russian sable coat! It is to die for."

"Sable? A fur?" Jo felt spots of heat rise to her cold cheeks. "I told her specifically—no dead animals at my wedding. I let her have everything the way she wanted it. I let her invite all those bigwigs, all those reporters and photographers. I let her stick us in these outrageous dresses. How could she do this to me?''

Maggie, dressed in the same outfit as Eliza but looking a little less comfortable in its excess, shooed their youngest sister toward the door. ''Stop causing problems, will you? Go help Alex and Kit fasten their buttons or something.''

''Oh, they're all dressed,'' Eliza said cheerfully. ''But Kit's not happy. She says she's too pregnant to be a bridesmaid and she looks like a whale.''

''Well, that's fitting. After all, Neil and I met over a whale. Do you remember Junior and the Fish Fest at Freedom Lake? Junior's the only one within a hundred miles not invited to this circus.'' The glazed look in Jo's eyes as she paced in her rustling gown made her sisters wonder if she was getting hysterical.

''Jo, snap out of it, will you?'' Maggie pleaded, while Eliza squealed about it being happily-ever-after time.

Maggie finally succeeded in getting rid of Eliza, and then she pulled Jo over in front of the mirror. ''Look at yourself, Jo. You're beautiful. What are you worried about?''

''I don't know.'' Jo plopped herself down on a satin bench in front of the mirror, refusing to spare a moment's concern for what sitting on it might do to her dress. It, too, was high-waisted and extremely full, with huge poufs for sleeves and a wide border of lace edging the off-the-shoulder neckline.

Jo wrung her hands, squinting at herself in the mirror. ''I feel so out of place, Maggie, in this Princess Di dress, with all those people waiting to stare at me. And I'm freezing.'' She raced on. ''There are winter storm warnings, did you hear? We may never get out of here! I should be getting married in the summer in a field of buttercups. Not in the dead of winter in a cathedral the size of Montana,'' she wailed, warming to her topic. ''And my feet hurt. You know how much I hate high heels.''

Tugging Jo up to her feet, Maggie smoothed the folds of the dress back into place. "The wedding will be beautiful and you know it, regardless of your dress or the people or the weather. I'm sorry things got a little out of hand, but what do you expect when you decide to marry a Hawthorne?"

"I don't want a Hawthorne. I want Neil."

"You're getting Neil," Maggie returned sensibly. "Now quit moaning and behave yourself. And take your shoes off if you don't like them. Nobody will see them anyway."

"Do you really think I could ditch the shoes?"

"Definitely."

"Thank goodness. I was so afraid I'd trip." Divesting herself of her satin pumps, Jo asked, in a fresh rush of anxiety, "Are normal people this nervous? Do you think this is a bad omen?"

Although she felt like laughing, Maggie bit her lip and answered calmly. "I've never been married, Jo, so I have no first-hand experience. But I saw Neil, and he didn't look nervous at all, so he probably cancels you out as a bad omen. Anyway, Kit was a basket case, and her marriage turned out fine. I'm sure it's perfectly normal to be nervous."

"Okay," Jo murmured, holding on to that thought. It was perfectly normal to be nervous.

A light tap on the door signaled the arrival of Kit's husband, Riley. "They've seated the mothers," he said with a big smile. "Maggie, you should go line up with the bridesmaids now."

Maggie turned to go, but caught a glimpse of Jo's round, uncertain eyes. With tears threatening her own vision, Maggie grabbed Jo, smashing her in yards of satin and an emotional hug.

"Thank you so much, Mags," Jo whispered. "I love you."

"Don't worry," Maggie whispered fiercely, squeezing Jo's hand and backing out the door. "It's the right thing."

Jo swallowed and nodded. "I know." She watched the back of her sister's gown recede down the hallway, and she blinked back the tears. She would never again live with Maggie and the others in the big old house by the park. That part of her life was over.

Taking a deep breath, she took her brother-in-law's arm, and stepped out into the hall to wait for her cue. There it was, the first bars of the new RoRo and the Boats hit, "Love You Forever."

Barefoot, desperately clutching a nosegay of wildflowers worth about fifty cents in the right season and an outrageous amount now, she held on to Riley and lined up at the end of the aisle.

In front of her, people murmured approval of the small bride in the beautiful dress, and they stood and smiled as she and Riley took the measured steps they had practiced. Jo didn't take in any of it—not the people or the music or her mother's tears or Riley's arm under hers.

All she saw was Neil, waiting for her, and she relaxed. He might be wearing a frock coat and an ascot and he might be too gorgeous for his own good, but he was smiling, and he was Neil. Everything was going to be just fine.

And then she was up with him and he took her hand, and the familiar feelings of love and longing glided from her fingers all the way down to her bare toes.

"I do," she said softly, smiling up at him.

"Me, too."

Neil gazed down at Jo, and he wanted to touch the undisciplined waves of her hair, to reassure himself that it was really her, and this was really happening.

In a blur of soft words and meaningful glances, of secret smiles and exchanged rings and a final passionate kiss that sent shock waves through the audience, they did it.

"We did it!" they shouted in unison. And then, "Let's get out of here."

With heavy snow pounding against the doors, Eliza and Alex cornered Jo. "You can skip the reception for all we care. But you *can't* leave without throwing the bouquet!"

Jo realized that she could get into an argument about the archaic nature of the tradition, but this was not the time or the place to make a fuss. Instead, she closed her eyes and heaved the bunch of wildflowers over her head into the crowd.

Alex and Eliza jumped for it, but it was Maggie, cool, independent Maggie, in whose hands the bouquet landed.

Maggie looked down at the flowers with a stunned expression. Jo blew her sister a kiss as Neil swung her up into his arms and hurried out the door into the beginnings of a blizzard. Quickly, he helped her into the back of a long limousine trailing streamers and pop cans.

"Do you believe it?" In the spacious back seat, Jo snuggled closer into the comfortable circle of his arms. She was still shivering but warming up quickly. "Of all people, *Maggie* caught the bouquet. She doesn't even date. I guess it just goes to show you should pay no attention to ancient customs."

Neil smiled and tightened his arm around his wife. "Never can tell," he said lightly, tapping the end of her freckled nose with his finger. "Maybe Maggie is just holding out for someone as good as her little sister got."

"Maybe." Chuckling softly, Jo ducked down and then pulled Neil over on top of her, squashing the flowers in her hair and letting the bulk of her wedding dress fan out around them. Lying underneath him, she tangled her arms around him and sighed with contentment. "Now where in the world could Maggie find someone as good as you?"

Take 4 NEW Silhouette Sensations FREE!

Silhouette **Sensation** is a thrilling NEW Silhouette series for the woman of today. Each tale is a full 256 pages long - a beautiful blend of sensitivity and sensuality. When you've enjoyed your FREE **Sensations** there's an extra treat in store!

You could go on to enjoy four more exciting new **Sensations**, delivered to your door each month - at just £1.35 each *(we pay postage & packing)*. **Plus** a FREE newsletter and lots more!

No strings attached - you can stop receiving books at any time.

EXTRA FREE GIFT
If you reply within 10 days

Post the coupon **NOW** and we'll send you this beautiful Digital Quartz Clock **plus** a surprise mystery gift!

FREE BOOKS CERTIFICATE

To: Reader Service, FREEPOST, PO Box 236, Croydon, Surrey CR9 9EL.

NO STAMP NEEDED

Please send me, **free and without obligation,** four specially selected Silhouette Sensation romances, together with my **FREE** digital quartz clock and mystery gift - and reserve a Reader Service Subscription for me. If I decide to subscribe I shall receive four new Silhouette Sensation titles every month for £5.40, post and packing free. If I decide not to subscribe, I shall write to you within 10 days. The free books and gifts are mine to keep in any case. I understand that I may cancel or suspend my subscription at any time simply by writing to you. *I am over 18 years of age.* *Please write in BLOCK CAPITALS.*

Name _____

Address _____

_____

_____

_____ Postcode _____

Please don't forget to include your postcode.

Signature _____ **EP48SS**

SEND NO MONEY - TAKE NO RISKS - POST TODAY.

Silhouette Sensation

COMING NEXT MONTH

COME HOME TO ME
Marisa Carroll

Special Agent Seth Norris and Laurel Sauder would
have one night together. And out of that one night
would come a baby, created out of loneliness and
love. But for Seth, too, that night was a beginning; he
felt that he'd found a home for his heart.

TAKING A CHANCE
Robin Francis

Paulette D'Amboise was charming, vivacious and
determined to make a shambles out of her landlord's
sober life. Paulette forcibly reminded Jonathan Day
of a tornado; she was turning his life upside down
and he didn't know how to deal with it — after a
while, he wasn't even sure he wanted to deal with it,
he was starting to enjoy the experience!

Silhouette Sensation

COMING NEXT MONTH

THE AMBER SKY
Kristin James

When Valerie de la Portilla first met Ashe Harlan she wasn't free to love, nor did his harsh assessment of her beauty and her morals bode well for a future relationship between them. So when Valerie appealed to Ashe, she wasn't surprised that he wouldn't help her. But she needed him. How could she make him believe that?

DOUBLE ENTENDRE
Heather Graham Pozzessere

Journalists Bret and Colleen McAllistair were chasing diamonds that had been missing for forty years. The jewels had led to the death of at least one man. Bret was determined to protect Colleen and he wanted to revive their marriage. His remaining time as a married man could be counted in weeks, unless he could convince Colleen that she was far more important than any story!

VOWS   *LaVyrle Spencer*   **£2.99**

When high-spirited Emily meets her father's new business rival,
Tom, sparks fly, and create a blend of pride and passion in this
compelling and memorable novel.

LOTUS MOON   *Janice Kaiser*   **£2.99**

This novel vividly captures the futility of the Vietnam War and the
legacy it left. Haunting memories of the beautiful Lotus Moon fuel
Buck Michael's dangerous obsession, which only Amanda Parr can
help overcome.

SECOND TIME LUCKY   *Eleanor Woods*   **£2.75**

Danielle has been married twice. Now, as a young, beautiful widow,
can she back-track to the first husband whose life she left in ruins
with her eternal quest for entertainment and the high life?

**These three new titles will be out in bookshops from
September 1989.**

W●RLDWIDE

*Available from Boots, Martins, John Menzies, W.H. Smith, Woolworths
and other paperback stockists.*